AN INNOCENT KISS

Captivating Kisses
Book 3

Alexa Aston

ARE YOU SIGNED UP FOR DRAGONBLADE'S BLOG?

You'll get the latest news and information on exclusive giveaways, exclusive excerpts, coming releases, sales, free books, cover reveals and more.

Check out our complete list of authors, too!

No spam, no junk. That's a promise!

Sign Up Here

www.dragonbladepublishing.com

Dearest Reader;

Thank you for your support of a small press. At Dragonblade Publishing, we strive to bring you the highest quality Historical Romance from some of the best authors in the business. Without your support, there is no 'us', so we sincerely hope you adore these stories and find some new favorite authors along the way.

Happy Reading!

CEO, Dragonblade Publishing

Additional Dragonblade books by Author Alexa Aston

Captivating Kisses Series
An Unexpected Kiss (Book 1)
An Impulsive Kiss (Book 2)
An Innocent Kiss (Book 3)

The Strongs of Shadowcrest Series
The Duke's Unexpected Love (Book 1)
The Perks of Loving a Viscount (Book 2)
Falling for the Marquess (Book 3)
The Captain and the Duchess (Book 4)
Courtship at Shadowcrest (Book 5)
The Marquess' Quest for Love (Book 6)
The Duke's Guide to Winning a Lady (Book 7)

Suddenly a Duke Series
Portrait of the Duke (Book 1)
Music for the Duke (Book 2)
Polishing the Duke (Book 3)
Designs on the Duke (Book 4)
Fashioning the Duke (Book 5)
Love Blooms with the Duke (Book 6)
Training the Duke (Book 7)
Investigating the Duke (Book 8)

Second Sons of London Series
Educated By The Earl (Book 1)
Debating With The Duke (Book 2)
Empowered By The Earl (Book 3)
Made for the Marquess (Book 4)
Dubious about the Duke (Book 5)
Valued by the Viscount (Book 6)

Meant for the Marquess (Book 7)

Dukes Done Wrong Series
Discouraging the Duke (Book 1)
Deflecting the Duke (Book 2)
Disrupting the Duke (Book 3)
Delighting the Duke (Book 4)
Destiny with a Duke (Book 5)

Dukes of Distinction Series
Duke of Renown (Book 1)
Duke of Charm (Book 2)
Duke of Disrepute (Book 3)
Duke of Arrogance (Book 4)
Duke of Honor (Book 5)
The Duke That I Want (Book 6)

The St. Clairs Series
Devoted to the Duke (Book 1)
Midnight with the Marquess (Book 2)
Embracing the Earl (Book 3)
Defending the Duke (Book 4)
Suddenly a St. Clair (Book 5)
Starlight Night (Novella)
The Twelve Days of Love (Novella)

Soldiers & Soulmates Series
To Heal an Earl (Book 1)
To Tame a Rogue (Book 2)
To Trust a Duke (Book 3)
To Save a Love (Book 4)
To Win a Widow (Book 5)
Yuletide at Gillingham (Novella)

King's Cousins Series
The Pawn (Book 1)
The Heir (Book 2)
The Bastard (Book 3)

Medieval Runaway Wives
Song of the Heart (Book 1)
A Promise of Tomorrow (Book 2)
Destined for Love (Book 3)

Knights of Honor Series
Word of Honor (Book 1)
Marked by Honor (Book 2)
Code of Honor (Book 3)
Journey to Honor (Book 4)
Heart of Honor (Book 5)
Bold in Honor (Book 6)
Love and Honor (Book 7)
Gift of Honor (Book 8)
Path to Honor (Book 9)
Return to Honor (Book 10)

The Lyon's Den Series
The Lyon's Lady Love

Pirates of Britannia Series
God of the Seas

De Wolfe Pack: The Series
Rise of de Wolfe

The de Wolfes of Esterley Castle
Diana
Derek
Thea

Also from Alexa Aston
The Bridge to Love (Novella)
One Magic Night

PROLOGUE

Beauville, Surrey—June 1803

PEREGRINE BEAUMONT ACCEPTED the reins from the groom and mounted his horse. He rode the length of his father's estate and then crossed onto the lands owned by Lord Tilsbury, his closest friend. The widowed viscount had served as an adviser of sorts to Perry ever since he had returned from university over a year ago. The two men both had a deep love of the land and military history, and Perry usually called upon Tilsbury twice a week and took tea with him.

He believed he was at a crossroads. He wanted to do more at Beauville, but his father, the Earl of Martindale, held all the power and authority over the country estate. Perry worked daily alongside their steward, Mr. Rankin, but he wished he could do more. Any suggestion he made to his father regarding the land or tenants was met with either silence or a quick refusal to change anything.

Once he arrived at Tilsbury Manor, a groom took his horse, and Perry cut through the kitchens, being so frequent a visitor that the practice was accepted.

Cook smiled brightly at him. "I've made that apple tart that you favor, my lord. I'll send tea up to you and his lordship soon."

"Thank you, Cook. When I become the Earl of Martindale someday, I may try to steal you away from Viscount Tilsbury."

She laughed heartily. "There'll be no stealing, my young lord. Now, behave yourself and go upstairs."

He came across the butler and greeted him before heading to

the study, where he knew he would find his friend. Rapping upon the door, he heard, "Come."

Perry entered the study and found Lord Tilsbury behind his desk, poring over a newspaper.

He took a seat in front of the desk, and asked, "What is the news today, my lord?"

Tilsbury looked grim. "Since we recently entered this war with Bonaparte, I fear the news will grow far worse before it ever gets better. The Little Corporal has a vision to dominate Europe. The papers report that he is preparing to invade England."

A tiny bit of alarm rippled through him. "You do not think Bonaparte would succeed with such an invasion, do you?"

"I certainly hope not. However, Britain will expend a plethora of resources and lose many good men in this upcoming fight. I see the storm raging across Europe, Perry. This war will last for many years. The cost we pay will be high."

Deciding it was time to test the waters and tell his friend what was on his mind, Perry cleared his throat. "I am toying with the idea of enlisting," he revealed.

Tilsbury cocked an eyebrow. "Enlisting? My boy, you are the only son to an earl. Your father would not grant you permission to go off to war."

Anger filled him. "I am of legal age, my lord. My father could not stop me even if he wanted to. Besides, what else am I going to do with my time?"

"Martindale will never pay for your commission."

Frustrated, he raked a hand through his hair. "I feel useless at Beauville. Mr. Rankin does a fine job running the estate without my help. In truth, I am floundering. I want to take a more active role in Beauville's management, but that is not something my father is eager for me to do. He may not care about Beauville and its tenants, but he refuses to relinquish any power to me. It forces me to be in a state of limbo."

"Are you truly that unhappy, Perry? So much that you would risk your life?"

Resolve filled him. "I am, my lord. And I do have a great sense of duty and loyalty to my country. England will need good men in this fight against Bonaparte. I might as well offer up and be one of them."

Tilsbury studied him a moment. "Promise me that you will not enlist. That if you truly believe that you are destined for the military, you will come to me. I will purchase your commission."

Knowing how expensive commissions could be, Perry shook his head. "I cannot ask for you to do that for me, my lord."

"You are a gentleman, Perry. The son of a peer. If you decide to go into the army, you should enter as an officer. I will provide the necessary funds if that is your final decision."

When he started to protest, Tilsbury said, "We shall call it a loan. Your father will not last forever. You will be the Earl of Martindale one day, and you could repay the loan when you come into your title."

Astonishment filled him, followed by a tenderness he felt for this man, who had just turned sixty years of age. In the past year, Lord Tilsbury had been more a father to him than his own had.

"Let me think on it, and then I will give you my answer."

"Swear to me that you will not act rashly. That you will speak to your father before you make any kind of commitment."

He snorted. "That will mean a trip to town. My parents are so rarely at Beauville. I will take heed and let you know of my decision, my lord."

Tilsbury rose. "Then let us go into tea. I hear Cook has made your favorite today."

Perry accompanied his friend to the drawing room, where the teacart was rolled in. They enjoyed an hour together, discussing the Battle of Thermopylae. It seemed every time they came together, they talked of some battle from history. He had always been a fine student, excelling in history and mathematics, and these afternoons spent in the older man's company meant a great deal to him.

He bid the viscount farewell and rode the three miles back to

Beauville.

When he entered the house, Foster came toward him. By the look on the butler's face, Perry knew it could only mean one thing.

His father had returned unexpectedly to his country seat.

"My lord, Lord Martindale is in his study. He asked to see you as soon as you arrived."

"Thank you, Foster. He didn't happen to mention why he has made a trip to the country, did he? After all, the Season is in full swing."

Foster looked apologetically at him. "He did not, my lord."

Making his way to his father's study, Perry tried to prepare himself for their encounter. It seemed each time he and his father spoke, the words grew harsh, and they parted on uncertain terms. Most likely, this time would not be an exception.

He knocked on the study's door and heard his father call for him to come in. Perry entered the room, one which he never went into out of respect. Not that his father had ever shown him any respect in return, but Perry tried to remain a dutiful son all the same.

"Sit," his father commanded.

He did as asked, waiting patiently to see what the topic of conversation might be. His father continued writing on paper for the next several minutes, acting as if his son were not present. It was a ploy his father often used, summoning his son and then making him wait, as if everything else in the world were more important. The one thing Perry had sworn to himself was when he had sons of his own one day, he would never ignore them, or make them feel small and insignificant. He would show them love, something he himself had never received.

Finally, the earl set down the quill. "I hear you have been visiting with Tilsbury this afternoon. What is the old goat up to?"

He wanted to point out that there were only a handful of years difference in the two men's ages, but he thought his father baited him—and he refused to bite.

"Yes, I had tea with our neighbor. Lord Tilsbury is in good health and was in good spirits when I left him."

"Why do you bother to spend so much time with him, Peregrine? Oh, I know the two of you yammer about history, but you should be with those your own age."

Here it came. Another lecture about him coming to town.

"You are a young man of one and twenty. You should be at the Season with your friends. Sowing your wild oats. Having the time of your life."

His father had never understood his son's nature. How Perry was a quiet man who enjoyed solitude. The earl did not share his son's love of the country nor his connection with the tenants at Beauville. His father had begun drinking and wenching his way through life during his university years—and had never stopped. Not even marriage had quelled his voracious appetite for women and drink. And apparently, he did not even recall how old his own son was, since Perry was three and twenty.

"I know that you and Mother enjoy the social whirl of the Season," he began. "I prefer life in the country, however."

"What the bloody hell do you do here all day, Peregrine?" his father demanded. "In town, you could be at White's with your friends. You could go to parties and balls. Attend the theater and the opera. There are numerous gaming halls. Why, you could even have a mistress. Or at least enjoy the sexual favors of a few women, if you do not want to be bound to one woman."

He was interested in none of those things. No matter what he said, though, his father would never understand that.

Perry decided the time had come and said, "You know Britain is at war now. They declared last month."

His father looked puzzled by the sudden turn of their conversation. "What of it?"

Summoning every bit of courage he possessed, he said, "I intend to enter the army to fight for king and country."

The earl gasped. "You will do no such thing!" he shouted. "You are my only son. My heir apparent. And what would your mother think of such nonsense?"

"Let me see," he mused. "What would Mother think? First, she would have to even remember that she has a son, much less one old enough to go away to war. Do you know I cannot even recall the last time I laid eyes on her? And when she is in residence at Beauville for brief spells, she never asks to see me. We never speak. Why, it has been years since we have held even the barest of conversations. You do not get to bring up Mother as a valid reason for me to remain in England."

His father snorted. "It is madness for you, my heir, to enter the army, Peregrine. Have you even considered that you might be killed?"

This was his chance. His father stood before him now. He would plead his case—and hope he was truly heard.

"Then help me to stay here, Father. Give me more responsibility at Beauville. I have lived here over a year since I graduated from university, and I still feel as if I have no purpose. Mr. Rankin does a fine job as our steward, but you hold all the cards. I have no authority. Relinquish some of it to me. Let me run Beauville as I see fit, especially since it will be mine one day. It should not matter to you. You are so rarely here, as it is."

"No," his father said emphatically. "That is simply not how things are done in this family. Why can't you be like I was and go to town? Enjoy your youth, Peregrine. Do not waste it, either buried in the country or fighting in some god-awful war. I came into my earldom at thirty years of age. I will continue to exercise full control until I am gone, just as my father and his father did before him."

His father's words let him know the only course of action available to him.

"Then I will return from war once you are dead and buried," he said bluntly. "I have no desire to tup every woman in the *ton* as you have done. You have been a terrible husband and an even worse father."

"How dare you speak to me in such a manner! You cannot

buy yourself a commission, you fool. They are far more expensive than you might believe."

With full confidence, he replied, "I already have the funds to do so. Our conversation now has helped me to make up my mind, Father. I will be leaving Beauville tomorrow. I would tell you that I would write to you and Mother, but neither of you have ever answered a single letter I have written to you over the years."

Perry rose, assured that he was making the right decision. "This is the last time we will speak, Father. The last time that we will ever see one another. I wish you the best."

Turning, he started toward the door, the earl berating him the entire way.

"You bloody ingrate!" his father shouted. "Go and get yourself killed. See if I care. You have always been such an odd duck. I have often wondered if you are even my blood since your mother has coupled with more men than I could ever count."

He shut the door behind him, the earl continuing to rage. Going upstairs to his bedchamber, he wrote a note to Lord Tilsbury, telling him that he had spoken with his father and decided leaving Beauville to serve in His Majesty's army was best for his future. He wrote that he would come to tell the viscount farewell tomorrow morning, and hopefully collect the promised funds he would need to purchase his commission.

Ringing for his valet, Perry waited until Grilley appeared, eyeing him with concern. All the servants must have heard the earl's tirade, and Grilley smiled sympathetically at Perry.

"Take this note to Lord Tilsbury at once." He paused. "I am leaving Beauville, Grilley. I will be purchasing a commission in the army. I can write a recommendation for you before I depart, though. You are incredibly good at what you do. It should be easy for you to obtain a position in another household."

The valet looked at him steadily. "I won't need one, my lord. I'll be coming with you. You'll need a batman." With that, the servant took the letter and left the room.

Perry took a seat in the chair by the window, looking out over the Beauville gardens. He would miss the serenity of this place terribly, but he could not languish any longer without a purpose in life. He would do his duty and serve England, hopefully contributing to ending the threat Bonaparte posed to its citizens.

He couldn't help but wonder, however, if he would ever see Beauville again.

CHAPTER ONE

Huntsworth, Surrey—August 1807

THE COACH TURNED up the lane, and excitement ran through Lady Drusilla Alington.

"Is it very far now?" she asked her brother.

Con, whose long legs were stretched out before him, his feet propped on the seat opposite them, smiled. "We should be at the main house in five minutes."

She couldn't wait to see her sister. Lucy had left Somerset last spring to make her come-out during the London Season, and she had wed the Marquess of Huntsberry in May. Lucy had written Dru about her marriage, saying that while she had been caught in a compromising position with Huntsberry, she was still pleased with the result. According to Lucy, she and Huntsberry were a love match.

Dru, a year younger than her sister and scheduled to make her own come-out next spring, couldn't fathom being wed, much less being in love. She had no interest in marriage or children and oftentimes, she preferred the company of animals to people. Still, she was thrilled that Lucy was so happy and eager to meet the marquess who loved Lucy so much.

"Are you relieved to have escaped seeing Mama?" her brother asked.

Lady Charlotte Alington was a most particular woman, one with firm opinions on any given topic and ready to share those opinions whether a person wished to hear them or not. Dru and Mama clashed often. Mama had a firm idea about how each of her children's lives should play out. While Con was her favorite, being the only male child, Mama paid little attention to Dru and Lucy—unless she was telling them what to do.

Thank goodness Lucy had finally escaped Mama's clutches. As a married woman and marchioness, Lucy actually outranked her own mother. She was free to make all her own decisions now, something Dru envied. It would be the only reason she would consider marriage, but she did not want to trade one jailer for another. Dru wanted to be free to come and go as she pleased. Pursue the things which interested her. Even wear what she wished, which usually meant breeches during the months Mama and Papa went to town for the Season. If she could find a husband who would grant her such freedom, only then would she contemplate marriage.

More than anything, Dru wanted to avoid being paraded about on the Marriage Mart next spring. She had no desire to wear new gowns and make small talk with people she did not know, with the goal of landing a husband. Mama's ideas of an eligible husband included one with a lofty title and a vast amount of wealth. She couldn't help but wonder what Huntsberry was like, and if Lucy had followed Mama's instructions to obtain a suitable groom. While Lucy had always been a good girl, meekly following Mama's instructions and advice, Dru had constantly quarreled with her mother whenever they were in the same room together. She couldn't imagine living with Mama for months, with a parade of suitors coming in and out, Mama evaluating which ones Dru should consider, and which ones should be discarded.

"What is Huntsberry like?" she asked. "Did he measure up to Mama's standards?"

Con chuckled. "Judson is quite wealthy, and you know he is a marquess, so that pleased Mama. He is an only child, however, so he does not have siblings who have married into other, socially acceptable families. You will learn when you make your own come-out next Season that social standing is a very important aspect when choosing a husband. Lucy is fortunate Judson compromised her, else Mama would most likely have seen to selecting a different husband."

"Well, she will not choose a husband for me," Dru declared. "I may not wed at all."

"Truly?" Con asked, removing his feet from the opposite bench. "Isn't that what all women want?"

"I have never wanted a husband. And the only babes I find the least bit tolerable are furry ones." She stroked Toby, who sat in her lap, and the cat began purring. "I simply cannot picture myself giving birth, much less caring for a babe."

"That is what a nursemaid and wet nurse are for," he said matter-of-factly. "They handle the daily things a babe requires. But some parents actually like their children. You will see when you watch Ariadne and Julian with Penelope."

Dru had met her cousin Ariadne years ago in town. For some unknown reason, the ten cousins had all been brought to London and introduced to one another. They had played together for a week and then went back to their homes. The Alingtons lived in Somerset in the west. The Worthingtons resided in Kent. The Fultons were far to the north in the Lake District. Of course, Uncle George had passed on just after that week in town, and his son had become the new Earl of Traywick. Dru wondered how ten-year-old Hadrian had felt, coming into his title at such a tender age after losing his father.

"I do look forward to seeing Ariadne again and meeting her husband and child."

"Julian might scare you upon first sight. He is a large man with an unusual background. He was not brought up in Polite Society."

"Ooh, I like him already."

"I am certain, given time, he would be happy to share his story with you. It is almost comical, though, to see a man of his size handle a babe so tenderly."

She frowned. "He holds his daughter?"

The thought seemed foreign to her. Dru and her siblings had rarely seen their parents when they were present at Marleyfield, and that did not count the spring and summer months Lord and Lady Marleyfield spent in town during the Season. The Alington children had been brought up mostly by their governess and tutor, along with various servants. Of course, Con had gone away to school and university, while she and Lucy had stayed home in Somerset.

"Julian is most unique. He spends time in the nursery and regularly brings Penelope to tea. She is the apple of his eye."

She laughed. "Can you picture Papa holding any of us, much less bouncing a babe on his knee while at tea?"

Her brother joined in her laughter, then he grew serious. "I think our generation will be different from that of our parents, Dru. Ariadne is the one who first brought it up with us. She also felt abandoned, as we did, every time her parents left the country for town and the Season. She deliberately brought Penelope to town with her this spring, and she and Julian have decided they will never leave their children at home. She has talked to Lucy, Val, and me about this. We have made a pact to, once we have wed and have children, to bring them with us to town each spring."

The idea stunned her—but she quite liked it.

"Ariadne regrets not having known all her cousins. She believes while the Season is known for its many social affairs, it is a time family can come together. Think of how different things might have been if we had come to town each spring and were able to see our cousins on a daily basis. That is what Ariadne wishes, to make up for the time we lost in our childhoods not knowing one another, and to allow our children to be brought up with their cousins, forming strong bonds of family and friendship."

"I think Ariadne is a very wise woman," Dru declared. "That is a marvelous idea."

"You will like her. Lucy and I do. And Julian and Judson have fast become good friends of mine." Con paused. "I only am sorry that Uncle Charles passed away last spring, preventing Lia and Tia from making their come-outs, and sending them and Val back to the country to mourn, along with Aunt Alice."

She knew Val was Con's closest friend. They were the only two of the ten cousins who had known one another since they went to school together. They had remained close throughout the years, even sharing rooms in university. With Uncle Charles' passing, Val had come into the ducal title.

"Did you know Aunt Agnes went to Millvale?" Con asked.

Her brother spoke of their uncle George's widow, mother to three of their cousins. "No. Why?"

"Apparently, she and Aunt Alice are very close friends and have always spent a great deal of time together each year during the Season. Aunt Agnes even sent for Verina and Justina, and they joined their mother in Kent. I am not certain how long they plan to stay, but I think it nice that Lia and Tia have spent time with two of their cousins, especially since they were so disappointed in not being able to make their come-outs."

Con paused, glancing out the window. "We are here."

"I am afraid you must go inside your basket, Toby," she told the tabby, removing him from her lap and slipping him into the basket before closing the lid. The cat wasn't friendly to anyone but her. He tolerated Lucy at times, but Toby hissed at anyone else who came near him. While she had to leave all her other animals at Marleyfield, it went without saying that Toby had to make the journey to Surrey with her.

Setting the basket on the seat beside her, Dru gazed out the window, seeing Ariadne's bright copper hair. All the Worthington siblings had varying shades of red hair. A tall man with dark hair and brows stood next to her, and Dru assumed it was Ariadne's husband, the Marquess of Aldridge. Her gaze turned to her sister, who smiled widely, waving at Dru. A muscular man, even taller than Lord Aldridge, had his arm about Lucy's waist. He was handsome, with dark brown hair, and as the vehicle stopped, even from the carriage, she could see his emerald eyes. This man had to be the Marquess of Huntsberry, her sister's new husband.

"Dru!" Lucy cried, slipping from her husband and running to the carriage.

The footman placed the set of stairs down and opened the carriage door. Con bounded out, handing Dru down, and she fell into her sister's arms.

"Oh, how I have missed you," Lucy told her.

"Not nearly as much as I have missed you." She kissed her sister's cheek and hugged her again.

Lucy stepped back, gesturing to her husband, who stepped forward. "Dru, this is my husband, Lord Huntsberry."

She saw the love her sister had for this man shining in her eyes, and immediately knew she would like him simply because he made Lucy happy.

Dru curtseyed. "My lord."

"Oh, none of that," Huntsberry proclaimed. "We are quite informal with family. I am Judson." He wrapped his arms about her and hugged her. "Lucy and I are delighted you agreed to come and stay with us."

"I am grateful for the invitation, Judson." It sounded odd to call a lord she had just met by his Christian name, but he was her host and family now, as well.

"Come here," Ariadne said, holding out her arms.

She greeted her cousin, who was even more beautiful than she had been as a child. "It is good to see you, Cousin Ariadne."

"This is Lord Aldridge, my husband," Ariadne said, pride in her voice and love in her eyes. "Call him Julian."

Dru saw it was true—both her sister and cousin had made love matches. She was happy for them.

Julian embraced her, as well. "Welcome to Surrey, Dru. And don't think you have to spend all your time at Huntsworth. Aldridge Manor is only but a couple of miles away. Ariadne and I hope you will come and stay with us a while, as well."

"Where is Penelope?" she asked, curious to see how he would

respond after what Con had told her.

The marquess' face lit up. "She is napping, else I would have brought her to meet you. In fact," he said, turning to his wife, "we should have Dru over for tea tomorrow. That way, she can see our estate and meet her little cousin."

"Speaking of tea," Lucy said. "Why don't you all come inside for some?"

"I asked Mrs. Worth to have us served on the terrace, love," Judson said.

Dru caught the endearment, as well as the tone her brother-in-law used in addressing Lucy. She saw her sister smile at her husband. Any doubts she'd had about their sudden union were totally dispelled. They were obviously deeply in love.

"Do you wish to freshen up a bit?" Lucy asked. "I will have Annie unpack your things while we are at tea. Come, let me take you to your room first. Ariadne, if you will see everyone to the terrace?"

"Of course, Lucy," their cousin replied.

She accompanied her sister upstairs. Lucy took her to a large bedchamber done in shades of the palest green, with accents of daffodil yellow.

"This is beautiful," she said, seeing her trunk already sitting at the foot of the large bed. She also saw Toby's basket and heard his low growls. Opening the basket, the cat sprang from it and curled up on the bed next to the pillows.

Taking Lucy's hands, she added, "I am so happy for you. I have never seen you so relaxed and joyful."

Her sister grinned. "Marriage to Judson suits me." She paused. "In fact, I wanted to tell you while we are alone that I am expecting a babe."

"Oh, Lucy!" she cried, hugging her sister tightly. "That is marvelous news."

"I wanted you to know before anyone else. Now that you do, I will tell the others at tea." She placed her hands on her belly. "This is something I have always wanted, even more so now that

I am wed to Judson. I always wanted to be a mother, but now I am blessed to have Judson as my husband and father to our children. He is such a good man, Dru. He understands me so well. Our love grows daily."

Taking Lucy's hands in hers, she said, "I am thankful you found one another. I wasn't quite sure what to think after reading that first letter regarding how you came to be engaged, but now that I see the two of you together, it is obvious how much you love one another."

"He treats me as an equal," Lucy said. "I never thought I would have such a marriage. Mama constantly told me what to do. I was so ready to break free and decide the path I wished to travel. With Judson, I have the perfect companion." She hugged Dru again. "And it means the world to me to have you here with us. Ask Judson, he will tell you. You are welcome to stay until next spring. I see no reason for you to travel so far back to Somerset and be under Mama's heavy thumb. Besides, you will want to also go to Aldridge Manor and spend time with Ariadne, Julian, and Penelope, as Julian suggested."

"If it does not put anyone out, I would enjoy staying." She hesitated. "Now, whether that means I leave here and go to town for my come-out, that is another matter."

Lucy looked at her with concern. "Are you still unwilling to do so?"

"Frankly, I do not see the point in any of it. I think all the balls and parties would bore me. I am not interested in finding a husband. Of course, Mama and Papa are ready to cast me from the nest and make me someone else's responsibility, as well as better their own social standing with my advantageous marriage."

"You do not have to decide anything now," Lucy advised. "If you decide the Season is not for you, I will do everything in my power to make Mama understand that."

Tears misted her eyes. "You would do that for me? Take on Mama's wrath?"

Her sister grinned. "I am quite daring these days. Just ask Judson. If Mama wants to wash her hands of you, I assure you that you will always have a home with Judson and me."

"I would never wish to impose—"

"You are my sister, Dru. Judson is eager to get to know you. He had no siblings, so he plans on making you his unofficial sister, whether you agree to it or not."

They both laughed.

"Oh, Lucy, you seem so lighthearted now. Marriage does suit you, as will motherhood."

"Take a few moments for yourself," her sister said. "I will wait for you at the bottom of the stairs."

"I won't be long," she promised as Lucy left the bedchamber.

She appreciated the fact that Lucy remembered how Dru liked to be alone when she relieved herself. She retrieved the chamber pot and quickly did her business, washing her hands with the fresh water in the basin. She checked herself in the mirror and saw all her pins were in place.

A knock sounded on the door, and she crossed the room to answer it, finding Annie there.

"It is good to see you again, Annie," she told the maid.

"Likewise, my lady. Your sister is so excited that you accepted her invitation to come to Huntsworth. I will be taking care of you during your stay. Doing your hair. Attending to your clothes. Your personal needs. Be sure to ask me for whatever you might wish."

"I will do so, Annie. Thank you."

She exited the room, returning the way she and Lucy had come, and went to the staircase, quickly descending the stairs. Her sister waited at the bottom, and Lucy slipped her arm through Dru's.

"Let us go enjoy our outdoor tea," Lucy said, taking Dru through a set of open French doors and onto the terrace, where a lovely tea had been laid out.

The rest of the afternoon passed quickly. She found Judson

and Julian both charming and friendly. Con entertained them with stories of the Season and the various mamas who had hoped he would end his bachelorhood and take on the shackles of marriage. Dru already knew that Con—and Val—had vowed not to wed until they came into their titles. Since Val was now the Duke of Millbrooke, she wondered if her cousin would be perusing the Marriage Mart next spring.

Ariadne and Julian left, and Dru spent the next hours with her sister and brother-in-law. The pair was quite open with their affection, which she knew would flabbergast her mother. Still, by the end of day when they said their goodnights, Dru was satisfied that Lucy had wed the man she was meant to be with.

As she crawled into her bed and snuggled beneath the bedclothes, Toby curled beside her, Dru couldn't wait to enjoy the freedom that would be hers for the next several months. She banished all thoughts of Mama and being pressed to make her come-out next spring, deciding she would enjoy each day, one at a time, and treasure this special time in her life.

CHAPTER TWO

T HE SCREAM WOKE Perry. Quickly, he buried his face into the pillow, which absorbed much of the noise. He got control of himself and rolled back over, sweat pouring from his body. At the same time, he shivered from a chill. He glanced about, not even knowing where he might be. Then it struck him.

He was at Beauville. Finally.

The darkness frightened him, so he rose from the floor where he'd slept and went to the windows, throwing back the curtains. At least this allowed in a little moonlight. This time of year, the sun rose early. He would leave the curtains open and welcome the light.

Padding barefoot across the room, he retrieved the pillow, placing it back on the bed, along with the top layer of bedclothes which lay bunched on the floor. When he had arrived late last night, all he had wanted to do was escape into sleep. He had headed for his old bedchamber, but Foster stopped him, taking Perry to the earl's rooms instead. They had not known when to expect him, only that he would arrive at some point now that the former Earl of Martindale was dead and buried.

Perry pulled the bedclothes up to his chin, trying to get the shivers to subside. He doubted sleep would come again.

He let his mind drift, thinking of the letter he had received from his mother, the first time she had ever written to him. It had been succinct, informing him that he was now the earl and that he should return to England with all due haste and take up his duties. Typical of her, she gave no details of how his father had died or when and where the death had occurred. He had notified his commanding officer of Martindale's passing and his intention to sneak out as quickly as possible. Having risen through the ranks quickly over the last four years and being a major stream-lined the process.

Perry had gone straight from the battlefield to Surrey. Though he had docked in London, he hadn't spent any time in the city. He supposed he could have gone to visit his mother while there, knowing she would still be in town because the Season had recently ended, and she had never been one to rush home after its conclusion. Most women would have taken a year to mourn a husband's loss, yet he doubted she had paused for any longer than a few seconds. He had learned through gossip at school just how promiscuous each of his parents were. While his father had mostly ignored his son, his mother had pretended he did not even exist. He felt no loyalty to her and assumed the marriage settlements signed at the beginning of his parents' union would now provide for her. As far as Perry was concerned, he didn't care if he ever saw her again.

He thought back to what a foolish lad he had been. He might have been book smart, but he was naive in the ways of the world, marching off to war full of idealism. He couldn't recall now why he had been so adamant to leave Beauville. Yes, he thought many things needed to be addressed to improve the property. He felt he had been cut adrift after graduating from university. The Beauville steward did the best he could in managing the estate without much support from his employer. Perry had wanted to make changes that both he and Rankin believed to be necessary for Beauville to thrive, yet neither of them had much authority to do so. He had thought by threatening to go off to war that his father, who cared not one whit for his country estate and its tenants, might cede a small portion of his authority and funds to allow Perry to make changes to better Beauville and help it to prosper.

Instead, his stubborn father had called his son's bluff and practically shoved him out the door. Oh, he had wanted to go to war. Wanted to make a difference. Felt the obligation to fight for his country. But the reality of war was far different from anything he'd ever encountered. There had never been a time he led his men into battle that he was not utterly terrified. He supposed he should go on the stage because he had masked his terror, acting the role of a brave officer.

Time after time, he had taken men into battle, seeing them fall all about him. hearing their gasps of pain. Their cries calling for their mothers and other loved ones. The stench of death surrounding him until it nearly drove him mad.

Some men could not handle the horrors of war. They froze on the battlefield—or worse—they fled. Perry had seen many an officer berate soldiers who had remained paralyzed on the battlefield, belittling them so they had no confidence. He had also witnessed soldiers rounding up men who had run, enacting court martials and sending these terrified, broken men to prison.

He had never spoken a harsh word to any man under his command. Ironically, Perry gained a respected reputation, even being known as Beaumont the Bountiful, because of his generosity with the men under his command. Others clamored to be assigned to his units, and even those who were the weakest of soldiers proved to be the strongest ones, putting their lives on the line, time and time again, not for Britain.

For him.

And because of that, he carried heavy guilt for each death that occurred under his leadership.

He pillowed his hands behind his head, knowing sleep was impossible. He only hoped no one had heard his cries of anguish. Nightmares were common amongst so many of the men who had fought. Knowing he was the only family member in residence, though, he doubted anyone was in this wing of the house in the dead of night.

Throughout his years at war, Perry had yearned for the tranquility of Beauville. War had been ugly. Brutal. He often questioned why he had joined the army and given up the solace of his childhood home. He knew now to cherish every moment of life, especially at a peaceful place such as Beauville.

Being the new Earl of Martindale not only gave him access to great wealth and authority, it also reminded him that he would need to provide an heir. Perry had never attended the Season, finding the idea of all the social affairs to be a waste of his time. Now, he would need to do so next spring so that he might peruse the Marriage Mart for a bride. Once he had done so, though, he intended never to go to town again. Beauville would be his refuge, a place he would gather strength.

Or would he have to go to town to find his countess? Surely, there must be some eligible young ladies in the neighborhood whom he might consider suitable for marriage.

He thought of his closest neighbor, Viscount Tilsbury. They had corresponded throughout his time in the army, and the last letter he had written to his friend had told of him selling his commission and heading home. He would call upon Lord Tilsbury soon, and his first act when he had returned to Beauville last night had been to send a message to his friend, along with the proceeds from the sale of his commission.

But who else lived in the area?

Perry recalled on the other side of Alderton, the nearby village, lay Aldridge Manor. The Marquess of Aldridge had wed several times, trying to get his heir. The last Perry knew, it was a third marriage which had proved unsuccessful in securing children. That meant no daughters of the house whom he might consider for marriage.

Adjacent to Aldridge's estate lay the lands of the Marquess of Huntsberry. Lord Huntsberry, who was close in age to Perry, had come into his title as a child. They had attended different public schools, though. In fact, he had known that Huntsberry attended Cambridge, as Perry himself had done, yet he had never laid eyes upon him during those university years. Where Perry had come home to Surrey and the land, Huntsberry never visited Huntsworth and remained in town exclusively. Even if Huntsberry had wed and sired a daughter during the years Perry was at war, she would be far too young to become Perry's countess.

He could not recall anyone else in the neighborhood but would explore the possibility of finding his wife close by because the thought of going to town and being around hundreds of others, forced to make small talk, made him ill.

Dawn finally came, light slowly seeping into this bedchamber, warming the room. He rang for Grilley, whom he had instructed to have bathwater brought up first thing this morning. Perry had been too tired to bathe last night. Oh, it would be such a luxury, sinking into a tub of hot water and scrubbing away all memories of the war. He could not recall the last time he had sat in a tub.

Grilley arrived, Perry's uniform draped over his arm. The valet said, "Hot water is on the way, my lord. I washed your shirt and breeches. Ironed both. I also brushed your coat. This will give you something to wear today. You'll need to visit the village tailor as soon as possible, though, for civilian clothes."

"I doubt fashion for men has changed so much that I cannot wear clothes I left in my wardrobe, Grilley," he teased.

An odd expression crossed the valet's face. "You no longer have any clothing here, my lord," Grilley said apologetically.

"I must," he insisted. "I left a good number of—" His voice trailed off. Without being told, Perry realized his father had expunged all signs of his son from Beauville.

Stoically, he said, "I will dress in my officer's uniform then. After breakfast, I shall ride into Alderton and see the tailor."

Grilley looked relieved in not having to explain the situation further.

Servants appeared with buckets of water. When the tub was full, Perry sank into it, his thoughts idly drifting. Grilley gave him a few minutes of solitude, and then the valet scrubbed him from head to toe. He stood and allowed Grilley to rinse the soap from him, the water sluicing down his body.

He appeared at breakfast in his uniform, and Foster asked, "What would you like for breakfast this morning, my lord?"

It startled him to think he had a choice in what to eat, much less that he could name whatever he wished, and it would appear upon his plate. He would need to work hard to erase the unpleasant years of army life.

"I will start with plenty of strong coffee. Three eggs and a rasher of bacon. Toast. With marmalade. That will do for now."

"Yes, my lord," the butler said, disappearing from the breakfast room to convey the order to Cook.

More than anything, he looked forward to drinking good coffee and tea. The ersatz coffee had never satisfied him, while the tea had been incredibly weak, the leaves used over and over until the water barely tasted of anything.

Foster returned with newspapers in hand. "If you would like to peruse these, my lord." The butler set them on the table.

Perry had always enjoyed reading, especially the newspapers, seeing what bills were being passed in Parliament and what went on throughout the country and Europe. He had not picked up a single newspaper since he had left Beauville and now almost dreaded what he might read about the war. After four years, he understood the fighting would go far longer than any British politician or the War Office predicted.

While waiting for his breakfast to arrive, he skimmed several articles, surprised at how much of the paper was dedicated to gossip from the Season. It amazed him how men and women could be dancing in ballrooms while their fellow countrymen were felled by bullets and sabers, not to mention diseases such as dysentery. At least Perry had returned home intact. Too many soldiers lost eyes. Arms. Legs. Many others never returned at all.

His meal arrived, and he ate with gusto. He would never again take for granted the availability and taste of good food. Once he finished eating, he went to the kitchens and found Cook. She looked startled by his appearance.

"I must thank you for the best breakfast of my life, Cook," he declared. "After four years at war, I look forward to dining upon more of your wonderful meals."

The old woman's wariness evaporated, and she broke out into a smile. "Do you still have the same favorites, my lord? You used to favor roast chicken and duck for special occasions."

"Food is scarce during a war, Cook. I will be happy to eat whatever you place before me, including roast chicken and duck."

"I understand, my lord," she said quietly. "If you think of anything you would care for me to prepare, only send word. I will be happy to make it for you."

"I know I will want fresh bread daily," he told her, thinking how that had been a luxury on the battlefield. The bread he did eat was usually moldy or infested with bugs and without fail, harder than a rock. "Perhaps a sweet or two every now and then, as well."

"It will be blueberry scones at tea this afternoon, my lord," Cook promised.

He salivated. "I eagerly look forward to those scones."

Perry went to the stables, finding only two horses there. He assumed the earl's coach and team were in town with his mother. That would be something he would eventually have retrieved. She could take a hansom cab to her various appointments and assignations. One horse he recognized as one Rankin had ridden regularly during the year before Perry had gone off to war. The other mount was new to him, and he supposed it would become his horse to get about the estate. He would need to meet with his steward soon, but he decided going into town and speaking with the tailor would be a much better use of his time. He may have worn his major's uniform with pride in the past, but Perry wanted nothing to do with it now. The sooner he could have a small wardrobe made up for him, the better.

Then he would burn the scarlet jacket and never look back.

A groom saddled the horse for him, calling it Zeus, and Perry rode into Alderton. The day was already a beautiful one, not a cloud in the sky. The fact that the only sounds he heard were birds singing with no firing of cannon made it a day in which to rejoice.

As he reached the outskirts of town, he came to the church and its graveyard. He decided to see if his father might be buried in the Beaumont section. Tying his horse to a low tree branch, he wandered through the graveyard until he came to his family's plots, finding the stone bearing his father's name and his birth and death dates. He stared at the last date, feeling nothing.

"Good morning, my lord," a voice called.

He turned, seeing a man dressed as a vicar approaching. Part of being an earl, in Perry's opinion, was being kind to others, and he would begin with this fellow.

"Good morning," he replied in return. "I am Martindale." He offered his hand.

"And I am Mr. Harper. I came to Alderton as vicar two years ago." He paused. "I see you are visiting your father's grave. Forgive me if I interrupted you at prayer."

Perry had prayed mightily during the war, never knowing if God heard his prayers. After what he had seen, he wasn't even certain he believed that God existed.

"No worries, Mr. Harper. I merely stopped on my way to town to pay my respects."

"I am sorry for your loss, my lord." Looking hopeful, the vicar added, "It would be lovely to see you in church tomorrow, Lord Martindale. Your father was so rarely in the country. In fact, I only met him once."

"I am not one for town life. I will spend a majority of my time at Beauville."

He wouldn't volunteer any funds now, but he knew it was up to titled noblemen such as himself to make certain he generously donated to the local church. Once he met with his solicitor, he would have a better idea of how much of a fortune he possessed. Then he would address the changes necessary at Beauville, as well as supporting the community about him.

A moment of worry struck him, knowing his father liked to gamble. What if the previous earl had lost all the estate's wealth? He told himself not to borrow trouble, at least until after he had met with his solicitor.

"Then I look forward to seeing you tomorrow, my lord."

The vicar left, and Perry returned to Zeus, riding the short way to the tailor's shop. He entered, spying Mr. Billings.

"My lord, it is so good to see you again back in Surrey, safe and sound."

"I am happy to be on English soil again, Mr. Billings. I find I am in need of a new wardrobe."

He saw the tailor assessing him. Not wanting to be gossiped about, he said, "My former clothing no longer fits me. I suppose my frame has changed during my years at war."

"Of course," Billings said. "Then we shall measure you. I will keep those measurements on file, my lord."

He spent a half-hour with the tailor, discussing his needs. For now, he could do with a smaller wardrobe since he planned to remain in the country, but he needed everything, from shirts to trousers to waistcoats and coats. Billings assured him he could handle most of his wardrobe needs, save for new boots and hats. While he could wear the Hessians he now had on as he traipsed about the land, he would need nicer boots not battered by war, as well as shoes and even a pair of slippers for the evenings.

"Come back in three days' time, my lord," the tailor told him. "I will have a few things made up for you by then. It will take another couple of weeks to complete everything."

"Add a greatcoat to the list," he suggested. "No need to work on it now, but I do want to be prepared for when winter comes. I plan to be out on my estate a great deal and wish to be warm on the chilliest of days. Thank you, Mr. Billings. I look forward to dressing as a civilian."

He stopped in at the shoemaker's, being sized for boots and shoes, and then thought to call at the milliner's, where he placed an order for two hats.

By now, it was past noon. He was famished, despite the breakfast he had eaten only a few hours ago. As a soldier, he had put aside hunger pangs, but now he was back in England, he swore never to go hungry again. He decided to stop at the local bakery, which also served as a sweet shop. If Mrs. Cadmann still ran it, he knew everything would be of good quality.

Entering the shop, he saw her, greeting her by name.

"Oh, Lord Martindale, how good it is to see you again!" she exclaimed.

He inhaled deeply. "Ah, the smell of your bakery was a favorite of mine as a boy. Things have not changed. Might I have some fresh bread with butter and a cup of tea, Mrs. Cadmann?"

"Coming right up, my lord," she said, beaming at him. "Have a seat. I'll bring the bread and crock of butter. A bit of jam, too, just in case you might favor some."

Perry took a seat. Minutes later, he was filled with contentment, sipping a strong cup of tea and trying not to gobble down his bread. He told himself to savor it. To never be in a rush again. No one was chasing him across a battlefield, bearing down on him, trying to snatch his life.

The door opened, and a woman with copper hair entered. Mrs. Cadmann greeted her.

"Good afternoon, Lady Aldridge. It's lovely to see you."

He did not recognize the woman, which meant Aldridge had wed again, hoping to sire his heir. This wife was far prettier than the previous Lady Aldridges had been, though.

"I have my husband with me. Lord and Lady Huntsberry, as well. And my cousin has come to stay at Huntsworth for an extended visit. They are finishing up some shopping. I said I would come ahead and order tea and cake for all of us."

"I will prepare it now, my lady. Any special cake?"

"I think your spiced cinnamon cake this time for us all."

"Coming right up, my lady."

She turned, spying him, and came over straightaway.

"You must be Lord Martindale. I am Lady Aldridge. My condolences on the death of your father."

"We were estranged," he said bluntly, not really caring to talk with another of Aldridge's wives.

"I know you have been at war for several years. Thank you for your service."

Her tone was genuine, and Perry regretted being harsh with her, recalling how he wished to be kind to all as the new earl.

Softening his tone, he replied, "I appreciate hearing that, my lady."

"My husband will be here soon, as will my two cousins and Lord Huntsberry. Would you please join us so we might welcome you back to the neighborhood?"

It would be churlish to turn down her kind offer, so he nodded. "I would be happy to do so, my lady."

The door opened, and two women stepped through it. Both had beautiful, tawny hair and even from where he sat, he noted their unusual amethyst eyes. They looked close in age and were obviously sisters, the cousins Lady Aldridge had referred to.

He rose to greet them, seeing two men following them into the bakery. Neither was the Lord Aldridge he had known from his youth, and Perry realized another death had occurred in the community, and a new Lord Aldridge had taken his title.

"Everyone, this is Lord Martindale from Beauville," Lady Aldridge said. "My cousin, Lady Huntsberry, and her sister, Lady Drusilla Alington. And Lord Huntsberry and my husband."

Perry saw the fond look she bestowed upon her spouse as she spoke.

He looked to Lady Huntsberry first. "A pleasure to meet you, my lady." He took the hand she offered. Turning to the other woman, he said, "And I am delighted to meet you, as well, Lady Drusilla."

This time, the gloved hand he squeezed gave him a different feeling altogether. His gaze met Lady Drusilla's. Her lips parted a moment. Then she smiled radiantly at him.

"It is so nice to meet you, my lord," she said. "You look quite impressive in your officer's uniform. I hope you might share with us a few stories about your time at war."

Immediately, he released her hand. "I will never speak of the war, my lady," he said adamantly. "It is in my past. I am only interested in the present—and the future."

He turned abruptly from her, speaking to the two gentlemen.

"Why don't we all sit?" Lady Huntsberry requested.

Perry found himself next to Lady Drusilla. As Mrs. Cadmann brought out a tray with slices of cake and distributed them, Lady Drusilla gently touched his forearm. Her touch brought a shiver which raced through him. He had never had a reaction to any woman before, much less one so strong.

"I apologize for upsetting you, my lord," she said quietly. "I must admit that I am a curious sort. I have spent my entire life in the country and have yet to even make my come-out." Her nose wrinkled. "I merely wanted to hear about your experiences because I follow the war in the newspapers. I realize it was wrong of me now to press you about such personal matters. I will think before I speak so rashly in the future."

He warmed to her, not just because of her words, but because of her mesmerizing eyes.

"It was not a pleasant time in my life, my lady," he told her. "I doubt I could repeat anything that happened to me without causing you dismay."

"Let me make it up to you," she said. Looking to her sister, Lady Drusilla asked, "Might we ask Lord Martindale to tea tomorrow, Lucy?"

"Since tomorrow is Sunday, why don't we make it the day after, my lord," Lady Huntsberry said.

Though Perry had thought he would relish solitude and not wish to interact with others now that he'd come home to Beauville, he found himself suddenly hungry for company. Even friendship.

And he wanted to know more about the intriguing Lady Drusilla.

"I happily accept your invitation, my lady," he replied.

Then he glanced at Lady Drusilla. She smiled at him, causing his heart to beat faster. Perhaps he wouldn't have to scour the neighborhood or go to London for the Season.

Because he might have found the woman who would make a perfect Countess of Martindale in Alderton's bakery.

CHAPTER THREE

ANNIE FINISHED HELPING Dru dress, and she thanked the maid before petting Toby, who lay curled on the bed, and heading to the breakfast room. Already, her stay at Huntsworth had been interesting. Lucy had given her a tour of the house, which was even larger than Marleyfield, proudly showing off some of the decorating changes she had made. Naturally, Lucy's favorite part of the house was the nursery on the top floor of the house. They had talked about things the babe would need, and Ariadne had said she could help in any way since she had learned so much about infants after Penelope's birth.

Penelope was a delight. Lucy and Judson had taken Dru to Aldridge Manor for tea. While she thought the house and estate beautiful, she had lost her heart to the tiny girl. Penelope had tufts of red hair, a softer shade than her mother's copper locks, and round, blue eyes, reminiscent of her father's. Though Dru had never been much interested in children and had never been around babes, other than for short visits to their tenants when she accompanied Lucy, Penelope was different. She would be six months soon, but she already was alert and loved to smile. She also had two teeth on the bottom and one on top. Gnawing on fingers was one of her favorite pastimes.

Still, one babe did not change Dru's mind about marriage. She could not see herself with a husband. She had never liked being told what to do, especially by Mama, and trading Mama for a husband did not seem like a wise decision. Dru valued independence more than anything. She told herself it wasn't necessary she have babes of her own. She could be the doting aunt to Lucy and Con's children. To her cousins' children, too.

Judson had taken her for a long ride about Huntsworth. The estate was vast and took several hours to ride. He introduced Dru to some of his tenants, and she saw the crops in the field and livestock grazing. Her brother-in-law was very intelligent and wanted to please Lucy in every way. He assured Dru that she was welcome to stay at Huntsworth as long as she pleased, even until next spring when she was supposed to make her come-out. She wondered how she was going to get out of doing so. The idea of dancing until the wee hours of the morning night after night seemed rather boring. While Dru did enjoy dancing, she did not think she would like all the courting that went with it.

"Good morning," she told Lucy as she entered the breakfast room, going straight to the buffet and filling her plate. She had always had a healthy appetite and was so active, she could eat whatever she pleased without consequences.

Settling into a seat to Lucy's left, she thanked the footman for bringing her tea, and then asked her sister, "Have you heard from Mama?"

"No." Her sister took a sip of tea. "Then again, I am not expecting to. I believe she said she and Papa were staying in town until the end of the month before they returned to Marleyfield."

"What about Con?"

After her brother had escorted her from Somerset to Surrey, he had returned to town.

"I assume he will stay in town for a bit," Lucy said. "He enjoys being there. Of course, with Val no longer his constant companion, he might go to Kent to see Val there."

"I always envied Con and Val being such close friends," she said. "They got to spend all those years together at school and university, and then they enjoyed being bachelors in town."

Lucy signaled for more tea. "Those days are over for Val,

with him now being the Duke of Millbrooke. Sons are not prevalent in our families. Val is the only boy of four. Con is the boy to our two. And Hadrian also has two sisters. If Val is going to get his heir and spare, he needs to wed and start his family."

"I hate that. It sounds so practical."

Her sister laughed. "I thought you liked practical. You have never been a whimsical female, Dru."

"And I never will be." Turning the conversation to a new topic, she said, "I really do like Judson."

Lucy's face grew dreamy. "Isn't he marvelous? He is the best husband I could have asked for, and I know he will be a wonderful father."

She had seen the interaction between the pair and knew for certain they were a love match for the ages. Ariadne and Julian were also most affectionate. While she was happy for her sister and cousin, she could never picture herself so enamored with a man.

Then thoughts of Lord Martindale invaded her mind.

The earl was certainly handsome, with his thick, blond hair and moss green eyes. She was tall for a female, but he was a good half-foot taller than she, with a long, lean frame.

Why on earth was she mooning over Martindale?

She had learned from talk at tea that he was a quiet sort. Though an only son, he had entered the army shortly after Great Britain declared war against Bonaparte. Intuitively, she knew the war had affected him harshly. It wasn't merely that he did not wish to speak about it. It was the way he said it. Something in his eyes told Dru he'd had a rough time of things. She supposed that was what living daily with men butchering other men would do to a soul.

Even though she had no intentions of wedding, she did wish to get to know Martindale a bit better. He had looked so vulnerable. She decided she would make a friend of him. Not that ladies and gentlemen were ever friends, but then Dru was no typical lady. If today were not one where they would attend church, she would be in her usual breeches. The thought made her glad she was not Catholic and having to confess her sins to a priest. Mama and Papa had no idea their daughter roamed the countryside alone in male attire while they were gone, much less that she had brought breeches with her for her visit with Lucy and Judson.

Her brother-in-law entered the breakfast room, bending to kiss his wife's cheek. His hand went to Lucy's belly, cradling it a moment. Dru couldn't see a difference in her sister, other than she glowed a bit, which Dru chalked up to Lucy being in love.

"Good morning to you both," Judson said cheerfully, helping himself to the food on the sideboard. "Anything planned other than church today?"

"Not that I can think of," Lucy said.

Dru caught the wolfish look Judson gave his wife and decided that the couple would be occupied this afternoon in their bedchamber. Lucy had admitted to her that she and Judson shared a bed each night, which Dru thought outlandish. Of course, she only had her parents to judge by, but she could no more see Mama and Papa sleeping together than she could see men walking on the moon. Lucy had told her it was an unusual practice, and that Ariadne and Julian did the same.

That would be another reason never to wed. It would be bad enough having to submit physically to a man, much less have him in her bed all night. To Dru, her bed was her sanctuary. She loved lying in it, reading, playing with Toby, even daydreaming. A husband would not be welcome in it.

They finished their breakfast, and Annie fetched bonnets for them before they climbed into the carriage.

"We walked to church last week because the day was nice," Lucy said. "Now that I am increasing, Judson says we will drive."

"I think walking would be good for you, Lucy," Dru pointed out, eager to test her theory that even men in love ordered their wives about.

"I do enjoy walking," Lucy said. "And it is not as if my belly is swollen and interfering with me walking."

Immediately, Judson rapped his cane against the ceiling in the carriage, and it began to slow.

"We will walk if that is what you wish, love," he said, such tenderness in his eyes that it gave Dru goosebumps.

"The day is warm," Lucy told her husband. "I would not want to arrive at church with a flushed face, perspiring."

A footman opened the door. "Do you need something, my lord?"

"No. Have the coachman continue on," Judson said.

The vehicle started up again, and Dru decided she was quite impressed. Lucy had said Judson looked upon her as an equal. She should have known that because he doted on his wife, he would do whatever she asked. She thought Judson unique, which was another reason she did not want a husband. Lucy and Ariadne had swept up two unusual, kind, thoughtful men. Dru doubted any more like them would be available for years to come. Even though she loved her brother, she did not see Con behaving this way with a woman.

Then again, she had never seen her brother in love.

They reached the village and climbed from the carriage. Entering the church, she saw it was filling. Judson led them to the front, where two full pews remained almost empty, save for Ariadne and Julian and an older gentleman sitting in the first one. She knew the practice of reserving plum spots in a church for titled gentlemen in the area and wondered if Lord Martindale might make an appearance this morning.

Drat! There she went again, her thoughts drifting to the handsome earl. She shouldn't call him handsome. That made her feel weak, and if anything, she was a strong-willed woman.

Judson indicated the second pew, and Dru went in first, followed by Lucy and then Judson. Ariadne and Julian turned to greet them.

Her cousin said, "This is Viscount Tilsbury. Lord Tilsbury,

this is Lady Drusilla Alington, my cousin, and Lady Huntsberry's sister."

The viscount, whose hair was as white as snow, gave her a welcoming smile. "Lady Drusilla, it is lovely to meet you. I hear you are from Somerset. So was my late wife."

He looked so sad, Dru wanted to wrap her arms about him in comfort.

"It is so nice to meet you, my lord. I am sorry you lost your wife. Where in Somerset did she reside?"

"Near Glastonbury, my lady."

"Oh, my father's country seat is near Taunton. It is probably twenty or twenty-five miles from Glastonbury. I will have to ask my parents if they knew her. Or you."

"I doubt it. Lady Tilsbury was quite shy. Some would term her a wallflower, but she was my everything. Once we wed, we never returned to town for the Season."

She smiled sympathetically. "I can tell you cared for her a great deal."

"We never had children. It was just the two of us. She has been gone almost ten years now, and I still miss her a great deal."

Dru liked this man. "Please do not think me forward, my lord. I am here visiting my sister for an indefinite period. Might I call upon you some afternoon? You could tell me about Lady Tilsbury."

Tears filled his eyes. "I would like that very much, Lady Drusilla. Perhaps you can come one day when Martindale calls. He recently returned to the neighborhood."

"You are friends?" she asked, curious about the earl's relationship with this man.

"Martindale is like the son I never had. He has been away at war and has now come home to take up his title."

"Yes, we met him at Mrs. Cadmann's bakery yesterday afternoon."

Just then, someone entered the pew, drawing her attention from the viscount.

It was Lord Martindale, still wearing his regimental colors. He looked every inch the military officer he had been, his posture erect, his countenance solemn.

"Might I sit here, Lady Drusilla?" he inquired, shaking hands with Viscount Tilsbury.

"Of course, my lord," she said.

"Lady Drusilla has promised to come see me, Martindale. I told her she could when we have tea together. Could the two of you come on Wednesday?" Tilsbury asked.

Lord Martindale turned to her. "Are you free Wednesday afternoon, my lady?"

"Yes, I am," she said, her voice suddenly small.

Lucy leaned over. "The service is starting."

A woman took a seat at the pianoforte, and soon the congregation sang *Come, Thou Fount of Every Blessing*. Dru noticed Lord Martindale did not pick up a hymnal, nor did he sing along. She, on the other hand, enjoyed singing very much, and did so with abandon, her low alto voice harmonizing with Lucy's soprano one.

She found it hard to concentrate on the sermon with Lord Martindale sitting so close to her. His shoulder and upper arm rested against her own, putting all kinds of unchristian thoughts into her head. They stood for a prayer, and she tried to nudge him a bit in the other direction so that when they sat, there would be a bit of space between them.

He only sat closer.

Frustrated, she leaned over to whisper to him to move some. Instead, she inhaled the wonderful scent of sandalwood, drawing a deep breath of it—and him.

Jarred by it, Dru turned her attention to Mr. Harper, who had begun his sermon. She forced herself to focus on his words but found by the time he finished speaking, she hadn't a clue as to what he had talked about. This was ridiculous. She had never been taken by any man. Then again, her experience was limited. She knew their neighbors, of course, and had been to assemblies in the village, where she had danced with young men close to her own age.

She wondered if Lord Martindale danced.

Huffing, she noticed Lucy staring at her. "All you all right?" her sister whispered, concern in her eyes.

"Never better," she replied, determined to keep all her thoughts pure—and not giving a second thought to Lord Martindale's sensual lips.

They sang another hymn and had a final prayer, and then it was time to adjourn. Dru had never been gladder that a service had ended.

She bid Lord Tilsbury goodbye and turned to leave. Suddenly, a warm hand grasped her elbow, stopping her progress.

"Aren't you going to say your goodbyes to me, Lady Drusilla?" the earl asked.

Dry-mouthed, she tried to swallow, hoping he didn't notice how nervous she was. The heat coming from his hand on her bare elbow had started a fire within her. It was something she didn't quite understand. All she knew was that she was attracted to this man—and did not want to be.

"Shall I call for you in my carriage on Wednesday when we go to tea?"

"We can discuss it tomorrow when you come to Huntsworth for tea, my lord," she told him, taking a step back.

He didn't let go.

"My lord?" she said, pointedly looking at his hand on her arm.

Martindale had the decency to flush and released her immediately. "I look forward to spending time with you tomorrow, Lady Drusilla."

For reasons she couldn't explain, she told him, "Please call me Dru. It is what my family and friends call me."

"That is kind of you to give me leave to use the diminutive form of your name, Lady Dru." He smiled. "I rather like it. It suits you."

His smile caused warmth to spread throughout her insides.

Suddenly, the church felt overly hot. She needed air. Now.

"I must go," she said abruptly, hurrying from the pew and down the aisle, catching up with Lucy and Ariadne.

Why the bloody hell had she told the earl to call her Dru?

She was afraid to examine the reason why.

CHAPTER FOUR

PERRY MET WITH Rankin the entire morning and for the early part of the afternoon, receiving the current overview of his estate, as well as how things had progressed during his years away. He felt blessed that Beauville had such an efficient steward. Rankin explained which crops were currently grown by the tenants and why, as well as the rotation of those crops and how to get the most yield from the soil. Perry was familiar with all the steward spoke about, having been involved with the estate for a year until he went off to war, but it was good to be refreshed on things.

"I had requested several times for Lord Martindale to consider raising livestock on a portion of Beauville," Rankin explained.

"I recall that you were rebuffed each time," he said, seeing the steward nod. "Give me your reasons why, and I will certainly consider doing so."

The steward laid out a solid case, and Perry didn't even need time to consider.

"I think your plan is solid. It will be an investment in Beauville's future."

That also meant an investment in his children's future, which led him back to Lady Dru.

He had spent a good deal of time mulling over the young woman. Yes, she was young, having yet to make her come-out, but she appeared quite sensible to him. He wasn't fool enough to offer for her right away. Perry would bide his time during her visit with her sister. See her whenever possible. Determine whether or not she would be a good fit for Beauville. Of course, even if she agreed that they would suit, she might not be willing to give up a London Season. From what he knew of Polite Society, a girl's come-out year was the pinnacle of her life, attending parties and balls.

Even if Lady Dru wished to make her come-out, it didn't mean she couldn't do it as a betrothed woman. Yes, the circumstances would be unusual, but he could see it occurring. Thinking ahead, if she did accept his offer, would he then be required to go to town and escort her about as her fiancé, or could he let her have her bit of fun while he remained in the country? He did not seek a love match. A marriage of convenience was the conventional choice of most couples. Ladies received the name and protection of a husband and in turn, they provided an heir. Husbands and wives usually led separate lives. Would it be so unusual to begin this practice before a marriage took place?

Perry chastised himself, putting the cart before the horse. He wasn't even certain he wanted Lady Dru as his wife, much less whether she would have him. He would let things play out between them and see if they had enough in common to agree to wed. If not, he would return to his original plan and attend the Season next spring. He did think she might look favorably upon a marriage with him because of the proximity she would have to her sister and cousin. Watching the interaction between the three let him know they were close. If the time came when he did offer for her, Perry would make certain to point out the advantage of Lady Dru having family in the area.

"We can pick up with this tomorrow, Rankin," he said. "I am expected for tea at Lord Huntsberry's soon."

They arranged a time to meet again tomorrow, and he went to the stables to claim Zeus. He saw no need to ready the carriage when Huntsworth was just the other side of Alderton. He rode through the village and exited the other side, reveling in the freedom he now had. For so long, the army had told him where to go and what to think, and he had parroted those orders to the men under him. It was liberating to be able to come and go as he pleased.

He rode straight to the stables and handed his horse off to a groom before starting toward the house. Though he planned to return to the front, he heard someone call his name and looked up, seeing Lady Dru waving to him from the terrace. She wore a gown of pale yellow, which complimented her tawny hair.

Making his way to her, he found his pulse sped up. It shouldn't surprise him. She was attractive, with flawless skin and those incredible amethyst eyes. She was taller than most women, her frame thin, with small breasts and an even smaller waist.

"I am glad I caught you before you made your way to the front of the house, my lord," she said as he came up the stone steps. "We are having tea on the terrace this afternoon since the weather is so pleasant."

"It is an excellent idea, Lady Dru," he agreed. "I have never partaken of tea outdoors."

"Would you like to have a seat? Lucy and Judson should be here shortly."

"Thank you."

He accompanied her to the table already set for tea and pulled out her chair, catching a whiff of orange blossoms wafting from her. Then he took hold of the chair next to her, but when he slid it back, he caught sight of a gray tabby sitting on it.

"Toby, what are you doing there?" she asked.

"It is all right," Perry said, lifting the cat in his arms and seating himself, placing the cat in his lap. He stroked the silky fur.

His companion's jaw dropped, and he asked, "Is something wrong, my lady?"

She didn't speak for a moment, and then she burst out in a rich laugh which washed over him.

"Not at all, my lord. I am most astonished. Toby cannot abide anyone other than myself. The fact he is not hissing at you and scrambling away is nothing short of a miracle."

He petted the cat, who looked quite content where he sat, the sun warming its coat. "I have always liked animals. They are sensitive creatures. I used to play with the cats in our stables. I never had a pet, though. How long have you had Toby? He must be special to you if you brought him all the way from Somerset."

Her eyes lit up. "Oh, I absolutely adore animals. Toby is two years old. He came from a litter of one of our cats in the stables." She smiled fondly at the cat. "He was the runt. You would never guess so now."

Lady Dru reached over and scratched the tabby between his ears. A blissful look appeared on its face, and a loud purr rumbled from the pet.

"I oftentimes like animals more than people," she confided. "People can disappoint you. Animals never do."

He wondered from her tone who in her life had let her down.

"If I had my way, I would have more than one cat, plus a few dogs. Not necessarily hunting dogs, though I do like ours. Just a couple to keep me company. I have a horse at home that is all my own, and I regularly exercise other horses in our stables." The words kept pouring from her, and she told him of the goats and sheep she spent time with. How she rescued injured birds and nursed them back to health and had helped mares in birthing their foals.

"Why, I have even taken a kit when their mother was killed, and fed them by hand until they were old enough and strong enough to be released back into the wild." She shuddered. "Every time I hear of a fox hunt in our neighborhood, I pray it is not one of the four I raised who meets their fate."

As she spoke, Lady Dru had grown more animated, which only made her more beautiful. Perry felt a strong attraction to her, idly wondering what it would be like to kiss her. He wondered if she had a childhood sweetheart who had already given her a kiss. The thought suddenly made him jealous.

"Good afternoon, my lord," Lady Huntsberry said, approaching the table with her husband by her side.

Her cheeks were flushed, while the marquess wore a satisfied look. Perry guessed they had been coupling. The idea of making love to a woman in broad daylight shocked him, but then again, he had already decided this pair was a love match, as were Lord and Lady Aldridge. A thought struck him.

What if Lady Dru also sought a love match?

That was something he could never provide her. While he wanted to like his wife and hoped they might have a few things in common, love would not be a factor in his decision to wed. If these two marriages were the example Lady Dru sought for herself, he doubted they could ever come to an arrangement. It was probably for the best. He was on the quiet side, always observing others. He preferred books to people, and his nature was that of a loner. Lady Dru sparkled. She was talkative and charming. She would need a husband who could help her shine.

With his war experiences and the way they had affected him, Perry could never be that kind of husband. For her sake, he decided to cast aside the idea of offering for her. The more he was around her, the more he realized how opposite they were. With her looks and vivaciousness, she would have no trouble finding a husband next spring. He only hoped he could land a wife in a single Season and not have to repeat the process more than once. If he could find his countess, one London Season would be more than enough for him.

His mind made up, Perry sat through the very pleasant tea, not saying much, simply enjoying the company of his neighbors. He hoped he would remain on friendly terms with them, as well as the Aldridges.

After an hour, their plates were empty, as were their teacups, and he knew it was time to depart.

"I cannot thank you enough for inviting me to Huntsworth today, my lady," he told his hostess. "I will have to return the favor and have you come to Beauville."

"We would be happy to visit you, Lord Martindale," the

marchioness said. "You really are someone special, you know."

He felt the tips of his ears grow hot. "Why do you say that, my lady?"

"Toby, of course. As a kitten, he attached himself to my sister, and Toby is her constant companion. He tolerates me, but only angry hisses come from him when he is near anyone else. The fact that Toby has sat in your lap this entire teatime, looking as if he has been in the cream, is remarkable."

Perry chuckled. "I do not think you can judge my character by Toby's response to me." He stroked the cat's fur absently. "But my invitation stands. With or without Toby," he added, smiling at Lady Dru.

She leaned over and plucked the cat from his lap. Rising, she said, "I will walk you to your horse, my lord. We should discuss our arrangements regarding tea at Lord Tilsbury's."

Lord Huntsberry offered Perry a hand. "Good to see you, Martindale. Do you plan to remain in the country?"

"I do. Even before I ventured off to war, I never went to town. I am firmly planted in Surrey, at least until next Season. I suppose I will have to choose a bride."

"My sister will make her come-out next spring," Lady Huntsberry said. "It will be good that the two of you know one another. She looked to Lady Dru. "Hopefully, Lord Martindale will sign your programme."

"You are assuming I will go to town, Lucy. Remember, that might not be the case."

He wondered what she might refer to. Tension filled the air. To break it, he said, "Again, thank you for your hospitality."

Perry walked alongside Lady Dru. When they reached the steps leading down, she kissed Toby's head and set the cat on his feet.

"Stay out of trouble," she admonished as the cat bounded down the stairs and took off.

He offered his arm to her to assist her down the stairs. She kept her hand in the crook of his arm as they strolled toward the stables.

"Do you always talk to Toby?"

Laughing, she told him, "I talk to all animals. For the most part, I find them far more interesting than people. Con, my brother, has always teased me for doing so."

"Where does your brother live?"

"Mostly, he is in town. He is best of friends with our cousin Val. They have been sharing rooms in town ever since they left university, but Val's father died suddenly last spring, just before the start of the Season. The mourning period prevented his sisters Lia and Tia from making their come-outs. Since Val is now a duke, he has more important things to do than be idle with Con. I am certain Val will come to town to find a bride when the Season starts up again next spring."

"So, your cousin will be there. I assume his sisters will also make their come-outs since theirs were delayed with their father's passing. And you have your brother. You should enjoy your come-out, my lady."

She stopped. "I may not make my come-out. Ever. Oh, I know it is what all girls are brought up to do. Go to town. Wear pretty gowns. Find a husband. Have his babes." She sighed. "If I may be candid, my lord, I will tell you I usually wear breeches most of the time. It is easier to ride and get around. I have no interest in spending months in town at boring social affairs, especially since I am a country girl at heart. I love my animals and riding and gardening. My mother is domineering, always trying to tell me what to do and how to think. I resent that. I cannot in good faith leave my father's house, only to go to that of a husband who would be even more overbearing than Mama."

She gazed at him, determination in her eyes. "I may be out of step with Polite Society, but I have no desire to join the Marriage Mart."

He looked at her, stunned by her pronouncement. "Is that even an option, my lady?"

She shrugged. "Probably not. I can see Mama dragging me by my hair to town, forcing me into fancy ballgowns and dictating whom I should wed. Lucy loves pretty gowns and was eager to make her come-out, but we are very different."

"Did your mother choose Lord Huntsberry as her husband?" he asked, curious.

She laughed, and again the sound made him want to make her laugh even more.

"No. If Judson had not offered for Lucy, though, I believe Mama would have chosen a husband for her. Thank goodness that did not happen. Lucy and Judson are very much in love. At least Mama is pleased because he is a wealthy marquess." She laughed. "Mama probably has rewritten history, telling others she was the one who suggested Lucy wed Judson."

Their gazes met. "If you think me odd, it is quite all right," she assured him.

"I do not think you odd at all," he said softly. "I believe you are a woman who knows her own mind and wants to write her own story. I admire that. I admire you, Lady Dru."

The urge to kiss her had grown stronger, and Perry gave into it.

He took her face in his hands, cradling it gently, and pressed a soft kiss against her lips. An innocent kiss. Not one of passion or flaming desire. Merely a harmless, chaste kiss.

Breaking the kiss, he told her, "I hold you in high esteem, my lady. Hold to your convictions. If a Season—or marriage—is not for you, do not be forced into doing something you would forever regret."

He dropped his hands. "I will come for you in my carriage on Wednesday at half-past three."

With that, Perry strode off, feeling her eyes on him as he went to the stables. Inside, he claimed Zeus, leading the horse outside and mounting him. Glancing around, he did spy Lady Dru in the distance, close to the house.

He shouldn't have kissed her. He knew that. But it was a sweet kiss, one of friendship. He hoped that they could be friends because she was a very interesting person.

Come Wednesday, he would know if there was the possibility they could be friends—or if Lady Drusilla Alington would outright reject him.

CHAPTER FIVE

F OR TWO DAYS, Dru had done nothing but think of that kiss.

Even in her inexperience, she understood it had not been one full of ardor. Why, Lord Martindale had barely touched his lips to hers. Yet the kiss had stirred emotions within her that she was curious about. At the same time, she was afraid to explore those feelings. She had no wish for a husband and knew the earl would have to wed in order to provide an heir to his title.

Should she ask him why he had kissed her? Did men and women even talk about such things? The longer Dru thought about it, the more she came to believe that the kiss was one of friendship, one which supported her. Lord Martindale had encouraged her to follow her heart and hold steadfast to her beliefs. It surprised her that she had even shared with him her reluctance to make her come-out and be paraded about on the Marriage Mart. After all, they barely knew one another.

Yet she liked him a great deal. He was different from most men. Quiet. Reflective. She wondered if that had been his nature before he had gone to war or if the war had changed the man he had been. Dru decided that she would not bring up the kiss when she saw him today. Best to ignore it and simply try to be his friend. She suspected he did not have many of them and hoped, once she left the neighborhood, that Judson and Julian would reach out to Lord Martindale. She would see if any friendship developed between the three while she was here. If she did not witness it, she would ask Judson to look after Lord Martindale when she was gone.

She rang for Annie and changed from her breeches into a gown, not wanting to shock Lord Tilsbury or Lord Martindale. Going down to Lucy's parlor, she found her sister knitting, her needles moving swiftly. Surprisingly, Toby sat in a chair, keeping Lucy company.

Joining Lucy on the settee, Dru asked, "What are you making?"

"A blanket for the babe." Her sister smiled. "Sometimes, it does not seem real to me yet, knowing I carry life within me. I have talked with Ariadne about it, and she felt the same. She said once my body shows more changes, I will feel differently. And when I can feel the babe kick, that will certainly change things."

"You can feel that? I had no idea. Of course, I was the youngest, so I was never around when Mama was increasing."

Lucy set aside her knitting. "Mama never spoke to us about much of anything. Thank goodness, I have Ariadne—and you have the two of us. We will be able to share with you all you need to know."

She assumed her sister meant what occurred in the marriage bed. She did not want to fight with Lucy now, though, and remind her that she was still reluctant about making her come-out. While she knew she had her sister's support and Lucy had even offered to speak to Mama on her behalf, Dru knew with Lucy expecting a babe and basking in Judson's love, Lucy would think every woman should wed and have children.

"I have noticed my breasts growing larger. Naturally, my belly will begin to extend. I still have not been ill, though."

"Babes make you ill?" Dru asked, fascinated. "Why?"

Lucy shrugged. "I do not understand why, but Ariadne says some women suffer nausea when they are increasing. She did. She would awaken each morning and retch for several minutes. That feeling passed, however, after a few months, and Ariadne said she felt healthy as a horse after that. I suppose I am fortunate

I have not been ill. Then again, with the next babe, it could be different."

"You want more than one? I assume you must try again if this one is not a boy."

"Yes, I will need to give Judson an heir. He and I do want several children. I see how good he is with Penelope when we visit Ariadne and Julian, and he even told me he does not care if this first child is a son or daughter."

"I think your husband is unusual in that aspect, Lucy. Most men would only want boys." She sniffed. "Even most women, based upon how Mama treated you and me."

Her sister nodded. "Mama definitely favored Con. It is the way of Polite Society. Sons are far more important than daughters. Sons carry on the family name and legacy. Daughters must be provided with dowries and then sent to other families, and their loyalties then lie with their new husbands and their families." Lucy paused. "I think Judson and I will value all our children. Ariadne and Julian are the same. It is Ariadne who has decided our families should change things."

"What do you mean?"

"She brought Penelope with her to town for the Season this past spring. You know from experience that we were always left at home in the country each year. Ariadne has chosen to bring her children to town each year. She asked Con, Val, and me to do the same. That way, not only do we get more time with our own children, but these cousins can also grow up together and form strong bonds."

"Con shared some of this with me when we were traveling to Huntsworth. I think it a wonderful idea," Dru said. "I cherished the brief time we were with our cousins in town. It would have been lovely to have seen them each year. I commend Ariadne for her idea."

"She also said it would give our generation of cousins time together, as well. As each cousin weds, she will approach them and share her idea, hoping they will agree. I already look forward to many happy times ahead with our cousins, as well as you and Con. When Con weds and eventually takes on Papa's title, he will be far away in the west country, while I will be here in Surrey. Coming to town for the Season each year will allow me to spend time with him and his wife."

Lucy patted Dru's hand. "The same with you. Your husband might live far away, so the only time I would see you would be during the Season." She paused. "That is, if you choose to make your come-out and wed. Remember, Judson and I will support you, no matter what you decide. You have options, Dru. You could delay your come-out until you are more comfortable with the idea. Or if you choose not to wed, we will stand firm with you. I know Mama will be angry, though, if you do not."

She couldn't begin to imagine what their mother would say.

"I appreciate your support of me, Lucy. Judson's, as well."

"Judson has said you will always have a home with us if you choose not to marry."

"Your husband is very kind. I am not certain I could do that, Lucy. Always having me underfoot? You might grow tired of me."

"You see how large Huntsworth is. And you would be beloved by not only us, but your nieces and nephews." Lucy squeezed Dru's hand. "No decision needs to be made now. You have months to think about what you wish to do. And Judson will help protect you from Mama's wrath. He can be quite convincing, you know."

"I appreciate that," she said, happy to have her brother-in-law champion her. Then she decided to ask her sister a question. "Why do you like kissing, Lucy?"

"What an odd question." Lucy paused. "Did the baron's son kiss you at one of the village assemblies? I have thought he had a tendre for you for the last couple of years."

Her cheeks burned. "No, he has not kissed me. I was merely curious, seeing as how I have come across you and Judson kissing numerous times. Sometimes, you haven't even been aware I am present, so I have quietly exited the room."

It was her sister's turn to blush. "Well, I will say that with the right man, kissing is one of the most wonderful things in the world. Perhaps we should talk about it."

Embarrassed, she said, "No. That is not necessary. I have no plans to kiss any man anytime soon."

"I think it is necessary to discuss," Lucy insisted. "I would rather have you prepared than not. My first kiss was unpleasant. It is something I have meant to share with you. Something that I did not want to confide in a letter, but rather speak to you about in person."

Lucy then told Dru of the evil Lord Eaton and how he had tried to ruin her last spring when Lucy made her come-out. Judson had come to her defense, ousting Eaton. He had also kissed Lucy, knowing the experience of kissing Lord Eaton had been distasteful.

"I was already attracted to Judson," Lucy admitted. "And his kiss was so very different from Lord Eaton's forced ones. In fact, it was divine."

Her sister then elaborated on kissing, shocking Dru when she explained how tongues were involved. She could feel her face growing hot.

Because she pictured doing that very thing with Lord Martindale.

"I wrote to you how we were caught kissing by a notorious gossip in the *ton*. That led to our rapid marriage," Lucy shared. "Neither Judson nor I wanted to be forced into marriage, but he did the honorable thing by offering for me and purchasing a special license. I almost did not go through with it, however. Minutes before the ceremony, I felt terrible, feeling I was trapping him in marriage." She paused. "Just as Mama did to Papa."

Shock ran through Dru. "What?"

"Mama admitted to me that she made certain there were witnesses to Papa kissing her. It meant she was compromised. Papa did the honorable thing and offered for her. It has made me wonder, however, about their marriage."

"Well, there is no love lost between them," she noted. "At least things worked out well for you and Judson. If I did not know any of this, I would assume you were a love match from the start."

"I am very satisfied with my marriage," Lucy said. "We quickly learned that we had feelings for one another, and we are not afraid to show our affection for each other. It is rare for a *ton* marriage since many of them are arranged. In fact, most marriages are ones of convenience."

A fierce look crossed her sister's face. "A love match is the only kind of marriage I would wish for you, Dru. I cannot imagine my beloved sister in an arrangement which is meaningless. If you choose to wed—and I hope you will—only marry for love."

"You and Ariadne have chosen two of the finest men in Polite Society to wed. I am not certain how many more men of such character are left. They may have run out," she said lightly.

A light knock sounded at the door, and the butler entered the room.

"Lord Martindale's carriage is approaching, my lady," Brown informed them.

"Thank you, Brown," Lucy said. Turning to Dru, she added, "I hope you enjoy a lovely tea with Lord Tilsbury. We have only spoken to him briefly at church, but he seems to be a very nice man. See if he would accept an invitation from us for tea. Or even dinner."

"He is a widower and has no children. He seemed lonely to me. That is why I volunteered to go and visit him. Lord Tilsbury mentioned that Lord Martindale has been as a son to him and suggested the two of us come to tea today."

"Let me say this, Dru. Things are different in the country. In town, you would not be allowed to be alone in a carriage with Lord Martindale, nor even in a room with him. Etiquette in Polite Society demands an unmarried woman be chaperoned at all times. Those rules are more relaxed in the country, however. I will still make a point of speaking to Lord Martindale about this. Come, let us go outside and greet the earl."

She wondered what Lucy might say to Lord Martindale. She definitely had not shared with her sister that the earl had kissed her. Again, she had felt no passion in the kiss and did not believe he was interested in her.

They went out the front door, Annie handing Dru her reticule as they did so. Lord Martindale drove a barouche up the lane. He brought it to a stop, exiting the vehicle and coming to greet them.

"Lady Huntsworth, Lady Dru. It is a lovely day."

"Thank you for escorting my sister to tea at Lord Tilsbury's, my lord," Lucy said. "I merely want to remind you that my sister is not even out yet, and that I expect you to be a perfect gentleman in every aspect."

Dru could feel her face burning as Lord Martindale said, "I understand how precious your sister is to you, my lady. I will take the utmost care of her. If you would like to send a maid with us to watch over her, I would be agreeable to that."

Lucy studied him a moment. "No, I do not believe that to be necessary, my lord. My impression of you has been favorable, and I do believe you are a man of honor."

"I will return Lady Dru straight after tea," the earl promised. Glancing to her, he said, "My lady?"

She took Lord Martindale's offered arm. "Goodbye, Lucy."

He led her to the barouche and handed her up. It surprised her he did not arrive in a carriage. Then again, a barouche was more of a summer vehicle, and the day was a pleasant one. She took a seat, worried they would once again be sitting directly beside one another. After being in close quarters at church, Dru wished their bodies did not have to be so close to one another. That one time had filled her with wicked thoughts, thoughts she did not care to have about the earl or any other man. She determined to keep her thoughts pure.

Looking to Lucy, she waved goodbye to her sister. Martindale took up the reins, and they began moving down the lane.

Before she could thank him for conveying her to Lord Tilsbury's, however, he said, "I think we need to address the kiss between us, Lady Dru."

CHAPTER SIX

PERRY SAW THE startled look on Lady Dru's face. He had determined not to bring up the brief kiss between them, but after hearing Lady Huntsberry's stern warning to him, he wanted to make certain that Lady Dru understood there was to be nothing romantic between them. Being young and impressionable—and most likely having never been kissed—it was imperative that he make things clear between them.

"I was not going to mention it to you, my lord," she said, quickly regaining her composure. "And do not think I told my sister of the kiss. Lucy was merely being overly protective of me. She likes you quite a bit, otherwise, she would not have given you leave to escort me to Lord Tilsbury's this afternoon."

"I should have apologized for kissing you yesterday, my lady," he said. "I do not want you to think I was trying to take advantage of you."

"Oh, no, my lord!" she exclaimed. "I never thought that. I may have never been kissed before, but I realized you hold no grand passion for me. You were merely being kind and asserting your support regarding whatever decision I make regarding my future. It was . . . a *friendly* kiss." She chuckled. "Believe me, I know exactly what a kiss between a man and a woman can consist of."

He frowned. "But I thought you just said you had never experienced a kiss before."

She laughed, that rich, deep, throaty laugh that sent a sizzle of desire through him.

"I have witnessed numerous kisses since I have arrived at Huntsworth. You have seen how affectionate my sister and brother-in-law are. Why, I have come across them kissing on the stair landing. In the drawing room. Out on the terrace. They are made for one another—and apparently, that means they enjoy kissing one another quite a bit."

"I see," he said, a little uncomfortable hearing about all that kissing. "Well, I wanted to clear the air between us, my lady. I have no wish to court you, much less offer marriage to you. The kiss was a mistake on my part, but you read my intentions correctly. I merely wanted to show that I do encourage you to make your own decisions." He hesitated. "And I hope that we might actually become friends during your stay in Surrey."

Perry saw the relief cross her face and for a moment, he was disappointed that Lady Dru did not share the same attraction to him as he did to her. Still, he knew he could put a muzzle on it and act as a gentleman in her presence.

"Do men and women form friendships between them?" she asked. "I have told you that I am not yet out in Polite Society, so I really have no way to gauge these matters."

He couldn't help but chuckle. "If you are not out, then neither am I. I have never attended a single Season."

"Why not? I thought that is what all gentlemen did."

"Usually, that is the case, but I am a bit diffident around others. I have always preferred books to people and was a studious sort with few friends. When I left university, I came straight home to Beauville. I had grand ideas of helping to run the estate."

"Was your father ill? Is that why you wished to assist in managing Beauville?"

"No. The opposite. Father was not interested in anything having to do with his country seat. Both my parents remained in town a majority of the year, leading very separate lives. I am ashamed to admit this to you, but my father was a womanizer and gambler. Since he showed no interest in the estate, I thought I could help Mr. Rankin, our steward, run it. There were improvements both Rankin and I wanted to see occur, and I was hoping my father would cede a bit of his authority to me so that I might help Beauville thrive.

"Alas, it was not to be."

Understanding dawned in her eyes. "That is why you went away to war. Usually, it is a second son who serves in the army. You felt stifled, however. Lacking in purpose."

Again, he was impressed by her insight. "Yes, you read the situation correctly, my lady. Rankin is an excellent steward, and he really did not need my help. I felt cast aside. Adrift. Not knowing what I should do with my time. I talked it over with Lord Tilsbury, who befriended me once I came home from university. Though we only knew each other for a little over a year as adults, the viscount always showed great kindness to me."

Perry glanced out the window, seeing they were past Alderton and fast approaching Tilsbury Manor.

"I confronted my father on one of his rare occasions at home, demanding that I receive more authority since Beauville would one day be mine, or I would do my duty to king and country and leave to fight Bonaparte. Britain had declared war the previous month, and I hoped I could be of service in the fight against the Little Corporal if I could not be of any use at Beauville." He shrugged. "Despite the fact my father cared little for Beauville, he was not willing to give an inch. I carried through with my plans and joined the army, thanks to Lord Tilsbury."

"What role did Lord Tilsbury play?"

"I had but a small quarterly allowance and could never have purchased the commission necessary to become an officer. Lord Tilsbury forbade me from merely enlisting. Instead, he gave me the funds necessary to purchase my commission, telling me to consider it as a loan that I could repay once I came into my title."

"I may not know much about you, my lord, but I can tell you are an honorable man. I know you served England well and that you repaid Lord Tilsbury the moment you returned home."

"As a matter of fact, I did. Even before having seen him. I only arrived home late last week, and I intended to call upon Lord Tilsbury this week. Seeing him in church, I was delighted when he invited me—and you—to tea."

Looking earnestly at her, Perry said, "I do hope we can be friends, Lady Dru. I am in sore need of one. Lord Tilsbury is my only friend in the neighborhood. I am afraid I had little in common with the other lads at school and am no longer in touch with any of my schoolmates."

"I would be honored to become your friend, Lord Martindale. Lord Tilsbury's, as well, if he will have me as one."

"We will arrive soon," he shared, and they both fell silent, until they pulled up in front of their destination.

The butler ushered them upstairs to the drawing room, where Lord Tilsbury greeted them warmly.

Taking Lady Dru's hand, the viscount kissed it, telling her, "Thank you for coming to see an old man, Lady Drusilla."

"You do not seem so old to me, my lord," she responded. "Besides, with age comes wisdom. I hope to learn not only of you, but also things from you."

The viscount beamed at her. "You are a delight, Lady Drusilla."

"Please call me Lady Dru, my lord. My family and friends do so."

Lord Tilsbury kissed her hand. "Then Lady Dru it shall be," he promised.

Releasing her hand, Tilsbury turned to Perry. Instead of shaking hands, he clasped him by the shoulders, saying, "I am both happy and relieved you have come home, Martindale."

Tilsbury pulled him close, clapping Perry on the back. When the viscount released him, Perry saw tears had sprung in the old man's eyes. He doubted his own father would have embraced him, much less cried at his return from war. Even his own mother had yet to write to him once she had informed Perry that he was the new Martindale.

Lord Tilsbury asked, "Shall we sit? The teacart should be here any moment."

When it arrived, the viscount asked for Lady Dru to pour out for them, and she agreed to do so. The viscount talked about the neighborhood, including various residents in the local village.

"I see that you have given up wearing your regimental colors, Martindale," Tilsbury said. "You looked quite gallant in them at church on Sunday."

"I went to visit Mr. Billings last week to be fitted for a new wardrobe. I had nothing to wear when I returned except for my major's uniform. Since I had sold my commission, it was time to dress again as a civilian."

He saw Tilsbury's brow furrow in confusion, but the viscount only said, "Mr. Billings has made up my clothes for years. You can always expect a quality fit from him."

"I went on Monday to try on a few completed items. They fit well, and so I left his shop with them. I will receive other pieces over the next several weeks as he completes them." He smoothed the coat's fabric on his forearm. "Billings did a fine job, and I am glad to cast off my uniform for good."

Perry neglected to mention he had done as planned and burned it.

"I have talked far too long," Lord Tilsbury told them. "Let me hear about you, Lady Dru."

"I am the youngest of three, my lord. My brother Con, Viscount Dyer, is the oldest and only son. He spends most of his time in town."

"Is your brother wed?" the viscount asked.

"No, my lord. Con and our cousin Val both decided to remain bachelors until they came into their titles. My uncle Charles passed away last spring, so I assume that Val will attend the next Season with the idea of finding his duchess." She glanced to Perry. "You would like Val. He has never met a stranger and is the type who would give you the shirt off his back."

She looked back to Lord Tilsbury. "You have met my sister Lucy, who is now Lady Huntsberry. She told me to convey to you her best wishes. She would like you to come to Huntsworth for tea—even dinner—sometime. I hope you will agree to do so, my lord."

"I would be happy to accept an invitation to either. Or both," the viscount said genially. "I would like to get to know Lord Huntsberry. He came into his title at such a young age, and then he did not return to Surrey after he left for university. I am glad to see he wed your sister and will be in the neighborhood on a more regular basis. But what of you, my lady?"

"I am a simple girl. I enjoy being outdoors. I like to ride, fish, and garden. I have already started advising Lucy's gardeners on how to bring the Huntsworth gardens back to life. Apparently, Judson's uncle neglected them when he served as the guardian of both Judson and the estate, and they turned wild during the years my brother-in-law remained in town."

"You should tell his lordship of Toby," Perry prompted.

"Toby is my cat," she said proudly. "As independent as they come, but he is ever so affectionate with me. He barely tolerates anyone's presence, but Lord Martindale met Toby the other day and even held Toby in his lap without any protest."

"Then I would say your Toby is a fine judge of character," Lord Tilsbury proclaimed.

"I have always been drawn to animals," Lady Dru continued. "It was hard to leave them behind in Somerset, but Judson has given me a fine mount to ride while I am visiting Huntsworth."

"Perhaps you might like to ride my estate, Lady Dru," Perry said impulsively. "I am very proud of the work we have begun on it."

"I would very much enjoy that, Lord Martindale. Being in the saddle is second nature to me."

She looked back to their host. "You have not spoken much of yourself, my lord. Tell me about yourself—and Lady Tilsbury."

Tears misted the old man's eyes. "We met during her second

Season," he began. "She had not chosen to wed at the end of her first, upsetting her parents a great deal. Her father and mine enjoyed partnering at cards, and they hatched a scheme between them to bring us together."

Smiling, Lord Tilsbury added, "We allowed them to believe it was an arranged marriage, when all along, it was love at first sight."

"You are very fortunate to have made a love match," Lady Dru said. "The same as my sister and cousin. My understanding is that is very rare within the *ton*."

The viscount nodded. "It is. I am grateful for every day I had with my wife. She had a child the first year after we wed. A son. He was stillborn." Sadness filled his face. "The doctor told us there could be no more attempts at a child. We clung to one another in our grief, but we had our strong love to continually sustain us for decades after that."

"Who is your heir apparent then?" she asked.

"My brother's eldest son. My brother passed away two years ago, so the title will go to my nephew upon my passing."

That news surprised Perry. "I did not know your brother was gone, my lord. You never wrote of it."

Pain filled the viscount's eyes. "I did not want to burden you while you were at war. You had enough to deal with."

"Then please accept my condolences now."

Lord Tilsbury shrugged. "I have lost those closest to me—and still endure."

"You mean a great deal to me, my lord," he said. "I do not think you understand the influence you have had upon me. I hope you will be around for many years to come, offering me advice, as well as your friendship."

"You are a good man, Martindale. I look upon you as a son."

The viscount pulled a handkerchief from his pocket and dabbed at his eyes. Brightening, he said, "Would you like to see some of Lady Tilsbury's paintings, my lady?"

"I would enjoy that very much," Lady Dru said. "I have no

talent in the arts. Although I do enjoy singing, I play the pianoforte abominably. My governess had me try my hand at painting, but it was an unpleasant experience. I admire those who paint and do it well."

"Then let me take you through the house. Her paintings are scattered in various rooms."

Lord Tilsbury first led them about the drawing room, showing them a few paintings hanging there, and then they left to visit other rooms throughout the house. He was glad Lady Dru had come with him today to visit Lord Tilsbury. Perry had never known Lady Tilsbury painted or that numerous paintings she had done filled the walls of the house.

They ended in a room on the ground floor, and Lord Tilsbury said, "This was my wife's parlor. Sometimes, I come and sit in here, just to feel close to her. I will close my eyes and convince myself that I catch the scent of the rosewater she used every day."

Lady Dru reached out and took the old man's hand. "You were blessed to have Lady Tilsbury in your life, my lord. Thank you for a lovely tea and more importantly, for sharing the viscountess' paintings with us. I quite admire her talent. They capture Surrey well, especially this miniature on the desk here."

Perry glanced at the small painting resting upon a stand. It captured roses in a garden.

The viscount picked it up, stand and all, a fond smile on his lips as he gazed upon it. Then he turned and handed it to Lady Dru.

"I would like you to have this, my lady."

"No, my lord," she protested. "I cannot take one of your beloved wife's paintings."

"Lady Tilsbury would have liked you, Lady Dru. She would want you to have it. Please, humor an old man and accept it."

She stepped to him and brushed her lips against the old man's cheek. "This will become my most prized possession," she proclaimed. "I cannot thank you enough for sharing your memories of Lady Tilsbury and giving me this painting of hers."

"Thank you for visiting me today." The viscount looked from one visitor to the other. "Both of you. You are welcome back anytime, no invitation necessary."

Lady Dru smiled brightly. "I will let my sister know that you are amenable to accepting an invitation from her. You will hear from her soon, my lord. Thank you for a most delightful afternoon."

They said their goodbyes, and Perry escorted Lady Dru to the waiting vehicle.

Once they were on their way, he said, "You were a balm to Lord Tilsbury's soul, my lady."

"I felt a strong connection with him. I cannot believe his generosity in giving one of Lady Tilsbury's paintings to me. I shall write him a lovely note once I get home. It can be included in the invitation that Lucy issues to him."

She had been looking out the window as she spoke, but she turned now, their gazes meeting.

"Would you also like to come when Lord Tilsbury visits us? He might feel more comfortable having you present since he thinks so highly of you."

"I am agreeable and will accept any invitation Lady Huntsberry issues to me."

They rode in companionable silence after that and soon arrived at Huntsworth. He climbed from the barouche and handed her down, where they were greeted by Lord and Lady Huntsberry.

"Here is Lady Dru, safe and sound," he told the couple.

"Lord Tilsbury is such a kind, wonderful man," Lady Dru declared. "He will eagerly accept any invitation to tea or dinner, Lucy. I think we should ask him for dinner so we can see more of him." She looked to Perry. "And Lord Martindale should also be included. Lord Tilsbury looks upon Lord Martindale as a son."

"I see," Lady Huntsberry said. She glanced to her husband. "How about tomorrow evening?"

"Whatever you want, love," the marquess told his wife.

Lady Huntsberry addressed him. "Then we would be honored if you would come to dinner tomorrow evening, Lord Martindale. Shall we say seven o'clock?"

"I will be there, my lady. Thank you." He looked to Lady Dru. "Until tomorrow night, my lady."

Perry returned to the carriage, settling back against the seat as his driver started up the carriage. He was grateful for the invitation because he did want to get to know his neighbors better.

Moreover, he was eager to spend more time in Lady Dru's company.

CHAPTER SEVEN

MEN KEPT COMING at him. Soldiers with rifles, shooting at him. Rushing at him with bayonets. Perry miraculous dodged every bullet. Every swipe of the knife's blade. He continually fired his pistol, never needing to stop to reload, even as he danced away from his attackers, plunging his own bayonet into them.

Weariness filled him. Sweat dripped from his brow into his eyes, stinging unmercifully, yet he hadn't a second to wipe it away, having to stave off a new attack. He called to his men, and they charged once more with him, following him blindly as the smoke from the cannon filled the air, obscuring everything in sight.

He continued to fight, his gut telling him it was a losing battle. He wanted to call a retreat, but the words wouldn't come from his lips. Halting in the middle of the field, the smoke began to clear. Then the eerie silence blanketed the scene.

Perry was the only man left standing.

Surrounding him were hundreds of bodies. Mangled. Bleeding. Soldiers crying out for help, blood rushing from their wounds, limbs sliced from their bodies. The scent of death permeated the air. He turned slowly, his eyes sweeping the battlefield, until he had completed a circle.

He was the only man left standing . . .

His scream broke the silence, shattering the area with its

volume, piercing his soul. Falling to his knees, another garbled cry sprang forth as he dropped his pistol and saber. He tore at his hair, tears streaming down his face, another hoarse cry emerging.

Suddenly, he awoke, feeling his fingers in his hair and the tears cascading down his cheeks. A low growl came from him, guttural, filled with pain.

Perry flipped to his stomach, burying his face in his pillow, screaming into it as his fingers grasped it.

When would the nightmares end?

Spent, he rolled to his side, shivering, pulling the bedclothes up around him. Each morning—and sometimes during the middle of the night—he woke from horrible dreams, his bedclothes drenched with sweat. The nightmares which had started during the last few months of the war refused to be vanquished. He had thought they would end once he reached safety in England. Instead, they plagued him more than before, and he assumed it was guilt at having left his men behind.

How could he, in good faith, take a wife when he was so troubled? Of course, he would not sleep with her. He would do his duty and visit her on a regular basis until she got with child, but he would always return to his own bed. As loud as he sometimes was when he awoke, it would be impossible to hide his nightmares from her. He prayed time would solve the problem. That by next spring, when the Season began, he would have vanquished his fears, and the horrid dreams would no longer plague him.

He couldn't tell anyone about them. He had no one he could confide in. Even if he did, he would only look weak in others' eyes. It was imperative to keep this to himself—and hope none of the servants learned of it. He wouldn't be able to stomach the pity in their eyes. Or worse, the fear that might appear, his servants thinking he had descended into madness.

Rising, he threw back the curtains, seeing that dawn was about to break. The light always helped. It seemed it was the darkness which he feared.

Perry returned to bed, not ready to ring for Grilley. Of anyone, his valet would understand since he had accompanied Perry to war as his batman. While Grilley had not been on the battlefield himself, he had assisted in surgeries and been one of those designated to dispose of sawed-off limbs, digging holes and burying arms and legs, covering them with dirt. He wondered if Grilley also suffered from nightmares, but couldn't bring himself to ask. If the valet did, they would both endure in silence as they tried to heal.

His thoughts turned to Lady Dru and tonight's upcoming dinner at Huntsworth. If he ever felt brave enough to speak of his problems, she would be the one he would seek out. She would be sympathetic without burdening him with her pity. Of course, he would never share with a woman the horrors of the battlefield, but Lady Dru had a caring nature.

She had been absolutely lovely with Lord Tilsbury yesterday, giving the old man her full attention. Perry knew she did not play the viscount falsely. She was genuinely interested in what he said, not pretending to care. Tilsbury had appreciated that, else he never would have given away one of his wife's paintings to the young woman.

Perry yearned to take Lady Dru into his confidence, but discussing his war memories and their effect upon him was not a line he would soon cross. He did want to be her friend.

"Liar," he said softly.

He should acknowledge what lay just beneath the surface.

He wanted her as his wife.

There. He had admitted it to himself. It was absolutely the wrong thing, but his desire for her grew the more he spoke with her. She was unpretentious. Sincere in her speech and actions. Candid. Straightforward. Perry had never met anyone quite like her.

She also had no interest in marriage. He respected that. Women in Polite Society had no choice, but Lady Dru seemed determine to forge her own path. What he knew of the *ton* was that a woman either wed or became a spinster—and spinsters were a burden upon their families. They sometimes served as companions to other relatives or even went to work as governesses. They were a part of a family and yet somehow set apart from the others. While he did not want this for Lady Dru, it was not his role to convince her to make a marriage. Besides, Lord and Lady Huntsberry seemed most kind. If Lady Dru chose not to wed, he could see them opening up their home to her. His gut told him the couple would not treat Lady Dru as an upper servant but more as a cherished family member.

But if she ever changed her mind, she would have men falling at her feet. Not only was she attractive, but she was also the type of woman who would only grow more beautiful over time.

Especially if she fell in love.

He had noticed a certain glow about Lady Huntsworth and Lady Aldridge. Both women were in love with their husbands, and the two marquesses were certainly smitten with their wives. Perry hoped that if Lady Dru changed her mind and decided to go ahead with her come-out, be it next year or another time, she would find a love match.

Thinking about next Season, he hoped it would not be awkward if Lady Dru did participate while he was in London at the same time, looking for a wife of his own. Would his heart be able to endure seeing her dancing in the arms of another man? Laughing over midnight suppers? Strolling arm-in-arm with a gentleman at a garden party?

Perhaps he would need to wait and see what her plans might include before he committed to attending the Season because already, jealousy sprang within him. It was mad because he held no claims upon her, yet it would cut him to the quick to see her with another man.

Perry doubted their paths would converge in the years to come, especially if she did change her mind and decide to wed. The chances of her making a match with someone nearby were slim. True, the possibility existed that she might visit her sister at

Huntsworth upon occasion, but it was more likely that the two sisters would merely visit one another while in town for the Season. Since he had no intention of every going to town again once he had wed, they would never see one another after her visit here in Surrey.

The light finally shone through the window, and he rang for Grilley to ready him for the day. Perry breakfasted and went through the post, pleased that he had received a response from Mr. Chapman, his solicitor. He had written to Chapman, asking him to come down to Surrey at his earliest convenience in order to discuss his affairs. His father had been a gambler, and Perry needed to see just how much of the family's fortune had been wasted on games of chance. He already had a good idea of the income Beauville brought in, based upon reviewing the ledgers and his conversations with Rankin, but it was important to meet with his solicitor regarding all his affairs.

He had also asked that Chapman bring copies of his parents' marriage contracts when he visited Beauville. Perry needed to know what they contained so that he could visit his mother in town and let her know about the income she could expect. He informed Mrs. Foster that the solicitor would arrive around noon the following day.

"I am not certain if he will stay overnight or return to town. Just in case, have a room made up for Mr. Chapman."

"Yes, my lord. I will also let Cook know we may have a guest for dinner tomorrow night."

After breakfast, he spent an hour with Rankin before going out on the estate for several hours.

When he returned to the house mid-afternoon, he was met by Foster. The look the butler wore did not bode well.

"My lord, I must inform you that Lady Martindale arrived a few minutes ago. She is in her rooms now, but she told me that she would be taking tea with you."

His gut roiled. "Have a footman come to my study in ten minutes. I must write to Lady Huntsberry and tell her I will not be able to come to dinner this evening."

"Yes, my lord."

Perry withdrew to his study, disappointment filling him at having to cancel his plans. He knew enough not to simply bring his mother to dinner with him as an unexpected, uninvited guest.

My dear Lady Huntsworth —

I regret to inform you that I will be unable to attend dinner this evening. I am sorry for this late notice, but my mother has arrived from town, and I should remain with her.

Thank you again for your kind invitation.

Your humble servant,
Martindale

He folded the note in half and dripped sealing wax upon the edge, pressing his signet ring into it. By then, a footman had arrived.

"Ride to Huntsworth and deliver this message to Lady Huntsworth," he instructed.

"Yes, my lord," the footman said, accepting the note and leaving.

Perry waited until another half-hour had passed. Then, as teatime approached, he made his way to the drawing room. Entering, he saw his mother standing at the window, looking out.

Crossing the room, he waited until he was closer before speaking. "Good afternoon, Mother."

She turned, her lips twitching in displeasure. He could not think of a single time she had smiled at him. They were, in effect, strangers to one another.

Leaving the window, she took a seat, and he did the same. A maid rolled in the teacart. Nothing was said while the servant was in the room, and once the maid left, the silence continued. His mother poured out, handing him a cup and saucer. Perry set it on a nearby table and placed a slice of cake and half a sandwich upon his plate.

"I suppose you are wondering why I am here, Martindale," she began, dropping a cube of sugar into her tea and stirring.

He remained silent, waiting to hear what she had to say.

She brought the cup to her lips and took a slip, setting it down. "I wish to speak to you regarding my marriage settlements."

"What of them?" he asked cautiously.

"I need to see a copy of them for clarification," she said crisply.

"As a matter of fact, Mr. Chapman, my solicitor, will be arriving at noon tomorrow to meet with me regarding my inheritance. I requested that he bring copies of your settlements for me to review. I fully intend to discharge my duty to you. You will not be tossed out onto the streets."

He saw his response rankled her, and she took another sip of tea. "I do not wish to be relegated to the dower house, Martindale," she said firmly. "I know that is what most marriage settlements indicate for a widow, along with a small allowance. That is *not* to my liking."

Now the reason she had come to Beauville in person was clear. "You wish to remain in town permanently."

"I do. I have never been fond of the country. Besides, my friends are all in town."

"And your lovers?" he asked, not bothering to hide his contempt.

"Martindale!" she exclaimed. "I did not raise you to be impolite."

Perry gazed at her steadily. "You did not raise me at all, Mother. There were times I could not even recall what you looked like because it had been so long since I had seen you."

"How dare you!" she exploded. "Why, you must—"

"Must what? Dance to your tune? In case you have forgotten, *I* am now the Earl of Martindale. You have no say as to what happens to you. It is up to me. I can honor the marriage settlements as they are written—or I can make other arrangements for you which are more to your liking. If I see fit to do so. I must first read what is in them before I decide what I shall do."

She started to speak and then quickly clenched her jaw. He wished now that he had not written to Lady Huntsberry and canceled his visit this evening, because he could not imagine sitting across from this woman and trying to make polite conversation over dinner tonight.

Then again, he didn't have to. He was the Earl of Martindale. He could order her to her bedchamber and have the servants serve her dinner there.

Over the next quarter-hour, Perry finished his food and drank the last of his tea, all the while watching his mother. She kept her gaze lowered, not daring to speak a word and alienate him.

Standing, he said, "You are welcome to stay in your old rooms for now. Especially since you were not expected, and the dower house has not been touched in a long time. And since you are tired from your journey to Beauville, I will have a tray sent to your room at supper."

Her head snapped up, fire in her eyes. He saw her struggling not to burst into one of her usual tirades.

"Thank you, Martindale. That is most thoughtful of you."

"I will let you know after I have read the marriage contracts what they contain. And what I plan to do about them."

Tears filled her eyes. "Please, do not banish me to the dower house. I beg you."

He wasn't about to tell her that if he had adequate funds, he would allow her to remain in town. Let her worry a little about her fate. As for him, having her remain in town was his best option. He did not want to have to see her, and that would be the case if she remained at Beauville. Perry couldn't picture her changing from the selfish creature she had always been to a loving grandmother to his future children. It would suit both of them to never be in one another's presence again.

"If you will excuse me," he said, starting for the door.

Foster entered. "My lord, the footman you sent to Huntsworth has just returned. Lady Huntsworth would be pleased if both you and Lady Martindale came to dinner this evening."

Perry cursed inwardly. If he showed up without his mother, there would be too many questions to answer, things he would prefer not to discuss with anyone.

"We are to have dinner at Huntsworth?" his mother asked, joining him and Foster.

"Yes," he said tightly. "I had canceled since you arrived, but Lady Huntsworth is a generous woman. Apparently, she will make room at her table for you this evening."

His mother's eyes shone with the small victory. "Then I must see my lady's maid and find something appropriate to wear."

He told her what time to be downstairs for them to leave, and she left the drawing room.

Turning to Foster, he said, "Never again give me a private message in that woman's presence."

CHAPTER EIGHT

PERRY DID NOT have any evening wear for tonight's dinner. In fact, he had yet to even order any from Mr. Billings. He hoped that, being in the country, the attire for dinner this evening would be less formal than what was expected in town.

He went to the foyer to wait for his mother, hoping she would arrive promptly. He didn't know if she was the kind of woman who liked to keep a man waiting, but he determined he would depart at the time he had given her, whether she was downstairs or not. Fortunately, he didn't have to make that decision because she arrived two minutes before they were scheduled to leave.

Most sons would do the dutiful thing and compliment their mother's appearance, but he had no relationship with this woman and wasn't about to start pretending they did now.

"Are you ready?" he asked brusquely.

She frowned slightly but was clever enough *not* to call him out, knowing she needed his goodwill as far as her permanent living arrangements were concerned. "Of course, Martindale."

Perry allowed a footman to hand her into the carriage and then followed, sitting across from her. He wasn't about to start a conversation, but he would be civil enough to respond if she asked a question of him. Now that she had come to Beauville in his carriage, he planned to keep the vehicle.

"I am surprised that we have been asked to dine with the

Huntsberrys. They wed quite early into this past Season. There was gossip about the speed of their marriage, but I saw them at several events throughout the summer. Huntsberry seemed besotted with his bride."

"From what I gather, they are very close," he said neutrally.

"I find it odd Huntsberry is in the country. I cannot recall him being here for many years. Of course, his father was so ill. We never had much to do with the poor man. He barely left his sickroom."

He didn't comment on her observations.

"So, tell me who will be attending this dinner."

"Obviously, Lord and Lady Huntsberry," he replied. "Lady Huntsberry's sister is also staying with them. She is Lady Drusilla Alington."

"Hmm. I do not recall a Lady Drusilla. I do know Lady Huntsberry is the daughter of Lord and Lady Marley."

"Lady Drusilla has yet to make her come-out."

"She will be at dinner?" his mother asked, sounding confused. "I think that a poor idea."

"Well, you are not in charge, are you? It is Lady Huntsberry's dinner party, and if she wishes for her sister to join us, it is her prerogative."

His mother sniffed. "I suppose things are more relaxed in the country. I am so rarely here. Who else, Martindale?"

"I know that Lord Tilsbury will also be present."

"Tilsbury? Why, I haven't laid eyes upon him in years. Once he wed, he and Lady Tilsbury never returned for a single Season. I simply cannot understand that."

"Just as you are drawn to town, there are others who much prefer the country. Lord and Lady Tilsbury were ones who did so."

Perry hated hearing his friend—or anyone—disparaged by his mother. He dreaded what this evening might be like, when all along he had been looking forward to it.

"Anyone else?" she prompted.

"It is possible that Lady Huntsberry's cousin and husband will be in attendance since they are close. That would be Lord and Lady Aldridge."

"Hmm. I saw the new Lord Aldridge last Season, but I was not introduced to him. So, Lady Aldridge is a cousin to Lady Huntsberry," she mused.

He said nothing, already tired of her prodding him.

Having received the information she desired, his mother ceased conversation for the short remainder of their journey to Huntsworth.

When they arrived, the butler met them. Perry saw another carriage already there. Another carriage pulled in behind his, and Lord Tilsbury got out. He watched the viscount's reaction as he caught sight of his neighbor.

"Lady Martindale. It has been many years since our paths have crossed since you do not frequent Beauville."

"My condolences to you on the loss of Lady Tilsbury," his mother said.

"Thank you. She was a wonderful woman."

"If you will follow me, my lords, my lady," the Huntsworth butler said, leading them into the house and up the stairs to the drawing room.

As they entered, Perry caught sight of Lord and Lady Aldridge, as well as his hosts. But his attention fell upon Lady Dru. She was wearing a simple gown of the palest blue, her hair arranged in a simple chignon. His heart began beating faster as their gazes met. He reminded himself that she was not the one for him.

Even as he approached her, he knew that was a lie.

She was the only one for him . . .

"It is so wonderful that you all could come this evening," Lady Huntsberry said. She looked to him, and Perry said, "I would like to introduce you to my mother, Lady Martindale. Mother, this is Lord and Lady Huntsberry, our hosts, and Lady Drusilla Alington, younger sister to Lady Huntsberry."

He also introduced the Aldridges to her. His mother greeted everyone appropriately, keeping all judgment from her voice, for which Perry was thankful.

"It is good to see young people starting to populate the neighborhood," his mother commented. "You have not been to Surrey in many years, Lord Huntsberry. I have seen you frequently about town, however. And you, Lord Aldridge, are new to your title. My husband and I were friendly with the previous Lord Aldridge."

Lord Huntsberry said, "I did not come to the country for many years, my lady, but I am happy to have returned to Surrey. My wife enjoys the country quite a bit, and I agree with her that it is even better than town." He gave his wife an intimate smile.

His mother glanced to Lady Huntsberry. "It seems that you will be raising children in the country rather soon, my lady."

Lady Huntsberry blushed. "Yes, I am increasing," she confirmed.

Lord Huntsberry slipped an arm about his wife's waist. "We are most happy about the news."

His mother turned to the Aldridges and said, "I heard you actually brought your infant to town this past Season. Is that correct?"

"We did," Lord Aldridge said, pride evident in his voice. "Penelope was born about six weeks before the Season began. We did not want to be parted from her."

Clucking her tongue, his mother said, "I assume it was too hard for you to leave an infant behind, Lady Aldridge."

"I would not have left my daughter behind, no matter what her age," Lady Aldridge boldly proclaimed. "My husband and I plan to always bring our children to town during the Season."

Perry covered his chuckle with a cough, seeing his mother's surprise. "But . . . children are to remain at home with their nursemaids. Their tutors and governesses. The Season holds so many events, there is not time to even see children."

Looking intently at his mother, Lady Aldridge said, "You may have chosen to leave your son behind, my lady, but that is something we will never do." She paused. "I am one of ten cousins, and I believe the Season is meant for families, not merely the social whirl. I have already spoken to several of my cousins, and we all plan to bring our children to town with us each year. We will attend some social affairs, but a good deal of our time will be spent with our extended family. That way, our children will grow up not only with their siblings, but their cousins."

"Why, that is the most outlandish thing I have ever heard," his mother sputtered.

Lord Aldridge smiled. "We are a new generation, Lady Martindale. Perhaps others will take notice of what we do and follow suit."

Perry glanced to Viscount Tilsbury, who was nodding in approval.

Drinks were served, and they sipped on them as they chatted about the neighborhood. Since his mother was never here, she contributed nothing to their conversation.

Then she turned her attention upon Lady Dru, whom he had taken a seat next to.

"I hear you have yet to make your come-out, my lady."

"I have not," she replied, not bothering to elaborate.

"You and your sister are Lord and Lady Marley's daughters, I believe."

"We are, my lady," Lady Dru said.

"I find your mother rather . . . opinionated."

Perry came to the rescue, saying, "You yourself are known for your strong opinions, Mother. I am certain you express them as freely as Lady Marley does her own."

Before she could reply, the butler announced that dinner was served.

As they rose, Lord Tilsbury offered his arm. "May I escort you into dinner, Lady Martindale?"

He gave his friend a grateful look and turned to Lady Dru. "May I do the same, my lady?"

"Certainly," she said, taking his arm.

They found themselves the last to leave the drawing room, and she said, "I see you are not close with your mother."

"No. She barely comes to Beauville. In fact, when she arrived this afternoon, it was the first I had seen of her in many years. Of course, I was away at war for four years, but before that? It had probably been five years or longer since we had laid eyes upon one another."

"Then why is she even here?"

"She has come to find out what I am to do with her. My solicitor is scheduled to arrive tomorrow at Beauville with a copy of my parents' marriage settlements."

"From what Mama has told me, widows usually move to the dower house. Since your mother is rarely in the country, will she be doing so?"

"She has already expressed her preference to remain in town. I do not want her at Beauville. Not only would she be bored to tears, she would most likely cause trouble for me. Yet I do not want her in my London townhouse. When I do go there for the Season, I have no wish to look at her every morning at the breakfast table. It will be enough trying to avoid her at social events."

"Could you give her an allowance? Rent her a place somewhere in town?" Lady Dru asked.

"I will learn if that is a possibility after I speak with Mr. Chapman tomorrow. He is to give me a better idea of my financial situation."

They arrived in the dining room, and Perry seated her. Lady Huntsberry indicated for him to take the seat next to her sister, and he did so.

As the soup course was being served, his mother said, "Thank you for accommodating me this evening. It was gracious of you to extend your invitation to include me, Lady Huntsberry."

"We were happy to have you join us," their hostess said. "Although I was not concerned with numbers, we were down a woman. You joining us this evening evened up our numbers."

Dinner conversation was lively, and Perry was glad his mother did not try to dominate the conversation, as she was wont to do.

When it came time for the ladies to withdraw, Lord Huntsberry said, "I would like for the gentlemen to join the ladies and forgo port and cigars."

"An excellent idea," seconded Lord Tilsbury. "I never understood that custom."

They retired to the drawing room again, where his mother asked, "Will any of you ladies be playing or singing for us?" She turned her gaze upon Lady Dru. "I would particularly like to hear you entertain us, Lady Drusilla."

Lady Dru's laugher bubbled up, spilling over. "I would not advise that, my lady, unless you have something to protect your ears. I can barely play the pianoforte. My sister and cousin are much more musically inclined than I am."

Frowning, his mother said, "You are quite frank for a young lady."

"I do speak my mind, Lady Martindale. Fortunately, my sister and brother-in-law encourage me to do so."

"I doubt your mother would approve, young lady," scolded his mother.

An uncomfortable silence filled the air before Lady Huntsberry said, "I will play a little something for us. Dru, would you turn the pages for me?"

"I would be happy to do so, Lucy."

The two sisters went to the pianoforte, and Perry's mother took a seat next to him.

"I hope when you choose your countess that you will find a young lady more docile than Lady Dru. In fact, I expect you to come to town this next Season and do that very thing. I already have a few candidates in mind to introduce you to, and they are most appropriate."

Coolly, he said, "Who says you will even be in town for the

Season, Mother? You might be residing in the dower house year-round."

A look of horror filled her face. "That would be impossible, Martindale. I would wither and die. You inherited the townhouse. It is large enough for us to live there together during the Season, even after you wed."

"It is large enough—but who says I want you there?"

He turned his attention from her and looked to Lady Huntsberry, who had begun to play. As he sat there, he could feel the waves of anger coming off his mother. She did not continue their conversation, though.

After playing two pieces for them, Lady Huntsberry rejoined them. Not long after that, their host indicated it was time for the evening to conclude.

Smiling, Lord Huntsberry said, "We keep to country hours, especially with my wife increasing. I insist that she get her rest. Thank you all for accepting our invitation this evening." He looked to Viscount Tilsbury. "It was delightful to get to know you better, my lord." Then he turned his gaze upon Perry's mother. "Thank you for joining us, Lady Martindale. I know your time here is limited, so I doubt we will see you again."

His mother smiled prettily. "Yes, my lord. I should be returning to town within the next few days. Thank you for your hospitality. I look forward to seeing you next Season."

Everyone walked out together, including their hosts. Perry found himself in Lady Dru's company.

"The invitation to ride Beauville with me is still open, my lady. Naturally, I will be tied up with Mr. Chapman tomorrow. Possibly the day after, as well. Would you care to join me on a ride the following day?"

Those magnificent amethyst eyes sparkled. "I am eager to see your estate, Lord Martindale. Thank you for the invitation."

"If Mr. Chapman leaves early, would you be able to ride the day after tomorrow?"

"Won't you still be entertaining your mother?"

"I hope to see as little of that woman as possible while she is here," he said bluntly.

Lady Dru leaned close, and he caught a whiff of gardenias. "I cannot say that I blame you, my lord. She is most odious."

The guests boarded their separate carriages, and the vehicles started up, one at a time.

His mother said, "Lady Aldridge is most opinionated. I cannot imagine insisting upon bringing children to town during the Season. I can almost understand why she did so this first year because her babe had just been born, but to think to do so year after year, much less convince her cousins to do the same? I hope you will exhibit better sense, Martindale."

"There are actually parents who love their children, Madam. Parents who miss their children when they are separated from them for months at a time. Lady Aldridge is one of those women. Her husband feels the same. Why, Lord Aldridge is well-known for his closeness to his infant daughter. He holds her. Plays with her."

"He does?" His mother looked horrified at the thought.

"Yes, he does. I find it admirable that Lady Aldridge insists upon bringing their children to town instead of leaving them in the country."

Her eyes narrowed. "You resent me, don't you, Martindale? You think I should have showered you with love. Or at least attention."

"It is natural for a mother to love her child," he said quietly. "Then again, you have never exhibited any maternal instincts where I am concerned."

He saw that she wanted to bite back at him, but he caught an inkling of fear in her eyes now, knowing he held her fate in his hands. Perry decided he would do whatever it took to wash his hands of her. Though he worried about any gambling debts his father might have, he decided no sacrifice would be too great to get this woman out of his London townhouse.

And out of his life.

If he didn't, she would ride roughshod over him and the wife he chose. He refused to be around someone so unpleasant.

They arrived back at Beauville and before they left the carriage, he told her. "I will let you know what decision I have come to regarding your status after I meet with Mr. Chapman tomorrow."

Then Perry left the carriage and strode into the house, leaving her to fend for herself.

CHAPTER NINE

THE NEXT MORNING, Perry breakfasted early and went to his study, glad his mother had not been at the meal. He supposed she would dine in her rooms in order to avoid seeing him.

He remained in the room until he saw his carriage returning from Alderton. He had sent it to the village to meet the mail coach Mr. Chapman would arrive on, and the solicitor exited the vehicle. Two minutes later, a knock sounded on his door, and Foster announced that Mr. Chapman had arrived.

"Show him to the room Mrs. Foster prepared," he instructed. "Allow him time to freshen up and then bring him back to me. Also, have Cook send some sandwiches and cider to us. Perhaps some fruit, as well."

"Yes, my lord," the butler said, leaving Perry to his thoughts again.

He had scoured the study, looking for any kind of financial records, finding none. His hope was that he had enough wealth to ensure that he never shared a roof with his mother again.

A quarter-hour later, Mr. Chapman arrived just as a footman brought a tray with tea and sandwiches.

"Leave it here," he said, indicating his desk, rising and shaking hands with the solicitor. "Have a seat, Mr. Chapman. I thought you could use a bit of refreshment after your trip from town."

"That is most thoughtful of you, Lord Martindale." Chapman

placed a satchel on the floor next to him and sat in the chair opposite Perry.

He handed Chapman a plate and while the solicitor filled it, Perry poured cider for them both. He placed two sandwiches and a pear on his plate and leaned back in his chair, sipping his cider.

"I am grateful for you making the trip down to meet with me in person."

"Not a problem, my lord," Chapman assured him. "Beauville is only a couple of hours from town. Now, if you had asked me to come up to York or out to Cornwall, I might have balked a bit."

"We can look at specifics once we have finished eating. For now, give me an overview of my holdings and their status."

"I thought you would like a more detailed account, and so I met with your banker, my lord. At some point when you are in town, you should call upon him, but he prepared a thorough report for your review." Chapman bit into his sandwich and chewed thoughtfully. "I can tell you that your father's debts have been paid. To his tailor. His wine merchant. That sort of thing. I made certain after his death that all accounts with merchants were paid in full and then closed."

"And his gambling debts?" Perry asked, trying to mask his worry.

The solicitor's brows shot up. "You are aware of them?"

"Only that they must exist. My father spent a great deal of time in town, and he let slip that much of that was at various gaming hells."

Chapman nodded thoughtfully. "You will pleased to know that all gambling debts have also been satisfied, my lord. There was a time, not too many years ago, when Lord Martindale had lost quite a bit at the tables. On horses and boxing matches. He curbed his habits for a while and when he returned to gaming, he actually had a long winning streak. Because of that, my lord, you are in good standing."

Chapman began speaking in broad terms regarding the estate's holdings and investments, and Perry was more than pleased to hear that it would not be necessary for him to seek a bride with a large dowry. In fact, he was so well off that a dowry would not even necessarily be a consideration.

They finished eating and got down to the business at hand. The solicitor pulled a large stack of documents from his satchel, going over each in detail with Perry. He began to gain a firm grasp regarding his financial situation, pleased with the information his solicitor was providing.

Hours later, the stack had dwindled to only a few sheets, and Chapman said, "The last matter to discuss, my lord, is the marriage settlements arranged for your parents' union. You had specifically requested to see a copy of those in order to meet your obligations to Lady Martindale."

He had almost forgotten about his mother as they had gone through so many records.

"Yes, I could not find a copy of them here at Beauville. In fact, I found no records at all."

Mr. Chapman grew thoughtful, and Perry believed the solicitor would carefully choose his next words.

"Your father, the previous Lord Martindale, did not care for matters of business. He left all documents either with my office or his banker." Almost apologetically, Chapman added, "The earl also had little interest in Beauville. In fact, I was the one who recommended Mr. Rankin to him when he found himself in need of a new steward."

"I have met daily with Rankin since my return from the army. He has kept meticulous records of all estate affairs. I owe you my gratitude for that recommendation. Without Mr. Rankin, I shudder to think about the state Beauville would be in."

He drained the last of his cider and then added, "I plan to be a much different earl than my father, Mr. Chapman. While I am grateful for all you have done for my family and will continue to retain your services in matters of business, I intend to be actively involved. Both in the running of Beauville and in regard to my business investments."

The solicitor nodded in approval. "I think that the wisest course, Lord Martindale. You seem the responsible sort, having been an army officer. I am grateful that you will continue to use my services. My son also works alongside me. The day will come when I am ready to retire, and I hope you will remain his client after that event occurs."

"Is that coming soon?" he asked.

Chapman chuckled. "Not if I can help it. I enjoy my work, my lord, and hope to continue on for many years. I merely wished to reassure you that if something happens to me, my son is more than ready to step up to any challenge."

"I most likely will not come to town before next Season, but I will make an appointment to stop by your office when I do. I would enjoy meeting the younger Mr. Chapman and getting to know him."

"I appreciate hearing that. Now, let us review the marriage contracts."

Chapman handed Perry a copy, and he had one for himself, as well. For the next several minutes, they looked over them, disregarding provisions for future children beyond the heir apparent. He had no need to review what had been promised to siblings he had never had. As he had suspected, it was the intention that his mother be allowed to reside in the dower house upon the death of her husband. A fairly generous allowance was also included in the settlements, but he doubted it would be enough to pay the rent on another property for his mother to live in while in London.

"I know these were drawn up before my parents' marriage. Were they ever updated at any point?" he asked.

"That would be quite unusual, my lord. The answer to your question is no. They were written and stand as is."

He took a deep breath and slowly released it. "The reason I ask is that over the years, my mother has spent little to no time at Beauville."

Chapman gave him a sympathetic look. "I am aware of that, my lord."

"If my mother were to be told she would reside in the dower house from this point forward, she would be most unhappy." He paused. "And she would make *me* most unhappy."

The solicitor's eyes lit with understanding. "Yes, I know Lady Martindale is fond of town and rarely visits the country. Naturally, it is up to you if you agree to have her reside in town. You are required, by law, to honor the settlements. You also have the ability to alter them if you choose to be more generous."

"Would she have to reside in my townhouse?"

Chapman's eyes widened. "Certainly not, my lord. All you owe her is shelter in the dower house and the allowance designated by the marriage settlements. Anything beyond that is up to your discretion."

He took a deep breath and slowly released it. "I would prefer having my townhouse to myself, especially once I wed. My mother is, shall we say, set in her ways. I would not want her to try and continue to run the household at the expense of my wife. I seek an alternative."

"You can tell from what you have seen that you are a wealthy man, Lord Martindale. If you choose to allow your mother to live in town instead of the dower house, it is your choice as to where she resides. If you believe she would make life uncomfortable— even impossible—for you and your future countess, my suggestion is to rent a house for her. Or you could even purchase one as an investment and merely allow Lady Martindale to reside in it until her death."

Perry decided that was what he would do. He couldn't see himself coexisting in the same house with her. She really was a stranger to him, and he would not have her intimidating his wife or ignoring his children.

He realized that he had been taken by the idea Lady Aldridge had mentioned, that of bringing children to town instead of leaving them for months at a time in the country. He wanted a close relationship with his children, without interference of his mother and her bloody opinions.

"Yes, that is exactly what I shall do, Mr. Chapman. May I leave this to your care? Talk with a leasing agent and see what might be available. It can be a house to rent or one to purchase."

"Do you have a specific area in mind, my lord?"

"Since it is a likely investment, let us say Mayfair to start. If you find something appropriate, buy it."

"Without you seeing it?"

"Yes. I trust your judgment."

"What of its size?"

"Something small, I would think. It is not as if an entire family will live within the property. If you would also look for a staff for it, I would appreciate that, as well. A cook and housekeeper. One or two maids and a footman. That should be more than adequate."

"What of a mews? A coachman and groom?"

Perry shook his head. "Those will not be necessary. My mother can beg rides from her friends or take a hansom cab to her destinations. The designated allowance from the estate is more than generous for her to do so."

Chapman rose, and Perry followed suit. "Then I will see to it straightaway, Lord Martindale. I will put my son in charge of this so you can see what he is capable of. Once he has found and purchased the property, I will have him come to Beauville and report to you regarding the matter."

The two men shook hands. "I had a room prepared for you in case you wished to wait and return to town in the morning," he told the solicitor.

"That will not be necessary, my lord. I can catch the last mail coach coming through Alderton. With sunset so late this time of year, I can be back in London before dark."

"Thank you again for coming to Surrey to meet with me, Mr. Chapman. My carriage will take you back to town." He glanced at the stacks of papers they had gone through. "You should collect these."

"They are all copies of documents already at my office, my

lord. These are for your benefit. I will merely take the extra copy of your parents' marriage settlements with me." The solicitor placed that document inside his satchel.

"Then I appreciate your thoughtfulness. And Mr. Chapman—have your son begin work on finding my mother a place to stay first thing tomorrow morning."

Biting back a smile, the solicitor said, "Of course, my lord."

Chapman left, and Perry glanced through some of the papers again. He would organize them tomorrow since it was almost teatime.

He went upstairs to the drawing room, where he found his mother pacing.

"I see Mr. Chapman just left."

"Yes, he did." Perry took a seat as a maid appeared with the teacart. "Would you care to pour out, Mother?" he asked genially.

"Of course, Martindale," she said brightly, looking optimistic about their upcoming conversation.

The maid left. He watched his mother act as hostess, accepting the cup and saucer she handed him. He placed a scone and half a roast beef sandwich on his plate and then took a bite of the sandwich, chewing slowly. He knew she watched him carefully, eager to hear what he had to say. Perry took his time, finishing his food and tea before engaging her in conversation. By then, she sat nervously, her hands fluttering about.

"Well? What say you?" she finally demanded. "What did the marriage contracts hold?"

"They were full of many interesting things," he began. "Much of it was devoted to the sons you would have beyond the heir apparent and the dowries for your daughters."

She waved a hand dismissively. "I did my duty to your father. I provided him with his heir. What of me?"

Leaning back in his chair, he casually crossed his ankle over one knee. "The settlements allow you to live in the dower house the rest of your natural life. With a small staff and an allowance, of course."

Her expression turned dour. "Surely, you do not expect me to languish in the country, Martindale? I have never been happy here."

He shrugged. "That is what was written into the settlements. I assume your father had a hand in them."

"He did," she reluctantly admitted. "But my papa would not want to see me unhappy. I was his favorite child."

Perry waited a full minute before saying, "I see no need for you to live in the dower house. You rarely come to Beauville."

"Thank goodness," she said, relief evident as her body relaxed. "What of my allowance?"

"We will get to that. Since you will not live in the dower house—by your own choice—it is up to me whether or not I provide you a place to live."

"Pish-posh," she said. "I can merely keep living in the townhouse. I have my rooms there."

"You currently live in the rooms of the Countess of Martindale, Madam. The moment I take a bride, you will become the dowager countess. And you should not expect to have those rooms any longer."

She pouted, her bottom lip turning out. "I suppose I can give them up once you wed. I could take rooms in the west—"

"You will not be living with me and my family."

Her eyes widened. "What?"

"I do not wish to be under the same roof with a stranger."

Visibly trembling, she said, "Oh, please, Martindale. We are not strangers."

"But we are. You never came to Beauville in the year I lived there after graduating from university. I never saw you any of the summers I came home from university because you were always at the Season. Other times when I returned to Surrey, you were never here. In fact, I am thinking, counting my years at war, it has been at least ten years since we have been in the same room. Frankly, I have no interest in you living in *my* townhouse."

Her posture stiffened. "Look here, Martindale. You must—"

"Must what? My only legal obligation is to grant you access to the dower house and your quarterly allowance. Since you do not wish to live there, you will live where I tell you to."

Anger burned in her eyes. "And where might that be?"

"I will arrange for you to have a house in town." Before she became giddy, he added, "A small house. I will pay for the house and the servants who staff it. I will also provide your allowance."

He named the amount and said, "You will pay for your personal expenses from it. Your gowns and hats. That sort of thing."

"I can do so," she said, somewhat mollified that he would provide her with a house and servants.

"In exchange for my generosity, I ask that you do not visit me. Either in town or here at Beauville."

Growing bolder now that she knew the arrangements, she said, "Why would I? It is as you pointed out. We are strangers. Sometimes, it is hard for me to imagine that you even grew inside me." She frowned. "You were a difficult child. Hard to love."

He refused to play her games. "You never cared for me. You dumped me in the hands of servants. They are who raised me. And now you are reaping what you sowed."

"I will return to town tomorrow," she said, spite in her voice. "I will stay in my rooms until you have found a place for me."

"Chapman and his son will be on that first thing tomorrow morning," he said. "He knows this is a pressing matter, so he should find something rather quickly in order to please me. Have your maid start packing your things. The moment I hear from him, you are to leave my townhouse." He paused. "And while I will allow my carriage to take you to town, it will return here. After all, it is my carriage."

She stood, spots of angry color dotting her cheeks. "I have a headache. Tell Foster I will take supper on a tray in my room."

Though he wasn't overly fond of her returning to the London townhouse, it would be best to have her gone from Beauville.

"Suit yourself."

Perry watched her cross the room and called to her as she

reached the door. "One more thing. I will be cordial if I come across you at an event next Season, but beyond a greeting, there will be no conversation between us. And you will have no say in my choice of a countess."

"But—"

"And if any rumors reach my ears that inform me you have spoken ill of me in any manner to any soul in London, the offer I have made you is rescinded. I will toss you from your house. You can either return to the dower house here at Beauville—or find somewhere else to live."

He saw her take in his words and recognized when she accepted defeat.

"Of course, Martindale," she said, gritting her teeth. "Why would I speak poorly of you, when you will give me a house to live in and servants to wait upon me? I wish you a good day."

She left. He hoped he would not see her again until next Season, and then, only for a brief moment here and there. In effect, they were now officially estranged, with him being most generous to her. He had no worries that she would try to damage his reputation because she would cherish the fact she was allowed to remain in town. She might hate him—but she would never say a word against him. Not only would it reflect upon her if she did so, but it would keep her from everything she loved.

Some might have thought Perry heartless and cruel for having done what he did.

But he knew this was imperative to his own survival.

He returned to his study and wrote to Lady Dru, asking if she wished to ride with him around Beauville tomorrow. If so, he would call upon her at the Huntsworth stables at ten o'clock.

Ringing for Foster, he gave the butler the note, requesting that a footman take it to Huntsworth and wait for a reply.

An hour later, a return message came.

Lady Dru would be waiting for him.

CHAPTER TEN

Dru was eager to tour Lord Martindale's property. She was at her happiest when outdoors, especially if she were riding or gardening. In fact, she had been the happiest in her life ever since she had come to Surrey, away from her mother and enjoying time with her sister. It was wonderful being at Huntsworth and seeing her sister so joyful. Lucy had always wanted to wed and have children, and her dreams were coming true. The fact that Lucy had such a wonderful husband in Judson only made the marriage richer.

She also liked being near Ariadne and Julian. Her cousin was kind and intelligent, and she had told Dru all about the orphanage she and Julian ran in town. Dru was hoping to go into town on one of the weekly trips Ariadne and Julian made so she could see Oakbrooke Orphanage and meet some of the children. It was fun getting to know Ariadne again after having met her so many years earlier.

That might be one good reason to attend the Season next spring. Val would be in attendance, and he would bring his sisters Tia and Lia with him, according to letters Ariadne had received from her three siblings and mother. Dru remembered how much fun Val was to be around, and the twins were only a year older than she was. Also, her cousin Hadrian, who was at university, would also come to town after he graduated, which she thought might happen next spring. That would make for a good majority of her cousins in town, which was reason enough to make her come-out. Dru reasoned just because she traveled to town and attended events of the Season, it did not mean she would have to select a husband.

Unless Mama chose one for her. From what Lucy said, that might very well have happened to her. It was only the unique situation Lucy found herself in that led to her marriage to Judson.

Could Dru risk going to town and enjoying the time with her cousins, along with the new friends she would make at the social affairs, and still remain unwed? She wished she knew more of what Mama had on her mind. Perhaps she could talk Con into wheedling the information from their mother. Mama had always favored Con over Lucy and her. If anyone could discern what Mama had in mind, it would be Con.

Her brother might feel lonely next Season because Val, his closest friend, would be hunting for a wife. Con did not want a wife until he came into his own title, and Dru couldn't blame him for that. If Con wed, he and his bride would most likely move into Papa's townhouse during the Season instead of residing in the rooms Con and Val had shared. They would also, more than likely, come home to Somerset and live at Marleyfield. That would be hard on the couple, with Mama's tendency to dominate everything. Con wouldn't have any authority on the estate, and his wife wouldn't be allowed to run any part of the household. No wonder her brother had decided to put marriage aside until he became the earl of Marleyfield.

She couldn't help but think that Lord Martindale would also go to town next spring to look for his own bride. Dru liked him quite a bit, even if he leaned on the shy side. She thought they were becoming friends. Goodness knew he needed some. He had already shared that he didn't have many friends while at school. Any friends he had made during his army days had been left behind.

And then there was his awful mother. Lady Martindale had a tongue even sharper than Dru's own mother, and she wasn't hesitant about using it—or letting her opinions be known. Something told her that Mama and Lady Martindale were not friends, or even friendly. They were too much alike.

That caused her to giggle as she climbed from bed and dressed for the day, Toby lazily watching her before he concentrated on cleaning his face with his paws. She didn't ring for Annie since she would be riding, putting on a shirt and breeches. Lady Martindale would be knocked over by a feather if she saw Dru's riding attire. Actually, so would her own mother. Mama and Papa did not know how she dressed during the months they were gone to town for the Season. It was an unspoken agreement that none of their servants tattled on her. They, along with Con and Lucy, had always been protective of Dru.

She hoped Lord Martindale wouldn't judge her harshly for her attire. He did not seem to be the type who would do so, but she would soon see. If he felt uncomfortable, she would come inside and change.

Sitting at her dressing table, she brushed out her long locks and then braided them in a single braid, tying a ribbon at the top and one at the bottom for a feminine touch. The last thing she did was slip on her riding boots, made just like a man's, and the most comfortable footwear she owned.

Dru went downstairs to the breakfast room, finding Judson and Lucy talking and eating.

"Are you going riding this morning?" her sister asked.

"Lord Martindale is coming over to meet me. He offered to give me a tour of Beauville."

Lucy studied her a moment. "You are enjoying being in his company, aren't you?"

She thanked the footman who placed a cup of tea before her. "Yes, very much so. He can be a little on the quiet side, but when it is just the two of us, he is more talkative." She paused. "I think the war affected him greatly. He is in need of a few friends. That is why I want to encourage Judson and Julian to start up a friendship with him, especially after I am gone."

"I would also like to see his estate," Judson said. "Perhaps I could go along with you today."

For a moment, disappointment flashed through her. Dru wasn't certain why it did.

"No, you cannot do so today," Lucy told her husband. "The doctor is coming to examine me for the first time around eleven o'clock. I want you here in case you have any questions for him."

He took her hand and brought it to his lips, kissing it tenderly. "You are right, love. I had forgotten. I suppose I can ask Martindale to take me about another time. Ask him about it if you would, Dru. Tell him I would return the favor and show him Huntsworth."

"I will do so," she promised, tucking into her eggs.

She finished her breakfast and went to the library, one of her favorite rooms at Huntsworth, and read for an hour before making her way down to the stables.

"Good morning, Harry. I am to ride with Lord Martindale today and see his estate. Would you please saddle a horse for me?"

"Right away, my lady," the groom said. "I'll bring the mount out to you."

She returned outside, thinking it a glorious day. Only a few clouds were present, with only the slightest of breezes. The temperature was mild, but it would definitely heat up as the day went on.

Scanning the horizon, she spied a rider and supposed it was Lord Martindale. Harry appeared with her horse, leading it to the mounting block, and Dru took hold of the saddle horn and tossed her leg over, sitting astride. Harry handed her the reins, and she waited for Lord Martindale to arrive.

The earl pulled up as he reached her. "You are . . . in breeches," he said, looking perplexed.

"Have I shocked you, my lord? I can always go inside and change if you are uncomfortable with my appearance."

A slow smile spread across his face. "No, my lady. In fact, I think it quite practical of you. That—and riding astride. Surely, it has to be more comfortable for your back."

"It is," she agreed. "I was taught to ride sidesaddle, but I soon learned riding as a man is infinitely better for both control and comfort. The same with breeches. I have worn them for years." She grinned. "At least, during the time my parents are away from Marleyfield."

His eyes crinkled as he smiled, making him quite attractive. "It reminds me of the famous idiom—while the cat's away, the mice shall play."

Dru laughed. "Exactly. I would never have Mama's approval to don breeches. The servants and my siblings are all in the conspiracy with me. No one has ever let the cat out of the bag, to use another famous saying."

"And how is Toby this morning?" Lord Martindale asked. "As long as we are speaking of cats."

"I left him on my bed, washing his face," she told him. "Sometimes, I place him in a sack for him to come riding with me. I decided to leave him behind today, though. Shall we go?"

"Certainly."

She nudged her horse and began to canter. Lord Martindale fell into place beside her. They rode in companionable silence across Huntsworth lands and into Alderton, traveling down its main thoroughfare. They slowed their horses to a walk in the village, picking up speed once again when they left. Soon, they were at the edge of Beauville.

Dru pulled up on the reins, stopping, and Lord Martindale did the same.

"How did Beauville come by its name? I would think your country estate would be Martinville. Or Martin Manor. Something to do with your title."

"My last name is Beaumont," he shared. "The place name must come from the family surname. That is a good question, though. I will have to check the estate's records and see if I can discover who named the property and when they did so. Perhaps you can come back to the house with me, and we might look together. There are all kinds of old books related to the estate in my library."

"You said the magic word," she told him. When he looked puzzled, she said, "Library. While I prefer being outdoors, my favorite inside hobby is that of reading. A library always feels like home to me."

"I told you I was a lover of books. I enjoyed reading about military history most of all, though I do have a fondness for Shakespeare's plays." He smiled. "Especially the history ones."

"I also enjoy Mr. Shakespeare's work. We will have to discuss it sometime. When it is a rainy day and we are stuck inside."

"Ah, that is the most polite hint I have ever heard, my lady. Come. I will take you to the mill first."

They spent a good three hours riding around the estate. Lord Martindale showed Dru some of the improvements that were being made on the property and told her of others in the works. She could tell he had a true love of the land.

"You are doing remarkable things at Beauville," she praised, slipping from the saddle and holding the reins as she led her horse to a stream for some water.

He sighed, following her. "Some of these things should have been handled years ago, but my father was never interested in Beauville. He visited on rare occasions, preferring to remain in town to gamble and drink. When I tried to get him to agree to changes, however, he turned stubborn and refused to do so, even if it would have improved the yield of the land and guarantee him more income. As I mentioned, it was the main thing that prodded me to leave England and go to war."

Impulsively, she reached for his hand, squeezing it. "You did the best you could, my lord. If your father was not willing to listen, nothing you could have done would have changed his mind. While I thank you for your service to England, I am sorry you were driven to go to war, especially since you were heir to Beauville and the title."

He clasped her fingers a bit tighter. "The war has stayed with me," he admitted. "I dream of the battlefields. The carnage. I thought returning to the green fields of Surrey would help me escape, but I seem to constantly be taken back to the horrors I saw."

She could see pain clouding his eyes, and her gaze met his. "We are becoming friends, are we not?"

"I believe we are."

"Then if you ever wish to unburden yourself, I would be happy to listen. I know enough not to try and give you advice. I merely want you to know you do not have to be alone in your suffering."

"You are most kind, my lady. While I would never speak of what I saw, just hearing that you are willing to listen to me is the kindest gesture I have ever experienced."

He brought their joined hands to his lips and brushed a tender kiss upon her fingers. The oddest sensation rippled through her, making her lightheaded, even as her heart beat faster. Even her belly tightened in an unusual manner.

Lord Martindale released her hand. The feelings subsided, but she still felt a bit breathless.

"Drink, Zeus," he urged his horse.

They met some of his tenants after that, and Dru could tell they liked their new lord very much. The earl listened quietly to a few of their concerns before offering some solutions. He even said he would speak to his steward, and the two of them would return tomorrow to discuss things with the tenants in greater detail.

"Shall we ride back to the house now?" he asked, tossing her into the saddle. "I could use something to eat."

"Definitely. Riding always makes me hungry as a horse." She laughed, feeling lighthearted. "Yet another idiom. We are full of them today, my lord."

He led her toward the stables, asking the groom who met them to feed both horses. Then he offered his arm and she took it, allowing him to guide her to the house. The butler gave Dru a perplexed look, and she realized it was because she wore her breeches.

"Perhaps I should not have come inside," she said quietly. When Martindale looked puzzled, she said, "My attire."

"Nonsense," the earl declared. "Foster, we are ravenous and in need of sustenance after several hours in the saddle. Have Cook make us something, including tea. We will be in the library."

"Yes, my lord," the butler said, leaving them in the foyer.

"He did look a bit judgmental," Lord Martindale ventured once the servant was out of earshot. "I suppose others can be shocked by your attire."

"I will admit that our servants in Somerset had to get used to it. I cannot recall when I started wearing breeches. It was that long ago."

"Come to the library. We will have several minutes before the food and tea appear."

They entered a large room with shelves filled with books covering three sides. Dru turned in a circle, taking it all in.

"This is amazing. Even better than Judson's library at Huntsworth and certainly larger than ours at Marleyfield."

"I have read every book on these shelves at one time or another," he said proudly. "And I plan to add to this collection. A man can never have too many books."

"Or a woman."

He chuckled. "Or a woman. Hopefully, my wife will enjoy reading and our children will, too."

"Are you eager to wed?" she asked.

The earl looked pained. "Not really, truth be told. I am a simple man. Before I left for the war, I had no thoughts of marriage. At war, marriage was the last thing on my mind. Now that I have returned and taken up my title, however, it is not a topic I can avoid."

"Providing an heir is important. You will have many women

to choose from next Season. That is, if you choose to go to town."

He blew out a long breath. "I suppose I must. How I will get the attention of some lady has yet to be determined."

"Why do you say that? You are most handsome, my lord. Intelligent. Thoughtful."

"You think me handsome?" he asked, clearly not believing her.

"I think you incredibly handsome," Dru asserted. "Your moss green eyes draw a person in, making them want to confide in you. You have excellent bone structure and wonderfully thick, blond hair, the color of summer wheat in the fields. Your posture is that of the officer you once were, and you haven't an ounce of fat on you. Altogether, you are well made, my lord. I doubt you will have one whit of trouble finding a bride on the Marriage Mart."

Suddenly, the air about them seemed to change. His eyes turned greener, heat in them. Her own heart began to beat rapidly.

Lord Martindale stepped to her, his body so close that it brushed against hers, causing her breasts to tingle. His hand moved to cradle her nape.

"I should not do this," he murmured.

And then he lowered his lips to hers.

CHAPTER ELEVEN

P ERRY'S HEAD AND heart warred with each other.
And his heart won out.

He knew it was wrong to kiss Lady Dru—but he did it anyway. One hand cupped her nape, while the other moved to the small of her back. Their bodies grazed against one another, even as their lips did. He would not rush this kiss. He would savor it.

Because it would be the last time he kissed her.

Slowly, he brushed his lips against hers. Soft. Ripe. He heard her breath hitch as he began pressing gentle kisses to her luscious mouth. Again and again, he touched his lips to hers, each time for a little longer. Then a little harder. He heard her sigh and felt as she moved closer to him, her breasts now pressed against his chest. His heart beat rapidly as he continued kissing her.

Knowing her only kiss had been the soft, easy one between them on a previous occasion, he took his time, letting the heat build between them. Then ever so slowly, he glided his tongue along her full, bottom lip. Back and forth. Back and forth. She stiffened when he first did so, but now she relaxed, snuggling closer to him, her arms reaching up, her fingers clasping his nape. She began toying with his hair, pulling slightly on it, murmuring something he could not discern.

Encouraged by her response, he ran his tongue along the seam of her mouth, gently nudging it open, gaining access to heaven. His tongue swept inside, tasting her sweetness, even as the faint scent of gardenias surrounded them. It was obvious that she did not know what to make of this kind of kiss because she stilled for a moment, letting him explore her leisurely. Then a whimper escaped from her, causing desire to surge through him.

He slid his hand down to her tight, rounded buttocks, squeezing one cheek, then letting his other hand glide along her spine to the other cheek. He kneaded her buttocks, causing her to mewl. Oh, how he wanted to strip the tight breeches from her and feel the bare skin, but he knew he could only go so far.

His hand moved up again, fingers splayed against her back, holding her in place. The other he brought between them, sliding it along her hip and thigh, reaching the place between her legs. As he kissed her possessively, his hand cupped her.

She gasped, breaking the kiss for a moment, her luminous, amethyst eyes meeting his, a question in them.

"Trust me," he whispered, his mouth covering hers again, the kiss deep and satisfying.

Slowly, he ran a finger along the seam of her sex, regretting that he could not plunge that finger into her. Still, he rubbed and caressed her lovingly, and she began to whimper, even as she moved against his hand. He believed he could get her to come and made that his goal as he deepened the kiss.

Her whimpers turned to low groans. He broke the kiss, his lips traveling down her throat, feeling her pulse jump. His hand moved faster now, his teeth grazing her throat. She began panting, her breath shallow and rapid.

"Let go," he urged. "Go with the feelings within you."

His lips moved to her earlobe, his teeth tugging on it. That was what drove her over the edge. Quickly, his mouth covered hers again, swallowing her cries of ecstasy, as she held on tightly to him, her hips moving, meeting his hand. They were so close he felt every beat of her heart as she pushed against him, her body trembling uncontrollably.

Then she stilled. She was the one who broke the kiss, turning her head to the side, breathing heavily. Perry kissed her hair, wanting so badly to have this woman in his bed.

And in his heart.

His hands went to her waist, steadying her. Their gazes met, and he saw she was dazed by the experience. She licked her lips, causing desire to flare within him again.

"Come. Sit."

He guided her to a chair, easing her into it. It looked out over the front lawn of Beauville. She gazed out the window, her eyes glazed and unfocused. Bending, he brushed a kiss against her brow and then took the chair opposite her. Neither spoke. He knew she must be trying to make sense of what had happened between them.

Hearing the door open, he glanced up, seeing a maid rolling in a teacart, thankful no servant had entered and seen them together. Perry rose, meeting the maid.

"I will take it. Thank you."

The maid left, and he rolled the cart over to the far side of the room, so that it was between them.

Only then did Lady Dru look up. Their eyes met, and he saw curiosity in them now.

"What was that?" she asked.

"Let's get a cup of tea in you, and then we can talk about it if you wish," he said lightly.

Instinctively, she began the ritual of pouring out. He made up a plate for them both, handing hers to her.

"Thank you," she said, accepting it. "I suppose I should also thank you for the kiss. Or was it kisses? I could not tell when one ended and another began."

"I do not think it is necessary to keep count," he told her.

"Lucy told me tongues were involved in kissing," she told him. "I did not really believe her." Her gaze met his. "But I do now. I know I have no experience in kissing, but I believe that you kiss divinely, my lord."

He felt the tips of his ears prickle. "Well, thank you, my lady.

You also kiss very well. I would call you a fast learner."

That caused her lips to curve in a smile. "I did pick things up rather well. It was the most enjoyable thing I have ever done. No wonder Lucy and Judson kiss so often," she mused.

Absently, she took a sip of her tea. He could tell she was still trying to think through what had passed between them. She ate an entire scone, her expression thoughtful, before she spoke again.

"What of the other. You know, beyond our kisses. I want to talk about that."

Though he knew it wasn't the most polite topic to converse about, he knew everything was new to her.

"The feeling you experienced is called orgasm," he explained. "The French have another term for it. *La petite morte.*"

"The little death," she echoed, translating the words. "Yes. I can understand that. It was almost as if I had died—and been reborn somehow." She frowned. "How could I let you feel the same?"

Now, his ears burned, and he thought them probably bright red.

"It is nothing for you to worry about, Lady Dru," he assured her.

"But . . . I felt so alive in that moment. As if I soared through the heavens." She paused. "Sometimes, when I ride astride, I have felt little pricklings in my core. You . . . touching me there . . . it made me feel invincible."

A bit of pride swelled within him. "I am glad you enjoyed it, my lady."

"Do all couples who kiss—"

"No," he interrupted, his tone firm. "In fact, I should not have done so. It is usually a practice conducted between married couples. Do not let another man touch you like that again until you are wed," he warned sternly.

Defiance flickered in her eyes. "And what if I choose not to wed, my lord?" she demanded.

"Then you can pleasure yourself," he told her. "You do not need a man to do what I did to you. You can do so yourself."

"I could never do that," she said, a blush spilling across her cheeks.

"You can," he said firmly. "You should. Especially if you do not decide to take a husband. It is something you can do in private."

She pondered his advice. "I suppose I could. With my bedchamber door locked so no servant might interrupt me." Frowning, she asked, "If this is something a wedded couple does, then why did you do it with me?"

Why, indeed?

"Because you have touched something deep within me, Lady Dru. You have been utterly kind, offering me your friendship. No, what we did is not something friends do, but I wanted to please you in the moment."

She chuckled, the sound making him smile. "Well, you most certainly did, my lord. I have never experienced such euphoria. And coupled with the kissing, why, it was simply incredible."

"It is not something you should speak of. Especially to you sister."

She shook her head vigorously. "No, I would think not. I am certain Lucy and Judson do so. Ariadne and Julian, as well. But I will not reveal what passed between us. Not even the kisses," she promised. "Lucy entrusted me with you. If I told her—or Judson—that we had kissed, I am afraid my brother-in-law might come and remove your head from your body. Slowly. And painfully." She giggled.

"And he would be within his rights to do so," Perry agreed. "I do not regret kissing you, Lady Dru. I thoroughly enjoyed it. As for the other? I think we should never mention it again."

"I agree. If I do agree to make my come-out, I will certainly kiss a fellow or two. Mostly to compare their kiss with yours, my lord."

"Are you leaning toward a come-out Season, my lady?"

She sighed. "It is possible. It would give me more time with Lucy and Ariadne. My other cousins, as well. I told you because of my uncle's death that Tia and Lia had to postpone their own come-outs. It would be fun to do so with my cousins. And Val will also be there, along with Con. I would like to spend time with all of them and even make a few new friends amongst the other girls making their own come-outs."

He watched her brow furrow. "What is it?"

"My only fear is that Mama will demand I wed. I told you she did not choose Judson for Lucy, but I did not tell you why. You see, they were caught in a compromising position. Kissing one another. Judson was gentleman enough to offer for my sister, who already had developed feelings for him. Come to find out, Judson also had feelings for Lucy."

"But you are wise enough not to go about kissing men and being ruined?"

"I would hope so," she said, laughing. "It does not mean I would not be agreeable to a brief kiss in the moonlight or while strolling some gardens. Thanks to Lucy's experience, I would be most careful. I have told you I am leery of marriage. Mama can be overbearing as it is. I do not want to go from her household to a husband who would be domineering and arrogant. I treasure having my freedom. If I do attend the Season, Mama might try and force my hand into marriage."

"You never mention your father. What of him?"

She shrugged. "Oh, Papa is a genial sort. He is quietly supportive of me—when Mama is not in the room."

"Would he stand up for you against your mother and allow you to make your own choice? Either of the gentleman you wish to wed—or the decision not to wed at all?

She sighed. "Mama has always made all the decisions in our family. She was a duke's daughter and is very opinionated, as your own mother pointed out. I believe Mama wishes she had been born a man so that she might have become the duke. I have never seen her back down from any challenge. She rules our household with a firm hand, and that includes telling Papa what he should do and where he should go."

He was concerned hearing this. "Both your sister and cousin have wed powerful, strong men. Could the four of them help you? And your brother?"

"That is what I am debating," she confided. "If those who support me would be enough to help me stand up to Mama."

"The Hardwicke Act should protect you, my lady," he explained. "You would have to give your consent and make your vows with no coercion for any marriage to be valid."

She brightened. "You mean that if I did not wish to marry a gentleman, I could simply refuse?"

"In theory, yes. No one can force you to speak your vows during the ceremony."

She shuddered. "I would hate to think it would take getting to the ceremony itself and refusing to speak at all in order for Mama to understand I did not wish to wed."

He reached and took her hand, ignoring the way it made him feel to do so. "If she tries to force you to wed, tell her you will not do so. Say the Hardwicke Act gives you the freedom from coercion. If she is wise, she would step back and not force the issue."

Brightening, she said, "This is a relief to hear, my lord. It gives me the confidence to go to the Season and enjoy the time with my family without dreading what outcome might come about, thanks to Mama's machinations." She paused, looking at him beseechingly. "And you will come next spring, won't you? You have said you wish to find a bride."

His heart heavy, Perry still put a smile upon his face. "Yes. I plan to do that very thing. It is important for me to find my countess and get an heir."

Lady Dru beamed. "Oh, it would be so wonderful to have you there. I would introduce you to all my family. I know you would like them. You already know Judson and Julian. Con and Val are also wonderful men. I know they could introduce you around and possibly even help you find a match."

A sinking feeling filled him. He had such tender feelings for Lady Dru, but she blithely only considered him as a friend. Perry told himself he should feel fortunate that he had a firm friend in her and, most likely, would also become friends with others in her family. It would be nice to have real friends, as well as find a wife.

Pushing aside his feelings for her, Perry said, "Then we should make a pact," he said. "We both go to the Season—or neither of us do."

She squeezed his fingers. "I like that idea. I can even help you in looking for your countess. I know men usually are only interested in a woman's looks or their dowry, but I can get to know the other young ladies and tell you about their character."

"I can do the same for you," he offered. "We can be one another's confidant. Give advice to each other."

"That is wonderful, my lord. You actually have me looking forward to the Season now," she declared.

He released her hand, no longer able to hold it without a deep yearning filling him. He had Lady Dru's friendship, which was something he cherished. He figured she would be a good judge of character, and she could help him find his wife.

Even as his heart broke.

"I am glad that is settled," he said. "Come, finish what is on your plate, then I will accompany you back to Huntsworth."

"Oh, I can ride by myself. I do so all the time at home."

"No," he said firmly. "Your sister has entrusted you to my care. I will deliver you home safely."

They finished eating and went to the stables. Despite his gloomy mood, he couldn't help but catch a bit of Lady Dru's joy. She had such a light heart and was a carefree spirit. Perry knew he did the right thing by not pursuing her.

He only hoped he could make it through the Season—and wed a woman who might help him forget this beautiful, spirited woman.

CHAPTER TWELVE

DRU DISMOUNTED AND gave her reins to the groom standing nearby. Harry led her horse away, and she looked up at Lord Martindale.

"Thank you for inviting me to accompany you about your estate today, my lord. Beauville is a lovely property. I know that you will be a good caretaker of it and that seeing it flourish will be very satisfying for you."

"Thank you for coming with me today, Lady Dru," he said. "I appreciate the suggestions you made regarding the land."

He hesitated, the tips of his ears turning slightly red. It was something she had noticed about him when he was embarrassed or uncomfortable, and she found it quite endearing.

"Then I hope we will see one another soon," she told him. "Perhaps next week we might go and visit Viscount Tilsbury again."

"Perhaps," he said non-committedly. "Please give my regards to Lord and Lady Huntsberry."

The earl wheeled his horse and cantered away. Dru stood watching him ride off, a slow, sinking feeling overtaking her gut. She wasn't ready to go into the house just yet. She needed time to ponder what had happened between them, and so she made her way toward the gardens, her favorite place to think.

Once there, she walked along the path, seeing how Judson's gardeners had cleared out the weeds and begun planting different flowers, based upon her suggestions. She came along a bench and took a seat upon it.

Alone, she said aloud what she could never utter in front of others.

"I think I might be in love with Lord Martindale."

There. She had acknowledged it. The last thing Dru had thought might occur in her life was to fall in love. She wasn't even certain what love entailed, having never witnessed any feelings of affection between her parents. Her stay at Huntsworth, though, had exposed her to the idea of love between a couple. Watching both Lucy and Judson and Ariadne and Julian had let her know that love within a marriage did exist. Still, Dru had never assumed she would be touched by it. After all, while she felt nurturing toward animals, she did not know if she possessed any maternal instincts. She had avoided the idea of a husband altogether because she hated being told what to do and knew once she spoke her vows, she would, in effect, become the property of her husband.

Yet seeing how Lucy and Judson treated one another as equals had opened her eyes to the possibility of a different world. A kinder world, filled with love and companionship. And yes, even children.

Might her future include a husband—and could it be Lord Martindale?

The more she was around the earl, the more Dru liked him. He made for good company. While she was outgoing and talkative, he was quieter and more introspective. Still, she thought there was a nice balance between them. They certainly had sparks between them. She had never thought of the idea of being physically attracted to a man, but she certainly had enjoyed Lord Martindale's kisses today. No wonder her sister and brother-in-law went about kissing all the time. Kissing brought a glorious feeling, not to mention what else had passed between her and the earl.

Dru felt herself growing warm, thinking of his hand pressed

intimately against her body and the feelings it had spurred. She couldn't help but wonder what it might be like without the barrier of her breeches. That thought caused her to go hot all over.

She knew he was attracted to her, just as she was to him, but he was being most respectful of her. Because she had confided in him that she was not seeking a husband, he seemed to have put aside the notion of the two of them being together on a permanent basis. That alone, coupled with other things she had observed about him, led her to believe that he might be a man she could commit to.

The question was how to voice this.

Yes, she could be bold at times, but Dru did not know if she had it within her to make her feelings known to Lord Martindale. It occurred to her that while the attraction between them was obvious, she might not be what the earl sought in his wife. He was a taciturn man, and he might believe her too emboldened to make for a good countess. The best course of action, in her opinion, was to do nothing for now. She would be at Huntsworth for weeks—possibly months. Dru saw no need to force the issue now.

Instead, she decided to let things play out between them naturally. If they were meant to be together, it would become apparent as time passed. Or she hoped it would. If Lord Martindale sought a different type of bride, then she hoped she could serve as a good friend and adviser to him. Dru believed him to be emotionally damaged by his war experience. Because of that, he would not be quick to commit to any woman. He had spoken briefly of dreams he had regarding the war, and she suspected those dreams were actually nightmares which haunted him.

Rising, she determined to continue as she had, enjoying her time here at Huntsworth. If nothing came of her budding friendship with Lord Martindale, Dru decided she would still attend the upcoming Season next spring. It would give her the opportunity to get to know some of her cousins better and let her gain a taste of Polite Society. Why, she might even find a gentleman cut from the same cloth as Judson and Julian. They were both strong men, physically and emotionally, dedicated to their properties and their wives. And if she could find no man in their same mold? She would revert to her previous plan of being a doting, spinster aunt. It would irk Mama to no end, but Dru had a mind of her own and would live her life as she saw fit. While she would never wish to be a burden upon Lucy and Judson, she did not think she would be.

Perhaps when Con wed someday, she might even spend part of the year with him and her sister-in-law. That is, if they were amenable to that plan. It was hard to picture her brother as a husband. He was such a carefree sort, much as Dru herself was. She would like to see a different side of Con. Going to town next spring would allow her to do so.

Leaving the gardens, she went inside the house and headed to the drawing room. When she arrived, she saw the teacart had already arrived and that Lucy was pouring out.

"There you are," her sister said genially. "I was not certain if you would make it back in time for tea with us."

"How did the visit with the doctor go?" Dru asked as she took a seat opposite Lucy and Judson.

Her brother-in-law beamed. "He thinks everything is going quite well."

Lucy chuckled. "Judson asked a good two dozen questions. I merely sat and listened. The doctor also recommended a midwife to use, and I will meet with her next week."

"Did he say it was unusual for you not to feel sick?" she asked, feeling Toby brush against her leg. She picked him up and placed him in her lap.

"It was as I suspected," Lucy replied. "He told us that some women become violently ill when they are increasing, while others only experience a mild nausea. Upon rare occasions, a woman is not ill in the slightest. I suppose that makes me very fortunate."

Judson took his wife's hand, entwining his fingers through hers. "He did warn us that each time is different, however. That simply because Lucy is glowing with good health now does not mean it would be the same with a second babe or beyond."

"I recall how Ariadne told me she was ill upon arising each morning and then some throughout the day," Lucy said. "The feeling subsided after a few months. And look at little Penelope today. She is the picture of health and continues to thrive."

They asked her several questions about Lord Martindale's estate, and Dru answered them to the best of her ability.

"Harvest will happen next week," Judson said. "I wonder when Lord Martindale's tenants will harvest their crops."

"Perhaps you should ask him to come that first day when the harvest begins," Lucy suggested. "He seems like such a kind gentleman. It would do you both good to spend time together. Lord Martindale might enjoy seeing how things are done here at Huntsworth."

Judson raised their joined hands, kissing Lucy's fingers. "A splendid idea, love. I will send a note around, asking him to do that very thing."

Just as tea concluded, Brown entered the drawing room.

"A note has arrived for you, my lady," the butler said, presenting a silver tray close to her.

"Thank you," Dru said, plucking the paper from the tray and opening it.

Scanning its contents, she began to smile.

"Ariadne has invited me to go to town with her and Julian tomorrow," she said excitedly. "I had expressed interest in seeing Oakbrooke Orphanage."

"Oh, you must go," Lucy encouraged. "Ariadne and Julian are doing such good work for the children who live there."

"Our cousin has invited me to come for dinner this evening and stay the night. We would leave for town early tomorrow morning."

"That would be more convenient," Judson said. "I shall have

the carriage brought around to convey you to Aldridge Manor."

"Wait a bit if you would, Judson," Dru said. "I simply must have a bath after spending hours in the saddle today."

"Go upstairs," Lucy said. "I will alert the kitchen to heat water and send Annie to you so that she might pack for you. I will also send a message to Ariadne to let her know you will accept her offer."

"Thank you, Lucy."

Dru went upstairs and while waiting for her bathwater to arrive, began sorting through her gowns, choosing a few to take with her. Annie arrived and began gathering other things Dru would need, from chemises to stockings to shoes.

She enjoyed her bath, Annie assisting her, and then the maid helped Dru dress again. She rang for a footman to carry her valise downstairs. Judson met her, saying the carriage would be ready at any moment.

Lucy came and kissed her goodbye. "Have a wonderful time while you are in town."

It struck her that she had not been to London but the one time, ten years ago. She might actually take in a few of the sights, as well as seeing the orphanage.

"I will accompany you to Aldridge Manor," Judson offered.

She thought it quite kind of him to escort her. They waved goodbye to Lucy, and the carriage began rolling along the lane.

"I dashed off a note to Martindale, asking him to come next Monday for the beginning of the harvest."

"How long does it take?" she asked.

"We should be done in two days' time," her brother-in-law told her. "If it spills into a third day, it will not be a problem. That third day, though, we will be celebrating at Huntsworth. There is to be a large, outdoor feast, along with music and dancing."

"That sounds marvelous, Judson. We never did anything such as that at Marleyfield."

"Different estates carry out various customs. I have been gone from Huntsworth for many years. This is something

Wayling, my steward, had the tenants engage in during my time away."

"You seem quite content now in the country after your years in the city."

He smiled. "That is all because of Lucy," he explained. "I did not have much of a home life, Dru. My mother died giving birth to me. My father was ill most of my childhood and died when I was but ten years of age. His brother, my uncle, became guardian of me and the estate after that."

Judson's mouth thinned, and his jaw tightened. "He was a harsh, cruel man. Once I left for university, I chose never to return home again. I did not have fond memories of Huntsworth and could not picture myself ever living there for any length of time."

He chuckled. "I thought I would have a marriage of convenience, leaving my wife buried in the country while I remained in town. Little did I know I would fall head over heels for your sister. While Lucy enjoyed being in town for the Season, she favors the country." He smiled. "And I favor my wife. I will go wherever she wishes us to be. Lucy believes raising our children in the country will be good for them. After being here with her and experiencing the happiness I already have, I heartily agree."

A deep yearning filled Dru. While she was thrilled that her sister had found such a good man, she was slightly jealous of their close relationship. Though Dru had thought of a husband as more of a jailer, she realized now that did not have to be the case. That she could share her life with a partner.

They arrived at Aldridge Manor, Ariadne and Julian greeting them.

Her cousin embraced her, saying, "Oh, I am delighted that you wish to come to town with us tomorrow. I cannot wait for you to meet Miss Darnell, along with the orphans who reside there."

"You have spoken so fondly of your work there. Thank you for extending the invitation, Ariadne."

"I must get back," Judson said. "Let me know when you return, and I will come and fetch Dru."

"Do not trouble yourself, Judson," Julian told him. "We will deliver Dru safely back to you and Lucy."

She went inside the house, a footman bringing her valise along and taking it up the stairs.

"I know Annie needs to stay to look after Lucy, so you and I will share my maid while you are here and we are in town," Ariadne told her.

Julian excused himself, and her cousin led them into a small parlor off the foyer, where they took a seat.

"Do you go often to town?" Dru asked.

"We try to do so once a week, now that Penelope has arrived. The carriage ride was a bit too much for me during my final months of increasing. It is a blessing that Julian's country seat is located in Surrey, putting us so close to town. It only takes a couple of hours for us to reach London. Because of that, we like to go as often as possible. Our commitment to the orphanage is strong, as well as a program we have started which helps provide clothing donations to the needy."

"Does Penelope go with you?"

"At first she did, but we have found it is best that she stay behind for the two days we are gone. She does better when she is kept to a schedule. Of course, it will be different when we return to town for several months when the Season starts."

"I have heard of your pact with my siblings. That you wish for them to bring their own children to town each spring."

"I look back on that magical week we ten cousins had together," Ariadne said. "It was ever so much fun spending time with all of you. Not only do I wish to have my own children with me and not leave them for months at a time, alone in the country, but I think it is an excellent idea for all my cousins' children to come together and share experiences with one another over the years."

Ariadne paused, scrutinizing Dru. "Lucy tells me that you do not seem to have an interest in a husband or bearing children. If that is your decision, I respect it. I only hope that you, too, will come to town each spring to share time with all of us."

"I have decided to go ahead and make my come-out," she explained. "I will not actively pursue a husband. Being at Huntsworth, though, and seeing how a good marriage can work may have changed my mind regarding the institution. I will admit, however, that it would need to take a very special man for me to enter the bonds of matrimony. I fear you and Lucy have snagged two of the best."

"I think it wise you will keep an open mind as you attend the Season," her cousin said. "And yes, there are numerous gentlemen who would not make for good husbands for you. Let me say this. You do not have to wed after your first Season. There are girls who come back two, three, even four times before they settle into marriage. Marriage is not to be taken lightly. I know you would never rush into anything. Simply be comfortable and enjoy the various social events." Ariadne smiled. "You never know when you will find the right one."

Dru wanted to say that she thought she had discovered a possible candidate, but she kept silent.

Only time would tell if she and Lord Martindale might suit.

CHAPTER THIRTEEN

THEY REACHED LONDON, and Dru suddenly recalled the bustling streets as Julian's carriage rolled along them. She remembered how she had never seen that many people before her only visit to the great city. The smells coming from food carts drifted through the air, causing her mouth to water. Other, not so pleasant odors, also mingled, and she shuddered.

"The warmth of the sun does exacerbate some of the more odious smells," Julian said. "I used to work on the London docks and thought I would never get the stink of fish from my nostrils."

She thought his statement odd. Why would a marquess—or at least the heir to a marquessate—be doing physical labor on the waterfront? Though curious, she didn't press him about it. Julian's past was not her concern.

"We will go straight to Oakbrooke," Ariadne told her. "Then the carriage will go to our townhouse. Tally will unpack for the both of us."

Dru patted her hair. "I like what Tally did with my hair this morning. Hopefully, she could teach Annie how to recreate this style."

"I will have her spend time teaching Annie how to do so once we return to Surrey," her cousin assured her.

For the next half-hour, she gazed out the window, looking at the buildings and people, while Ariadne and Julian talked of their work at the orphanage and why it was so important to them.

"I came from the lower classes," Julian shared. "Worked on the docks long hours and then served as a clerk to a solicitor. I had no idea I was the son of a marquess. The legitimate son," he added.

Now, his words made more sense to her, and she wondered how Julian had discovered his true heritage.

Ariadne snuggled against her husband. "I would have wed you no matter what you did. It is nice, however, to have a wealthy husband who has a heart for the poor and is willing to part with some of that wealth in order to do good for so many who are in need."

Dru could picture Julian as a laborer, based upon his physique. She also thought him quite honorable, giving both time and money to the poor.

They arrived at Oakbrooke Orphanage and sent the carriage along the way, with the coachman promising to return for them late in the afternoon. She had no idea what they might do for all those hours, but she was ready to take part in whatever Ariadne and Julian suggested.

As they entered the building, the large hall was empty. Her cousin said that classes were in session now, but that a school-wide assembly would begin shortly.

"We should make our way to the dining hall," Julian said.

Once they reached it, Dru caught sight of a woman setting up a few chairs at the far end of the hall's entrance.

"Who is that?" she asked.

"An angel in disguise," Ariadne quipped. "Come and meet our Miss Darnell."

She was introduced to the headmistress of Oakbrooke Orphanage and learned that Miss Darnell had been a teacher before assuming her current position.

"But I still do a bit of teaching," she told Dru. "I cannot ever see myself totally leaving the classroom."

"What is this assembly like, Miss Darnell?"

"It is a daily gathering of the orphans. We always refer to

them as students. I do not like to remind them of being orphans. Many times, they have already had a hard life before they reach us. We open with a prayer, and then I speak to them briefly. Sometimes, I let them know what is occurring in London and beyond. I believe an informed citizen is a better citizen. Also, an educated citizen can better understand his or her place in the world."

"That is followed by students sharing with others," Julian told Dru. "Sometimes, they will hold up their artwork so others might view it. A few are learning how to play a musical instrument, so they sometimes play a tune for us. One of the teachers has quite a good voice, and once a week, she will teach the group an English folk song. The children really enjoy learning those."

"It is a time to come together and bolster their spirits," Ariadne concluded. "They do spend a good deal of their day in a classroom, learning to read and write and do sums. We also offer classes to help train them for service. A good many of them will go into service in the great households in the city or at country estates of titled noblemen."

"The children also help take care of their environment and the orphanage itself," Miss Darnell continued. "They rotate various housekeeping activities, based upon their age. The younger ones are given simpler tasks. The students at Oakbrooke learn to cook, clean, and sew."

"All of them learn these things?" she asked.

"Yes," the headmistress confirmed. "Some of the great chefs in Europe and Asia are men. Even though I doubt we have a world-class chef in the making, I think it is important for each student to learn how to take care of themselves. That includes learning how to feed themselves and sew on a button. How to wash their clothes. Ironing is a very important skill, and it is something all Oakbrooke children learn to do. Not only do they learn how to iron clothes, but they also iron linens. Even newspapers. Many noblemen prepare to read a pressed newspaper at breakfast."

"We hope as they mature, Julian and I might hire some of them to come to work for us, either at Aldridge Manor or here in town," Ariadne said. "I will probably ask my siblings and cousins to hire some as the years go by and everyone starts establishing their own households."

Dru noticed children starting to enter the dining hall. They were in neat lines and moved silently as they took their seats on benches which had been placed on both sides of the long tables filling the dining hall. She saw the smiles these children broke out in as they caught sight of Ariadne and Julian. Glancing to her cousin, she saw love in Ariadne's own smile for these orphans.

For three-quarters of an hour, the assembly progressed. Miss Darnell introduced Dru, and they responded politely and in unison, saying, "Good morning, my lady."

After the assembly ended, most of the children remained seated, but several of them left the room.

"Where are they going?" she asked Miss Darnell.

"Students are assigned a various day of the week in which they serve others seated at their tables. A student must be ten years of age before they can become a server. We do not want little ones carrying trays of food and dropping them because they are too heavy."

"We would like to assist in this if you are willing to do so," Julian said.

"Of course. I would love to help," Dru said enthusiastically.

The three of them went to the kitchens, where food was dished onto plates and set upon trays.

A bright-eyed boy introduced himself. "I am Joseph, my lady. You can work alongside me if you'd like."

Joseph took her to a table, having Dru set plates in front of children on one side of it while he did so on the opposite side.

"We'll be back with the rest in a moment," he promised those who had yet to receive their meal.

She decided this must be the orphan Ariadne had spoken so fondly about previously. With his positive attitude, Dru thought the boy would go far in life.

Gathering another tray, she accompanied Joseph back into the dining hall, serving the rest of the table.

"You may go and sit with the teachers, my lady," the boy said, taking her tray. "I will see that you receive your meal promptly."

"Thank you, Joseph," she said, heading toward the front of the room where several adults already sat.

Ariadne and Julian joined her, and Julian said, "Joseph is very special. He is one of the oldest in the orphanage, and Ariadne and I are eager to have him come to work for us."

"He is a delight," she declared.

Moments later, Joseph returned, serving Julian, Ariadne, and Dru. They all thanked him politely. After that, she listened to the teachers discuss a variety of topics and accepted an invitation from one to come and work with students on their sums once they finished their meal.

"Have you ever thought of having any animals at the orphanage, Miss Darnell?" she asked. "I have a cat named Toby, and he is my true companion. I left him behind in Surrey because he can be a bit of a handful around others, but it might be fun for the children if they had a cat or dog to play with."

"I had not thought about that before, my lady," the headmistress mused. "It would teach some excellent lessons, having the children learn to care for animals."

"If you have room outside, you could even build chicken coops and raise hens for eggs," she suggested. "The little ones could gather the eggs each morning and scatter feed to the chickens."

"I like that idea," Miss Darnell declared. "And I believe our students might even be able to build the coops with a bit of supervision."

"I can help there," Julian volunteered. "I will look at the space you have available now and even go and purchase the wood." He looked to Ariadne. "You and Dru can stay here while I do so."

After their meal, Ariadne went off to teach students their letters. Dru enjoyed her time working with small groups of students. Two groups worked on addition, while another learned about subtraction. A third group of more advanced students were even learning multiplication, and she taught those students a song her governess had taught her, feeling both merry and useful.

The last hour she was at the orphanage, Dru read to various groups of children. Miss Darnell had told her that while it was important for the students themselves to read aloud, it was imperative that they had good reading modeled for them. She chose a story with talking animals, changing her voice each time a different animal spoke. By the end, she had the children in her care laughing, and they were imitating the various noises the animals made.

She bid a fond goodbye to the students, some even hugging her, which touched her deeply.

"I see you have the same heart for children as Lord and Lady Aldridge do," Miss Darnell praised. "You are welcome to call at Oakbrooke Orphanage anytime, Lady Drusilla."

"Thank you," she responded. "I have never really been around children. I am the youngest in my family. It is a bit surprising to me how much I enjoyed myself today."

"You will make a fine mother someday, my lady," Miss Darnell told Dru.

In the carriage, she couldn't stop talking about all she had seen.

"I cannot thank you enough for inviting me to come today," she told Ariadne and Julian. "I never thought I would be so comfortable around children, but I find I like them quite a bit. As much as I do animals," she teased.

"I hope you will join us again tomorrow," her cousin said.

"I would be happy to. After all, I want to come and watch Julian as he teaches the older children how to construct a chicken coop."

"The materials will be delivered first thing tomorrow morning," Julian said. "Not only the wood but saws. Hammers. Nails. I think your idea a fine one, Dru. The children will enjoy caring for the hens, and the eggs will be a wonderful addition to their meals."

"I spoke to Cook about that," Ariadne said. "She was thrilled that she would have access to fresh eggs on a daily basis."

Dinner was wonderful that evening, and Dru retired to her room with a book she had chosen from Julian's library. She was distracted, though, finding it hard to concentrate on reading.

Today had been enlightening. It had awakened something within her. She had always thought she wouldn't care for having children. Instead, after her experience at Oakbrooke Orphanage today, she was ready to accept the fact that she could see having her own children in the future. For that to happen, though, she would need a husband.

That brought her back to Lord Martindale. Dru thought he would have enjoyed spending time at the orphanage today. She also believed it would be good for him to be around others. It would be something she would suggest to Ariadne. Her cousin took great pride in the orphanage, and Dru knew she wouldn't mind showing the place to the earl.

Or perhaps even she could do so herself.

She marveled at how much and how quickly she was changing on this visit to Surrey. While she was still stubborn in nature, a few weeks ago she had wanted neither husband nor children, much less a come-out Season. Now, she decided all three would do. It was good to be open-minded. Just because she had believed she knew what her future held, she saw it could change—and for the better.

The question would be whether or not Lord Martindale might be a part of it.

Chapter Fourteen

D RU CARRIED TOBY to the French doors and opened one, setting the cat down. He scampered away happily. The tabby seemed to have taken to Huntsworth easily. While he still hissed upon occasion, Toby was much better behaved than he ever had been at Marleyfield.

She closed the doors and made her way to the breakfast room, happy to be back at Huntsworth after her two-day sojourn to town. Judson greeted her as she took up a plate and went through the buffet. She was ravenous this morning and filled her plate accordingly.

Taking a seat, she asked, "What are you doing today?"

Her brother-in-law chuckled. "What am I not doing today?" he countered. "With the harvest occurring in two days' time, I will ride the estate with Mr. Wayling a final time and meet with the head of my tenants, seeking his suggestions. I know Lucy will also spend time with Cook today, going over the menu for the harvest festival. While all the tenants' wives bring various dishes to the celebration, we here in the main house contribute heavily to the meal, especially because the servants are also encouraged to come to the celebration, and they have no means of bringing prepared food."

"Did you ever receive a reply from Lord Martindale? Will he come and observe the first day of harvesting at Huntsworth?"

Judson nodded. "Yes, he is most eager to do so. While he has told me that he has full trust in his estate's steward and even observed an autumn harvest before he went off to war, he wants to learn as much as he can from others."

Dru was happy to hear that and glad to know Lord Martindale would be joining them. She did hope he and Judson would strike up a lasting friendship since they were neighbors.

Lucy entered the breakfast room. Immediately, Judson shot to his feet and went to her, guiding her to a chair and seating her.

Smiling fondly at her husband, she teased, "I am not made of glass, you know."

"You are precious in my eyes, love. I intend to spoil you, not only while you carry our child, but for decades to come."

Lucy blushed prettily, and once again, Dru felt the slightest tinge of jealousy at the couple's closeness. Lucy had always been her closest friend and companion. While that would never change, she knew Lucy's allegiance was to her new husband and the family they would grow together.

It still amazed Dru how much her feelings had changed toward the institution of marriage. Then again, it would take a special man to convince her to enter it. She believed she did want that now, though, as well as children. After having spent two days at Oakbrooke Orphanage, she had absolutely fallen in love with the children there and was now eager to birth some of her own. Mama would gloat mightily, learning of the changes in her youngest child's opinions.

"What do you have planned today, Dru?" her sister asked.

"I am eager to be back in the saddle. While I thoroughly enjoyed my trip to town and meeting the orphans, I always find myself a bit restless if I have not been riding or outdoors for any length of time."

"Would you mind running an errand for me today in the village? I have just learned that one of our tenants is also increasing and will give birth a month before I do. I would like to start working on a blanket for her child, but the yarn I have is already designated to complete the blanket for our babe."

"Of course," she replied. "Is there anything else you might need, Lucy?"

Her sister frowned in thought. "Yes. Some stitch markers, along with the new yarn."

Having never knitted, Dru had no idea what stitch markers were, but she assumed they would be located near the yarn.

"Go to Mr. Brown's shop. He will direct you to where the yarns are inside it. If Mrs. Brown is there, she can help you as she is a great knitter herself."

"Do you have any specific color—or colors—in mind for the blanket?"

Lucy chuckled. "I have always wished there could be a way to learn the gender of a babe before it was born because I would knit a pink or blue blanket for them with that knowledge in mind. You know I like to keep the colors neutral, however."

"Yes, I have accompanied you many times when you have delivered a blanket you have made to one of Papa's tenants. I am glad you are keeping up that custom here at Huntsworth."

Dru recalled the blanket Lucy currently worked on for her own child, a combination of beige, pale yellow, and moss green.

The same shade of green as Lord Martindale's eyes.

"I will do my best in choosing wisely for you," she promised, chastising herself for constantly thinking about the earl.

Upon finishing breakfast, Dru excused herself and returned to her bedchamber. She rang for Annie, changing out of the breeches and shirt she had already donned for her morning ride. Going into Alderton meant she must dress more conventionally. Judson had been so kind to her, and she would not see him embarrassed or gossiped about due to her choice of garments. She accepted Annie's help in changing into the riding habit she had brought along in case she needed one, but Dru left her hair in the single braid, finding it more comfortable.

She went to the stables, where Harry saddled a horse for her, and then she rode about Huntsworth for an hour, enjoying the mild weather of the early September day. She had certainly taken to this part of England and hoped that Mama would not call her home anytime soon. She doubted that would happen, though. Her mother rarely gave a thought to either of her daughters, so Dru believed she would be safe from Mama's notice for now. Con always went home for Christmas, however, and if Mama demanded Dru's presence for the holiday season, then her brother would be happy to escort her back to Somerset.

Deciding it was time to head to the village, she turned her horse and rode straight to Alderton. The village was larger than Swanford, the one which was closest to Marleyfield, and Dru found it quite to her liking. She stopped at Mr. Brown's shop, tying her horse to a post located outside it. Upon entering, she introduced herself, telling him that her sister was in need of yarns and stitch markers for her knitting.

"Right this way, my lady. I have a large selection of yarns for you to peruse for Lady Huntsberry's needs."

Dru chose the same three colors of the blanket which Lucy was working on, but she also added a soft red, a deep purple, and a cream color to the mix. That way, it would give her sister a bit more variety when knitting the new blanket.

"I will place this on Lord Huntsberry's account," Mr. Brown said. "Is there anything else you might need, my lady?"

"No, thank you, Mr. Brown. I appreciate your help."

The shopkeeper wrapped the yarns and stitch markers in brown paper, tying it with string before presenting it to her.

As Lucy left, she felt a bit parched and decided to leave her horse where it was and call at Mrs. Cadmann's bakery for a cup of tea. She strolled down the street, greeting those she passed, and reached the bakery. Mrs. Cadmann smiled as she entered the shop.

"Good day, Lady Drusilla. How nice to see you again. Might Lord and Lady Huntsberry be joining you?"

"No, I simply came into the village to run an errand for my sister. I found myself needing a spot of tea, though."

"Have a seat, my lady. I will bring you a pot straightaway."

The owner paused. "Might you also like a scone to go with it?"

"I had not planned on doing so, but the wonderful aroma in your shop has weakened my resolve, Mrs. Cadmann. Yes, bring me a scone. Whatever flavor you suggest is fine with me."

"I took out a batch of fresh blueberry scones not ten minutes ago. I think you will fancy one of those."

Dru took a seat at one of the handful of small tables inside the bakery, leaning the brown parcel against the wall beside her feet. Mrs. Cadmann brought her a plate with a fat scone upon it and a dollop of Devonshire cream next to it, as well as a pot of tea.

"Let that steep for a few minutes, my lady," Mrs. Cadmann said cheerfully. "And here is some sugar and cream if you care for it."

She sat contentedly, waiting for the tea to be ready to drink. The bakery's door opened, and in walked Lord Tilsbury with another gentleman she did not recognize. There was a similarity between the pair, however, both in build and facial features, and she had a suspicion that this might be the viscount's heir.

"Lady Drusilla," Lord Tilsbury called out jovially. "How delightful to find you here."

He approached her, the other gentleman in tow.

Dru rose and said, "It is so nice to see you again, my lord."

"I must introduce you to my nephew and heir apparent. Lady Drusilla Alington, this is Mr. Hollis, the elder son of my deceased, younger brother."

Mr. Hollis took the hand she offered, and Dru quite liked his friendly, handsome face.

"It is delightful to meet you, Lady Drusilla. My uncle has sung your praises, and I was eager to make your acquaintance."

Lord Tilsbury turned to Mrs. Cadmann. "Bring us something sweet to eat, Mrs. Cadmann. If Lady Drusilla does not mind, we will share her pot of tea."

"At once, my lord," the bakery owner said.

The three took a seat at the table, and Dru asked, "How long will you be visiting your uncle, Mr. Hollis?"

"That is yet to be determined, my lady. Uncle is trying to convince me to remain at Tilsbury Manor permanently."

"Oh. Where do you usually reside?" she asked.

"I am a solicitor in London," he said proudly. "Uncle Tilsbury was kind enough to pay for my university education, since that would have been beyond my own father's means. I now practice in town."

The viscount looked at Dru, his eyes twinkling. "While I know my nephew enjoys his work, I am not getting any younger. I am trying to convince him to stay at Tilsbury Manor and learn all he can about the estate. Perhaps you can help me to persuade him to do so, my lady."

She turned her gaze back to Mr. Hollis. "Even though you have had a satisfying career in town, sir, perhaps it is time to look to your future. Viscount Tilsbury would be a wonderful teacher, Mr. Hollis, helping you to learn all you need to know about running a large country estate. In fact, he also has helped to guide another of his neighbors, Lord Martindale."

Mr. Hollis nodded, "Ah, my uncle has mentioned the earl and that they are close. I should very much like to meet him."

Mrs. Cadmann brought additional cups and saucers, and Dru began pouring out for them, asking each how he liked his tea.

"Where do you reside, Lady Drusilla?" Mr. Hollis asked.

"I live with my parents at Marleyfield, which is in Somerset."

"My, you are certainly a long way from home."

"I have come to visit my sister. Lucy recently wed Lord Huntsberry. They reside at Huntsworth, which is just the other side of Alderton from Tilsbury Manor. I would think, though, that you would sooner meet Lord Martindale since you are neighbors. His estate is adjacent to your uncle's."

"Beauville, Lord Martindale's estate, is large," Lord Tilsbury added. "Martindale served as a major in the army until his father passed and the title went to him."

"It seems I have several people to get to know in the area," Mr. Hollis said.

"My cousin also lives in the neighborhood," she volunteered. She is wed to Lord Aldridge of Aldridge Manor. I will mention to my sister that you have come to visit, Mr. Hollis. I am certain she will invite you to tea, along with some of our other neighbors. Better yet? We will be hosting an autumn festival after the harvest is collected. It will be this coming Wednesday. I hope you and Lord Tilsbury might considering attending. There will be food and dancing outdoors."

"That sounds marvelous, my lady," Mr. Hollis said. "I came specifically at this time to see a harvest in action since I have yet to witness one."

He turned to his uncle. "Would us going to this interfere with your own harvest, Uncle?"

"My steward tells me that we will start ours the week after next. It should take two to three days to complete. I see no reason why we could not travel to Huntsworth to join in their celebration. I have never hosted something of this nature, so I would be curious to see it myself."

"Then it is settled," Dru declared. "I will let Lord and Lady Huntsberry know that you will be joining us for the festivities."

They spent a pleasant half-hour over their tea and scones, Dru telling them about her recent trip to town and the orphanage sponsored by her cousin and husband. In turn, Mr. Hollis told a few amusing stories about previous clients of his. All in all, she had a marvelous time with the pair.

"I must be getting back to Huntsworth," she said, retrieving her parcel and rising.

The two gentlemen did the same, and Mr. Hollis inquired, "Might we offer you a ride to Huntsworth?"

"I rode into town. I merely need to reclaim my horse, which I left outside Mr. Brown's shop."

"Then let me escort you to it, my lady," Mr. Hollis offered. "I will return shortly, Uncle."

Mr. Hollis took the package from her and then offered his arm to Dru. She accepted it and they left the bakery, traveling down the main thoroughfare to Mr. Brown's shop. When they reached the horse, Mr. Hollis tossed her into the saddle and handed up the parcel.

"I cannot say how happy I am to have made your acquaintance, Lady Drusilla. I believe my uncle has been lonely ever since my aunt's death. He has spoken highly of you and your visit to him. I must thank you for going to see him."

"I enjoy Lord Tilsbury's company." She paused. "You could help curb his loneliness, Mr. Hollis, by deciding to reside permanently at Tilsbury Manor. It would do the viscount good to have your company. In return, you would be well prepared once you took up the title."

He gazed at her intently, causing her to grow warm at his scrutiny. "Perhaps I have found the reason I should do that very thing."

Dru guessed he might be speaking of her, and she found herself blushing.

Clearing her throat, she said, "I will make certain that you and Lord Tilsbury receive a formal invitation to the harvest celebration Wednesday night, Mr. Hollis. Good day to you."

She turned her horse, traveling down the center of the lane and leaving the village behind. A man had never so quickly shown an interest in her, but Mr. Hollis had been almost blatant in doing so. While she had never paid much attention to her appearance, she now thought perhaps she was a little bit pretty. Lucy had always received so many compliments on her looks that Dru had considered her sister to be the beauty of the family, not her.

The harvest celebration was turning into quite the event, and Dru looked forward to seeing more of Mr. Hollis.

CHAPTER FIFTEEN

PERRY RUBBED HIS eyes, tired of looking at the figures in the ledger. He closed the book and leaned back in his chair, pillowing his hands behind his head.

His tenants would bring in the autumn harvest this coming week. He had committed to go to Huntsworth on Monday in order to observe the first day of his neighbor's harvest. He had only been present at Beauville when a single harvest occurred, being away at school and university and then the army. It would do him good to refresh himself as to what happened during one. Although he knew Rankin had things well in hand, this would be the first time the Earl of Martindale had been present at a harvest in decades. It was important to him to have a visible presence at this important time. His father had never cared enough to be in the country during harvest times. Perry wanted to be a different kind of earl than his father.

He also hoped to see Lady Dru sometime during his visit to Huntsworth on Monday. Perry had learned from Lord Huntsberry that she had gone to town for a few days with Lord and Lady Aldridge, who supported an orphanage there and visited it frequently. He was curious as to what she thought of the orphanage.

Hell, he was curious about anything having to do with Lady Dru Alington.

Perry reminded himself that they were simply to be friends. It would be hard enough to burden any woman with him as a husband, but he could never intentionally encumber Lady Dru. His nightmares only seemed to worsen with the passage of time. It would be hard enough to hide them from whatever wife he chose. Lady Dru was far too perceptive. It would be impossible to keep anything from her. That was why he needed to let go of this fantasy of making her his wife. She was a fine woman and had been kind enough to offer friendship to him. He believed she would do her best to help him choose a bride next spring, as well as introduce him to other members of her extended family. Already, he liked Lords Huntsberry and Aldridge quite a bit.

He glanced out the window when he saw movement and saw a rider had stopped in front of the house. A footman hurried out to speak with him and motioned the stranger to the house, even as the footman led the horse by the reins around the house, most likely to the stables. Perry was not expecting anyone and wondered who this man might be.

A brisk knock sounded at his study's door, and he said, "Come."

Foster entered. "My lord, it is Mr. Chapman here to see you. The younger Mr. Chapman, that is. He said he was not expected but asked for a few minutes of your time."

"Certainly. Show him in, Foster."

Perry supposed a property had already been found for his mother and that Mr. Chapman was here to discuss the purchase of it with him.

The butler showed the solicitor into the study, and Perry rose to greet him.

"Good morning, Mr. Chapman," he said offering his hand.

Chapman shook it. "Thank you for seeing me without an appointment, my lord."

"Sit. Would you care for tea?"

"No, thank you. I hope to conclude our business quickly and return to the village to catch the next mail coach back to London."

"I am afraid that is not for several hours. What brings you to Beauville? Have you found a house for my mother to live in?"

"I have, my lord." Chapman reached into the satchel he carried, removing a sheaf of papers and handing them to Perry. "Things went rather quickly, I am pleased to say. I had a client whose husband had only passed last week, and she had me put their house up for sale since she intended to move to Bristol and live with her sister and brother-in-law. From what my father shared with me, I thought this house would be most suitable for you as an investment. I called upon my client and made an offer on your behalf. She accepted it on the spot, and I drew up the papers. By the end of the day, the matter was put to rest."

"That is most efficient of you, Mr. Chapman. I see you are as capable as your father," he complimented.

A pained expression crossed the solicitor's face. "I wish I could accept your praise, my lord, but we have a problem. My client left the next morning on the mail coach, having shipped those personal items she wished to keep to Bristol, leaving the rest of the house furnished. I did factor that in to the offer I made. Since Father said you were eager to have Lady Martindale take up residence in her new home, I made an appointment to see her that very day."

Perry suspected what had occurred. "You are here to tell me that she was unwilling to vacate my townhouse."

Chapman nodded slowly. "Lady Martindale was, shall we say, uncooperative. Totally unwilling to move to the new property. I told her that, as your representative, I had your full authority and was making your wishes known. That a house had been found for her to reside in, and she was to go there immediately. I suggested that she have her lady's maid pack and retain that servant's services, and I was willing to assist her in hiring the small staff which you and my father agreed upon."

Naturally, she would balk. He shouldn't have expected anything less.

"I am quite good at my job, my lord, but I have never been

asked to evict a countess from what had been her home. Father let me know that you wished your townhouse to be free of her presence. Other than physically picking her up and tossing her out onto the pavement, I was in a quandary regarding what to do."

Chapman raked a hand through his hair. "I hope you will not hold this against my father, my lord. I would hate to see him lose you as a client because of my incapability to . . . to . . ."

"Oust a noblewoman?" he supplied. "No, Mr. Chapman, I hold your father in high esteem. I am certain I will do the same with you. I am thrilled you were able to solve my problem so quickly and find a suitable house."

"It is an excellent property, my lord, in a plum part of May-fair, and it has been kept up well. Property in that area will only increase in value in the coming years." The solicitor sighed. "I am only sorry I could not fulfill all my obligations and see Lady Martindale relocated."

"She is more than stubborn," he shared. "Moreover, she dislikes me—and the idea that she will no longer live in my London townhome."

"If I may speak freely, my lord, I will say that after what I have seen of her, you are making the correct decision in expelling her. Why, Father told me how generous you will be with her, providing the house and staff, along with a liberal allowance." He winced. "She thoroughly rebuked me. I have not been scolded like that since my early schooldays."

"My mother had no right to castigate you, Mr. Chapman. She is a selfish, bitter woman and took out her anger at me on you." He rose. "I will accompany you back to town and see her to her new home."

The solicitor stood. "I hate to ask you to do so, my lord. I know that would be most inconvenient."

"No, I wish for the matter to be settled. I will have the carriage prepared at once. I saw you arrive on horseback."

"Yes. I rode the mail coach to Alderton and then rented a

horse from a Mr. Abel's stables in town."

"Return the horse to Mr. Abel. I will stop in Alderton for you."

Smiling, the solicitor said, "Thank you, my lord."

Perry rang for his butler and instructed Foster to have his carriage readied, saying that he had been called to town unexpectedly.

"When will you return to Beauville, my lord?"

It was Saturday. He needed to be back early Monday morning so he could go to Huntsworth. He also did not want to pass up the opportunity to see Lady Dru at church. Yes, it was foolish on his part, but he would be in church by her side on the morrow.

"Either late this evening or first thing tomorrow morning. Tell Mrs. Foster to be prepared for either, but I most likely will be home tonight."

"Shall I summon Grilley to accompany you?"

"No. That will not be necessary."

He could see no need for his valet to accompany him to town. He would go straight to his townhouse and speak directly with his mother, making certain the servants packed her things. Perry would even escort her to the new property himself. It would be good for him to see the house in person this one time because he doubted he would ever enter it until after her death. With sunset around half-past seven this time of year, the horses could easily rest for several hours until they conveyed him to Surrey again.

Perry climbed into his carriage, telling his coachman to stop in Alderton at Mr. Abel's stables in order to pick up another passenger before they made their way to town. During the journey, he got to know the solicitor better and found he liked him a great deal. When the time came for the elder Mr. Chapman to step away, Perry believed it would be a seamless transition.

They reached town shortly after noon, and Chapman asked to be dropped at his father's offices.

"Thank you again for locating a house so quickly," he said. "I appreciate your efforts in this matter, Mr. Chapman."

With a grateful look on his face, the solicitor said, "And I certainly appreciate you not firing me—and my father's firm—because I could not get Lady Martindale to vacate the premises." He swallowed visibly. "I will do better next time, my lord. I promise."

"I will hold you to that," he said, his tone light, conveying he held no grudge against Chapman.

Perry instructed the coachman to take him to the new property. He wanted to view it without his mother in tow. It was but a few blocks from his own townhouse, so he told his driver, "Take the horses to my mews. Feed and water them. I would like to leave town at five o'clock. Will five hours be enough rest for the team?"

"It should be, my lord. If not, we can always change out horses on the way to Surrey. I can then return later for them."

"Very good. See to them now. Unless you hear otherwise, be prepared to leave no later than five."

The carriage left, and Perry used one of the two keys Chapman had given him to enter the house. It was on a fashionable street, sandwiched between two much larger townhouses. He toured the ground floor first, finding a parlor, dining room, kitchen, and two rooms off the kitchen which could be used to house a cook and two maids. Upstairs, he found three bedchambers. One was as large as the other two put together. In the attic were two additional servants' rooms. A footman could stay up here. This would be all the house his mother needed. Because of its size, he thought she could forgo a housekeeper and merely instruct the two maids what to do herself.

Returning to the ground floor, he locked the door and pocketed the key, walking the short distance to his own townhouse. He had only been to it once, immediately after he finished up at Cambridge. His father had instructed him to come to town, and Perry had done so. He had stayed a couple of days, only seeing his father once, still slightly drunk the next morning. He hadn't seen his mother at all. Though his father had told him it was essential to remain in town and partake in the Season, Perry had turned down that request and retreated to the country.

He approached his own door, knocking upon it since he hadn't thought to bring a key. A footman opened the door.

"Yes, my lord?" he politely inquired.

Glancing past the footman, Perry saw Lufkin, who had been the butler during his past visit.

"Lufkin," he called.

The butler turned, his eyes widening. "Lord Martindale! We were not expecting you. Or rather, we were—because your carriage and coachman arrived." Quickly, he hurried to the door. "Let his lordship pass," he ordered the footman, who looked nonplussed at Perry's arrival.

"Is Lady Martindale at home?" he asked.

"She is, my lord," Lufkin replied. "In her parlor with Lady Parmley."

He recalled the name, and a vague impression of a woman who had come for a brief visit to Beauville formed in his mind. From what he remembered, the woman was a malicious gossip.

"Thank you."

He started toward the parlor, and Lufkin quickly joined him. "Will you be in town long, my lord?"

"No, not long at all," he said breezily. "Not even for dinner. Tea, perhaps. I will be returning to the country once I have spoken with Lady Martindale. I will inform you that I have decided to attend next Season, however. I will send a messenger to let you know my plans closer to that date."

"Very good, my lord."

"And Lufkin? Lady Martindale will be departing shortly. For good. My horses will not be ready yet to take her to her new residence. Would you have a footman summon a wagon or two so that her trunks might be transported? And have Lady Martindale's maid to commence packing immediately." He thought a moment. "Also, have a hansom cab waiting in front. Pay him extra for any time he has to wait."

The butler's eyes widened. "I will do so, my lord."

Lufkin then hurried ahead and knocked on the door, opening it. "Lord Martindale, my lady." The butler turned back to Perry.

And smiled.

He sauntered into the room, seeing the startled look on his mother's face and the sly one on Lady Parmley's. "Good afternoon, ladies," he said genially.

"Martindale! I did not expect you," his mother said. Then quickly recovering, she said, "It is lovely to see you. Do you recall Lady Parmley?"

He took the woman's hand. "I do indeed." Perry left it at that, turning his attention back to his mother.

Obviously, she did not want Lady Parmley to be party to any conversation between them and said, "I am so sorry to have to ask you to leave, my dear. With Martindale here, I simply must give him my full focus."

Disappointment filled Lady Parmely's face. "Of course, darling." She kissed her hostess' cheeks. "Do call upon me tomorrow. We can share tea."

He waited until the other woman left the room before taking a seat. His mother turned to him and hissed, "Whatever are you *doing* here, Martindale?"

"Do I need a reason to be in my own townhouse?" he asked drolly.

She wrung her hands together, knowing she had been caught disobeying him. "No. Of course not."

"Why did you not do as Mr. Chapman requested, madam?" he asked quietly, his gaze boring into her.

Her hands fluttered nervously now. "Oh, that young whippersnapper? I did not think he was truly serious, Martindale. After all, you are not even in residence now. I saw no harm in my staying a while longer."

His tone even—and deadly—Perry said, "He is my solicitor. And had my full authority." Pausing, he let her squirm a moment.

"I told you I was having a house found for you. That you were to leave this townhouse once that occurred."

"But it happened so fast," she protested. "I have resided here for decades. There would be so much to organize before I left."

"I instructed you to have your maid pack because I knew it would be quick," he countered. "The house is ready for you. I have seen it. It is fully furnished."

"But it might not be to my taste," she told him, obviously searching for any excuse to delay her departure.

"That is of no consequence. You have the furnished house. I have instructed Mr. Chapman to place the funds for your quarterly allowance in your account. The only thing left to be done is to hire your servants. You may hire a cook, two maids to clean, and a footman."

She frowned. "You had mentioned a housekeeper, Martindale," she said.

"I changed my mind since you did not move when requested to do so."

Her eyes flashed with anger, but she held her tongue, knowing she might suffer further consequences if she did not fall into step with his plans.

"I have already instructed Lufkin to have your maid pack. I expect you to be ready to leave in two hours' time."

"Two hours? Why, that is not—"

"That is what I am giving you. Take it—or leave it, madam. The choice is yours." He looked at her a long moment. "Besides, other than your wardrobe, you will be leaving everything else behind."

In defeat, she suddenly looked her age. He could not bring himself to find an inkling of sympathy. She reaped what she had sown. She had never had any feelings for him, and he felt likewise about her. He was not being cruel, going above and beyond the marriage settlements by providing her a house and servants in town, as she preferred.

She stood. "Excuse me."

"I will be in the library. Come find me when you are ready to depart."

Perry watched her leave and then went to the library. It was barely adequate, and he knew he would take pleasure in filling it with all kinds of books. A part of him wished that Lady Dru and he could do this together, but he was a practical man. He would find a wife who enjoyed reading, and they would complete this task together over many years.

He lost himself in a book and only realized his mother had entered the room when she cleared her throat.

"Are you ready?" he asked politely.

"I am. If you will summon the carriage."

"The horses are still resting from their journey from Beauville. I have arranged for transportation. It should be waiting outside by now."

Perry accompanied her downstairs, where two footmen were loading one of her trunks into a nearby wagon.

She gasped. "You expect me to ride in . . . this? How humiliating!"

"I can either walk with you the few blocks to your new residence, or you can accept a ride in this hansom cab."

He withdrew one of the two keys and handed it to her, giving the cab driver the address.

Her face was red with fury. "So, this is it?"

"This is it," he said calmly. "And remember, if I hear even the faintest bit of gossip that you have disparaged me, I will remove you from the house I am so generously allowing you to stay in. You can then move to the Beauville dower house for good."

She shuddered. "I will keep to this devil's bargain."

Perry refrained from laughing. "See that you do, madam."

He did the polite thing and handed her into the hansom cab and watched her set off, her head held high, her back stiff. One of the two wagons, which was already full, starting out after her. He waited until the hansom cab turned the corner before entering his house again, finding Lufkin and Mrs. Lufkin waiting anxiously in the foyer.

"Lady Martindale is not to enter the premises again. If she has forgotten something, give it away."

"Yes, my lord, "the couple echoed.

"Might I have a tour of my townhouse now, Mrs. Lufkin?"

The housekeeper beamed at him. "Certainly, my lord. If you will follow me."

At the conclusion of the tour, he took tea in the library and then said goodbye to the Lufkins before heading to the mews.

"Are the horses ready to travel?" he asked his coachman.

"Aye, my lord."

"Then let us return to Beauville."

Perry climbed into the carriage and settled against the cushions, satisfaction filling him. He was pleased to have taken a stand against his mother, and he did not fear her as he had as a child. The tour of his London home had shown him what a lovely place it was, and he was coming to terms with returning in the spring to find his bride.

With Lady Dru's help, of course.

CHAPTER SIXTEEN

DRU DECIDED SHE would give her full attention to Mr. Harper's sermon this morning. Last Sunday, she had foolishly been mooning over Lord Martindale instead of listening to the vicar's words. Although she still had feelings for the earl, she did not believe they would ever suit, and she needed to look to her future instead. She hoped they would continue to explore a friendship between them while she was visiting the neighborhood, one that would continue on to next Season. She was eager to introduce him to Con and her other cousins, knowing that he was a bit of a loner. And while it would hurt somewhat, she would do what she could in order to help him secure a bride.

They reached Alderton, and Judson handed both her and Lucy down from the carriage. Immediately, she spied Ariadne and Julian talking with Viscount Tilsbury and Mr. Hollis.

Lucy asked, "Is that Lord Tilsbury's nephew whom you spoke of?"

Once she had returned from her errand of buying yarn for her sister, she had shared with Lucy that Lord Tilsbury's nephew had come for an extended visit with his uncle.

"Yes. We should go meet him," she suggested.

Judson escorted them to where the other four stood, and Mr. Hollis smiled warmly at Dru in recognition.

"Lady Drusilla, how lovely to see you this morning."

"Good morning, Mr. Hollis. Might I introduce my sister, Lady

Huntsberry, and her husband, the Marquess of Huntsberry?"

Mr. Hollis greeted the couple, and Judson said, "We hear you are a solicitor but that you might be considering staying in the neighborhood."

Mr. Hollis laughed, a deep, rich laugh. "I believe it is a conspiracy, my lord. I fear my uncle has talked to all his friends, far and near, and that they are trying to persuade me to remain in Surrey and give up my London practice."

Julian spoke up. "It would be a good idea, Mr. Hollis. After all, you will hold the title one day. This could be a time of learning for you, at the hands of an expert, as you get to know your future tenants."

"I am finding reasons to stay, Lord Aldridge," Mr. Hollis said, glancing at Dru and then away again.

Was Mr. Hollis becoming enamored of her? She had thought him quite friendly at the bakeshop yesterday and had wondered if he were interested in her. Now that it seemed apparent he was, Dru wasn't certain how she felt about this sudden change of events. On the one hand, it would be lovely to be close to Lucy and Ariadne.

They had only met, and here she was thinking of marriage with the man. She pushed the thought aside, thinking she was putting the cart before the horse.

"We should go into church," Ariadne told the group. "I think almost everyone else has already done so."

They made their way inside and up the aisle to the first couple of pews. A flash of disappointment swept through Dru, seeing Lord Martindale was not present. She wondered how he fared and hoped she might be able to speak with him tomorrow when he came to the first day of harvest at Huntsworth.

As they filed into the pews, she realized Mr. Hollis would be sitting on her left. She decided to keep an open mind about the gentleman, just as Ariadne had encouraged her to do so.

Suddenly, someone slipped into the other side of the pew, taking the seat on her right.

It was Lord Martindale.

Dru's heart skipped a beat, and she reminded herself that the earl needed a much different lady than herself as his countess.

Wanting to be friendly, however, she turned and smiled at him. "Good morning, my lord."

Already, she caught a whiff of his cologne, wishing she could move closer to him, then thinking herself ridiculous for such a fanciful notion.

"Good morning, Lady Dru," he responded, looking curiously to her left, where Mr. Hollis sat.

Before she could introduce the two gentlemen, Mr. Harper approached the pulpit. The congregation rose as the opening hymn began, and she was pleased to see it was "Amazing Grace," one of her favorites.

The last verse of the hymn ended, and they remained standing as Mr. Harper led them in prayer. Dru deliberately concentrated on the vicar's words, quite liking what he spoke of in his sermon this morning. She had always felt solace fill her anytime she entered a church, and she was determined not to let either gentleman sitting beside her change that.

Today, Mr. Harper spoke of the importance of loving your neighbor as yourself. She had never given much thought to loving herself. Yes, she liked who she was and tried to be the best person she could be, but the vicar's words resonated more with her than ever before. She accepted that she was different from most other young women in Polite Society. She hoped she could find a gentleman who would accept her as she was, one who would not be ashamed of her but proud to call her his wife without trying to change her.

Mr. Harper concluded his sermon, and there were more prayers and songs before the service ended. Once it did, Mr. Hollis said to her, "That was an inspiring sermon. Didn't you think so, my lady?"

"Mr. Harper certainly gave me much to think about. I would like to introduce you to a good friend of my family's." She turned and saw the earl solemnly studying Mr. Hollis. "Lord Martindale, this is Mr. Hollis. He is Lord Tilsbury's nephew and the viscount's heir apparent."

They shook hands, and Lord Martindale said, "It is good to meet you, Mr. Hollis. I have the utmost respect for your uncle."

Mr. Hollis brimmed with enthusiasm, saying, "Uncle has told me so many wonderful things about you, my lord. Might I thank you for your service to king and country as you fought against Bonaparte?"

Dru saw Lord Martindale flinch slightly, but he quickly recovered. "I merely did my duty, Mr. Hollis. No thanks are necessary. Unfortunately, I think it will take many years of numerous campaigns to defeat the Little Corporal."

By now, people were filing from their pews, and Mr. Hollis turned, following Lucy and Judson from the row.

She did the same, waiting at the end for Lord Martindale, asking, "You are still coming tomorrow for the harvest, aren't you?"

"I am," he confirmed. "Lord Huntsberry extended the invitation to me. My own tenants will begin their harvest this coming Wednesday."

Spontaneously, Dru asked, "Would you care to also come to our harvest celebration? It is to be held outdoors on Wednesday, starting around six o'clock."

"Will Mr. Hollis be there?"

"Yes. I invited both Lord Tilsbury and Mr. Hollis to join us. Lord Tilsbury has never held such a celebration at the conclusion of a harvest, and Mr. Hollis is new to what happens on a country estate, as he is a solicitor in town."

"If it is acceptable to Lord and Lady Huntsberry, then I will accept your invitation, my lady."

They reached Mr. Harper, who stood just outside the door to the church, shaking hands with him.

"I quite enjoyed the topic you spoke on today," she shared. "Learning to accept—and love—myself is something I hope I can do more of."

"We are all God's children, my lady," the vicar responded. "God made us in His image, and He loves each of us a great deal. Be happy with who you are. Once you have accepted yourself, it is easier to accept, and even love, others."

She and Lord Martindale moved to where the others stood, and Dru heard Judson say, "If you are not otherwise engaged tomorrow, Mr. Hollis, my steward, is beginning our autumn harvest. Lord Martindale is coming to view our process. I would be happy to have your company, as well."

Mr. Hollis turned to his uncle. "Would that be acceptable to you?"

"Go and learn all you can, Edward. It would be good for you to see how Huntsworth takes on the task and compare it to what we do on Tilsbury lands next week."

Mr. Hollis looked to Judson. "Then I am happy to accept your invitation, my lord."

Lucy spoke up. "My sister told me that she asked if you could join us for the celebration after the harvest is completed, Mr. Hollis. It will be an outdoor harvest ball for our tenants to celebrate the end of the growing season. There will be plenty of food, along with music and dancing. Lord and Lady Aldridge will be attending, as well." Lucy looked to the earl. "And we would be honored if you, too, would join us, Lord Martindale."

"I would be pleased to accept your kind invitation, Lady Huntsberry."

"Uncle Tilsbury and I look forward to attending, as well," Mr. Hollis declared.

"I am an old man," the viscount said. "My dancing days are over and done."

"You could still come and enjoy watching the dancing, my lord," Dru encouraged. "And I know you will enjoy the many dishes prepared by Cook and the tenants' wives."

"Perhaps I shall, my lady."

"We must be going," Ariadne said. "Penelope will be waking from her morning nap soon." She smiled at Mr. Hollis. "That is our daughter. Penelope will be seven months soon, and she is the apple of our eyes."

"I am quite fond of children," Mr. Hollis declared. "My younger brother already has two. Being an uncle has proven to be most delightful. I look forward to having children of my own someday."

They said their goodbyes and began heading to their various carriages.

Once inside their vehicle, Lucy said, "My, Mr. Hollis is most handsome and so well spoken." Her gaze met Dru's. "What do you think of him?"

"I think you are trying to play matchmaker," she replied, causing Judson to burst out laughing.

"And what if I am?" Lucy asked. "I merely wish for my beloved sister to be as happy as I am with my own husband. Mr. Hollis is not married, and he even mentioned that he looks forward to having children. He may not hold the title yet, but one day he will be a viscount."

"A viscount who conveniently lives but a few miles from us," Judson teased.

"I see nothing wrong with simply pointing out to my sister that Mr. Hollis is an eligible man. Besides, if something did come of their pairing, it would mean Dru would be close to us."

"Lord Martindale is just as close," Judson pointed out. "I have yet to see you try to match the earl with Dru."

Dru felt her face grow hot. "Enough talk about marrying me off, Lucy," she protested. "You are beginning to sound like Mama. Let me merely enjoy my visit to Huntsworth."

Her sister shrugged. "All I am saying is that there are two eligible bachelors in the neighborhood for you to consider. Why, Mama would have an apoplexy if you did become betrothed before you even made your come-out."

"Promise me, no more talk of husbands," she said firmly. "We can discuss the harvest festival instead."

Lucy mentioned some of the food she had asked Cook to

prepare, as well as talking about some of the tenants who played musical instruments and would do so for the dancing on Wednesday evening.

"I am interested in seeing some of the harvest tomorrow, Judson," Dru told her brother-in-law.

"You are more than welcome to ride out with me and watch some of it, along with our guests."

"Then I will plan to do so," she said, eager to see what would happen—and perhaps interested in seeing both Lord Martindale and Mr. Hollis again.

CHAPTER SEVENTEEN

PERRY AWOKE WITH a start, terror filling him so much that even the scream was trapped in his throat. He gripped the bedclothes about him, feeling them soaked in his sweat. He told himself over and over that he was safe. In England. At Beauville. Not on the blood-soaked battlefields. Gradually, his racing heart calmed, though he felt drained from the nightmare, the second one of the night. He had never experienced two in a single night and worried his condition was deteriorating instead of improving.

He also worried at the lack of sleep he had gotten, especially with today being a big day at Beauville since dawn would be the start of his own tenants' harvest. He had spent Monday at Huntsworth, bringing Rankin along with him so that he and his steward might observe how the harvest was conducted at Lord Huntsberry's estate. Immediately, Rankin had paired off with Wayling, the Huntsworth steward. Mr. Hollis had also been present, as had Lady Dru. He had not known for certain that she would be there, but she said she was interested in observing how a harvest worked since she had never viewed one during her years growing up at Marleyfield.

After a day at Huntsworth, Perry had learned quite a bit, adding to his knowledge about harvests in general. What stayed with him most was how Lord Huntsberry had been eager to pitch in and encouraged both Perry and Mr. Hollis to do the same. All three men had discarded their coats and rolled up their shirtsleeves, joining the tenants in the field. Lord Huntsberry said he knew the men and women who worked his land spent long hours doing so, and he wasn't above a bit of physical labor himself in order to help them bring in the crops. Perry was ashamed that he would never have thought to physically participate in a harvest and vowed that he would model himself after Lord Huntsberry and do so today with his own people.

One thing had been obvious to him, and that was the fact that Mr. Hollis was quite taken with Lady Dru. The man made no secret of his admiration for the young lady and had dominated her time on Monday. Beyond greeting her when he first arrived, Perry had not exchanged a single word with Lady Dru through-out the long day.

He supposed a possible match between the pair would be a good thing for her. Hollis would take over his uncle's title and lands someday. If he wed Lady Dru, she would become an active part of the neighborhood, enjoying the fact that she was so close in proximity to her sister and cousin. If Mr. Hollis pressed his suit, Lady Dru might not even need to make her come-out next spring. Hollis seemed a decent fellow and would most likely make for a good husband. The had even mentioned his interest in having children.

Wedding Lord Tilsbury's heir would give Lady Dru the best of all worlds, something Perry himself could not do. Just look how he had awakened this morning. He would never escape the damage to him caused by his years at war. Though mightily attracted to Lady Dru, he refused to saddle her with such a burden. No, he would do what most every gentleman in Polite Society did. Find a bride on the Marriage Mart and make a marriage of convenience. Get an heir and a spare off his chosen wife. Lead a very separate life from her.

It would be hard to do so, however, when his heart belonged to another. If Lady Dru did wind up marrying Hollis, Perry would need to spend the majority of his time in town. He didn't think he could stay in the country, running into her often, seeing her happily wed to another man. Jealousy ran through him, thinking of her body swelling with Hollis' babe inside her. No, if she were to remain in the Surrey countryside, he would need to avoid Beauville at all costs. How ironic that he seemed to be destined to spend the bulk of his time in town, much as his own father had done. Perry could not see himself following in his father's footsteps, though, bedding women left and right and gambling and drinking far into each night.

Knowing a busy day lay ahead, he decided to rise. He did not ring for Grilley and merely dressed in breeches, a shirt, and waistcoat. He found his boots and put them on before making his way down to the kitchens as the clock struck five.

He spied Cook sitting at a table by herself, a cup of tea before her, along with a steaming bowl of oats.

She sprang to her feet. "My lord! Whatever are you doing here?"

"It is the first day of harvest time, Cook. I plan to work alongside my tenants. I could do with a bit of breakfast sticking to my ribs before I head out, however."

She smiled at him approvingly. "What might I make for you?"

"I will have the same as you, Cook."

He took a seat at the table as she bustled about, first pouring him a cup of strong tea. He sipped on it while she dished up a hearty portion of oats, hoping he wasn't stealing the breakfast of another servant. They chatted easily, the usual barrier of class nowhere evident.

"Thank you for a hardy breakfast," he told her once he had finished eating.

She beamed at him. "This is first time I have had the pleasure of dining with nobility, my lord."

"I went to Huntsworth this week to observe the beginning of their autumn harvest. I have been invited tonight to come to a celebration, as well. While the tenants will bring many dishes for this feast, the Huntsworth cook also provides a good portion of food. Might this be a task you would be willing to take upon, Cook?"

"I'd be happy to do so. What might you wish me to prepare for Beauville's tenants?"

"I will have a much better idea after seeing this evening's feast. I could meet with you tomorrow morning and discuss some of the foods which were served."

"It would be a wonderful tradition to begin, my lord. Your servants and tenants already revere you."

Left unspoken was how they had not felt the same about his father.

"Then we shall talk again tomorrow morning," he promised. "Mr. Rankin tells me he thinks we can harvest everything in two days. That would give you all tomorrow and the next to prepare. I hope that might be enough time."

She frowned slightly. "If I had another day, it might be better. Then again, if the other tenants' wives all bring dishes, that would help."

He thought a moment. "I will make certain that Rankin and I spread the word this morning, but the workers may be too tired to celebrate if we try this tomorrow night. Why don't we have our feast and dancing come Friday instead?"

"I am grateful for the extra day of preparation, my lord."

"Thank you for agreeing to do this, Cook. I hope it will be a tradition which will continue for many years."

Perry excused himself and went down to the stables, finding his steward there, saddling his own horse.

"You are up early this morning, Lord Martindale."

"I am ready for the harvest. I hope you do not think that I believe you have been remiss in performing your duties, Mr. Rankin. I merely wish for us to go to Huntsworth to observe how harvest is organized there."

"I have found you are a man who speaks your mind, my lord," Rankin replied. "If you were unhappy with my performance, you would have spoken up by now. I appreciated being able to see firsthand what Mr. Wayling does at Huntsworth. He is young but has excellent ideas. I think we will both learn from one another. We plan to stay in touch now that we have been introduced."

"Good. I did speak to Cook now about providing some food for us to hold our own harvest feast. She was agreeable to the idea, but she will certainly need help from the tenants' wives. If you would help me in spreading the word regarding our celebration, I would love to host the feast Friday evening."

Rankin smiled broadly. "The tenants will be excited to hear about this. It will give them something to look forward to after their hard labor. In fact, if you are amenable to doing so, we might do it twice because we will also harvest our apple crop come October."

He had almost forgotten that the apples needed a few extra weeks on the branches and they would not be a part of today's gathering.

"Excellent idea, Rankin."

Perry saddled his horse, and the two men set out for the fields. By the time the sun had risen, both men had joined the farmers, and they put in several hours of work, stopping at noon when the other farmers did. He ate and drank his fill of bread, cheese, and cider, provided by the wives. Several of the women told him they were excited to hear about the upcoming celebration and even described to him several dishes they would bring to the feast.

They returned to work, and Rankin said to him, "Thank you for participating in the harvest today, my lord, and not merely observing. It means a great deal to your people. This is not something they are used to seeing at Beauville, but it lets them know how invested you are in them and the future of the estate."

"I am happy to work side-by-side with them," he replied. "It will be interesting to tally things and see how productive this harvest is."

"All in good time. I am already keeping a count, both in my head and on paper, so we have an idea of what has been gathered. I believe this will prove to be the most productive autumn harvest Beauville has seen in many years."

He worked for several more hours before excusing himself. While the workers would continue toiling until sunset, Perry needed to return to the house in order to clean up for tonight's festivities at Huntsworth. He entered the kitchens, asking that water for a bath be heated and sent to his bedchamber. In his room, he stripped off his dirty, sweat-stained clothes, leaving them in a heap on the floor as he rang for Grilley.

His valet scrubbed him from head to toe and then shaved him, something needed since he had two days' growth of beard. Grilley then dressed Perry, and while sore from today's strenuous labor, he felt a deep satisfaction within him.

"I most likely will return late, Grilley. No need to wait up for me. I will undress myself and place my clothes over the chair."

"If you are certain, my lord."

"I am. Take a little time for yourself."

Grilley grinned. "In that case, I might go into the village and have a glass or two of ale. There's a pretty barmaid at the tavern who is interesting to talk with."

Perry laughed aloud. "Enjoy yourself, Grilley. You don't do that often enough."

The servant said, "I would say the same to you, my lord. I know the war was hard on you, but being back at Beauville has done both of us a world of good. Enjoy the food and dancing this evening."

The valet left the room, while he went to the stables. He saw no need to have his carriage prepared and merely asked a groom to saddle his horse for the short ride to Huntsworth.

He arrived at Lord Huntsberry's stables and Harry, one of the grooms, greeted him.

"Ready for the feasting, my lord?" he asked cheerfully.

"I most certainly am. I helped harvest my own crops today and am ravenous. Will you be attending the celebration?"

The groom nodded enthusiastically. "Lord and Lady Huntsberry said tonight is not only for their tenants but their servants, as well. The entire staff will be heading out to eat and make merry." Harry added, "There's a scullery maid I've had my eye on for quite a while. I hope I will be able to dance with her tonight."

"Then good luck to you," Perry said, leaving the stables and heading toward the lawn in front of the house. He yawned, realizing he was exhausted, and decided he would stay long enough to eat and then make his way back to Beauville and his bed. His aching muscles would thank him for a bit of extra rest, and he prayed he was fatigued enough that the night would be free of dreams.

The first thing he spied, other than the large crowd gathering, were numerous tables laden with food. He took the time to walk up and down the various rows, making note of what dishes were being served to the crowd. Lady Dru joined him, causing his heart to speed up.

"Good evening, Lord Martindale. I am delighted you made time to celebrate with us this evening. You seem particularly interested in the food being served."

She was wearing a pretty gown of pale pink, having abandoned the breeches he had seen her in on Monday. Perry almost preferred her in breeches because they showed off her long legs and rounded buttocks to perfection.

"I am perusing the items being served because I spoke with my own cook today about Beauville hosting a similar type of celebration to recognize the gathering of our crops. I am to report back to Cook tomorrow morning about what was served this evening."

"Would it be helpful if our cook sent a list to yours? I know she and Lucy met several times and discussed what would be served tonight."

"That would be very helpful, my lady."

"Then I will copy Cook's list first thing tomorrow morning and ride over to deliver it to your cook."

"You do not have to do so. Send a messenger with it."

She smiled at him, a radiant one which warmed him from the inside, spreading through him slowly. "You know I enjoy riding. It would be my pleasure to bring the list in person. Perhaps I might even stop and see—"

"There you are, Lady Drusilla," Mr. Hollis interrupted, nodding at Perry. "Lord Martindale."

The buoyancy Perry had felt left him. "Mr. Hollis," he said, keeping his voice neutral because he did not like this fellow. Oh, it wasn't that. Hollis was a good enough sort and would most likely make for an honorable viscount. It was merely jealously rearing its ugly head that caused his dislike of this man.

"Did Lord Tilsbury come with you?" Lady Dru asked brightly.

"He did indeed, my lady, and he is asking for you. If you would like, I can escort you to him so that the two of you might speak with one another."

She glanced to him. "Would you excuse us, Lord Martindale?"

"Certainly, my lady."

Perry watched her leave, seeing her slip her hand through the crook of Hollis' arm. He told himself he must let go of all feelings he possessed for her. A match with Hollis would be ideal for Lady Dru. He could not stand in the way. He simply was not worthy of her. His soul had been damaged beyond repair. She needed a man who would not hold her back or dim her spirit, not one lacking in so many ways, as he was.

Lord and Lady Huntsberry joined him, and the marquess said, "Thank you for coming this evening, Martindale, especially since I know you began your own harvest this morning."

He was growing fond of the marquess and smiled as he said, "We did, my lord. My aching muscles can attest to that. I must say that I followed your example and worked in the fields with my tenants. They seemed appreciative of my presence. I am weary, however, so I will only stay for a short while this evening."

The couple excused themselves, and Perry went back to looking over the food items to be served, knowing his knowledge, along with the list from the Huntsworth cook, would aid his own cook in putting together a decent feast.

A few minutes later, Lord Huntsberry addressed those gathered, thanking everyone for their hard work, and then raising his mug of cider, offering a toast for a bountiful year and for years to come.

Perry joined others in the line, heaping food upon his plate, and then he went to sit with Lord and Lady Aldridge at a nearby table. Lord Aldridge had a babe sitting upon his knee, looking perfectly at ease.

"Ah, good to see you, Martindale," the marquess said. "I would like to have you meet our daughter, Lady Penelope Barrington."

The babe looked at Perry with wide, curious eyes. Then she cooed in such an engaging manner that he felt his heart melt.

"She is quite beautiful," he told the couple.

"Penelope is also very smart," Aldridge said, causing his wife to laugh. "Well, she is," he insisted.

"Forgive my husband," Lady Aldridge said. "He is besotted with his child. I think I am going to have to give him more simply because I do not wish for Penelope to be utterly spoiled by her father."

The marquess gave his wife such a heated look, it took Perry aback.

"We can go home now, my love, if that is what you wish."

Again, Lady Aldridge laughed. "We shall stay long enough to dance at least once, my lord. *Then* we will see." Her eyes lit with mischief.

The powerful love between this couple was palpable. And it only made Perry more miserable, wishing he could have this kind of relationship with Lady Dru. If only he weren't so marred by his war experiences, he would leap at the chance to woo her.

He did enjoy the time he spent in the Aldridges' company,

however, and answered the marquess' questions about how Beauville's harvest had gone today.

"My steward thinks we can easily finish by the end of tomorrow," he shared. "Of course, we have a large grove of apple trees, and those must be plucked come October."

"Oh, I do love a good apple tart," Lady Aldridge said. She looked over her shoulder when a fiddle sounded. "I believe the dancing is about to begin. The musicians must be tuning their instruments."

Lord Aldridge asked, "Would you hold Penelope during our dance, my lord? We did not bring her nursery governess along." He grinned. "I wanted my two loves all to myself tonight."

Perry had been surprised by the fact that the babe had remained in her father's lap the entire time they ate and was even more surprised that the couple had not brought along a servant to watch over the infant.

Lady Aldridge must have sensed his hesitation. "It is quite all right if you are not comfortable doing so, my lord."

"No," he assured her, knowing she deserved a dance with her husband. "Though I have yet to hold a babe, I have watched your husband do so. I think I can manage Lady Penelope for a few minutes on my own."

The child was growing sleepy, blinking, taking longer each time to hold her eyes open.

Lord Aldridge stood and passed his daughter to Perry, instructing him how to hold her head in the crook of his arm and to always support her back and neck.

"Go have your dance, Aldridge," he encouraged, watching the couple leave the table, even as Lady Aldridge turned over her shoulder and mouthed a thank you to him.

For his part, Perry was enthralled as Lady Penelope drifted off to sleep. She was warm in his arms and had a unique smell he had never encountered before. Her long lashes rested against smooth, porcelain cheeks. Everything about her was tiny and perfect.

The music started, and he glanced up, seeing a few farmers

with instruments in hand. Groups of couples had come together for the country dance the musicians played. His eyes were drawn to the set of four couples Lady Dru was a part of. Naturally, Mr. Hollis had partnered with her, and Perry tamped down the instant envy that rose within him.

They were a handsome couple as they danced together. Lady Dru was tall for a woman, only a few inches shorter than Mr. Hollis. Both were energetic and excellent dancers. Wistfulness rose within him, knowing this woman could never be his.

Glancing back to Lady Penelope, he told the babe, "I hope you will find a gentleman to love you as much as your papa loves your mama."

And as much as I love Drusilla Alington . . .

He kept his eyes fastened upon the babe after that, finding it hurt too much to watch Lady Dru enjoying herself so much with another man.

The tune ended, and the Aldridges returned to him, the marquess possessively lifting his daughter from Perry's arms.

"See, she did not break," his wife teased. "Thank you, Lord Martindale, for allowing us a dance. It is time for us to leave so Penelope might go to bed."

From the look he saw in Lord Aldridge's eyes, the marquess would be eager to take his daughter to the nursery in order to spend the rest of the night with his wife.

He bid them goodnight, ready to head home himself, when Lady Dru appeared before him. Perry rose quickly.

"You did not dance, my lord," she chided gently.

"I had better things to occupy my time," he said lightly. "I was watching over Lady Penelope while her parents had a dance together."

Her eyes softened. "That was kind of you to do so."

He couldn't help but chuckle. "Well, it offered a new experience for me. I had never held a babe before. I found I could do so without breaking her."

"See, if you put your mind to it, you can accomplish anything," she teased, laughing, and he joined in. "Come, my lord. You must dance at least once with me."

"I am fatigued, my lady. I have been up since well before dawn and spent the day in the fields at Beauville, assisting my tenants in the harvest. I should be going."

"One dance," she begged.

And Perry knew he could not resist.

"One dance," he agreed, leading her to where groups were forming.

He promised himself this one dance, and then he would leave. If something were to develop between Lady Dru and Mr. Hollis, tonight would be a good time to encourage that flame be fanned. He did not wish to stand in their way.

The music began, and Perry was lost in the music—and Lady Dru's eyes.

CHAPTER EIGHTEEN

DRU HAD ALWAYS enjoyed dancing, and tonight was no exception. Though there had been an abundance of food, she had eaten sparingly so she could dance without being miserable. Mr. Hollis had asked her to dance first. While she found that she liked him a good deal, she had found her gaze wandering as they danced, looking for Lord Martindale. He had been nowhere to be seen, so when the first dance had ended, she had excused herself and gone looking for him.

It had surprised her that he had offered to hold Penelope while Ariadne and Julian danced, but then again, he seemed most kind. She only wished she could have seen him doing so. Or perhaps not. Already she was far too fond of the earl. Seeing him with a babe in his arms might have been disastrous, as far as her heart was concerned.

Still, she wished to dance with him and was glad she had sought his company. While she could understand his being weary after a day spent laboring in the fields, he might have slipped away unnoticed, causing her to miss this opportunity. She had him now as a partner, though, and would make the most of it.

The dance was lively, and she moved with abandon, enjoying every moment the music played. When she joined with Lord Martindale, those delicious shivers rippled along her spine, something that had not occurred when she partnered with Mr. Hollis. Dru made the most of the time she had with the earl, and he twirled her about as the lively music played on.

All too soon, it came to an end, and it was as if she could see him withdrawing from her. She wanted to help him, but she knew he would refuse to talk about his experiences during the war, what she believed to be the root of his troubles.

He took her hand and placed it on his sleeve to guide her away from the other dancers. She recalled seeing his bare forearms, his shirtsleeves rolled to his elbows when he had helped in the Huntsworth harvest on Monday. Those forearms had been a thing of true beauty. If she were a painter or sculptor, she would have pleaded for him to be her model so that she might capture them on canvas or in marble for eternity.

The earl did look weary as he told her, "I must be off, my lady. I still have another day of harvesting tomorrow, as well as my own estate's celebration to attend the following day."

Their gazes met and held. She did not want him to leave.

"Stay," she whispered.

He shook his head. "I cannot." He did capture her hand and bring it to his lips for a tender kiss. "Enjoy the rest of your evening, Lady Dru. Perhaps you can even get Lord Tilsbury to dance with you," he teased.

Then he was gone, and Dru felt cut adrift. Her heart grew heavy.

"Ah, Lady Drusilla," a familiar voice said.

Turning, she saw Mr. Hollis before her. "Might we dance to another tune? I so enjoyed our first dance."

"I thought I would see if your uncle might dance with me," she said. "Perhaps later, Mr. Hollis. My brother-in-law suggested I dance with some of our tenants."

Disappointment filled his eyes, but he stoically said, "Of course. I hope to see you shortly."

Dru found Viscount Tilsbury, sitting in a chair, tapping his foot to the music, which had started again by this time. She took the seat next to him.

"I saw you dancing, my lady. You do so with such joy, just as

Lady Tilsbury did."

"I am flattered to be compared to your wife, my lord. Have you danced since her passing?"

The viscount sighed. "I have not. And I vowed I never would—until we are united again and can dance together in the afterlife."

"That is a pleasant thought. I never thought about dancing once I am gone."

"Oh, I think about what comes after death all the time," he told her. "It is because I am closer to my time of passing than you are. I believe we are reunited with our loved ones when we leave this earth, and that we do all the things with them that brought us joy. For me, that would be dancing with my wife." He paused, his eyes misting. "Just think, an eternity with the woman I love in my arms. Now that, Lady Drusilla, is what heaven is all about."

She laughed merrily. "I like your version of heaven better than ones I heard about from some vicars."

"God is good," Lord Tilsbury said. "He knows what pleases us. Being with my wife was heaven on earth. Why wouldn't I have the same in the true heaven?"

"Why not, indeed?" she mused. "Very well. I shall go dance with others then."

He took her hand. "I saw you dancing with Edward. I think he enjoys your company a great deal."

She hesitated and then said, "I believe he might."

"And your feelings?"

"I am a little confused about that, my lord," she admitted.

"Not everyone falls in love, my lady, much less as quickly as I did with Lady Tilsbury. I hope that you are lucky enough to do so. If you are not, then my wish for you is that you will find a gentleman whom you can call friend and companion. One who will be someone you enjoying being a wife to."

She lifted his hand to her cheek and held it there a moment. "We will have to see what my future holds."

Dru excused herself and danced with several others. Lucy had told her to feel free to dance with anyone, be that a guest or one of the tenants. She danced with two farmers, Mr. Wayling, Judson's valet Tim, and even Harry, her favorite groom at Huntsworth.

By now, it had grown dark, and Mr. Hollis approached her again, a cup of lemonade in hand.

"Might I offer you something to drink, Lady Drusilla?"

"Thank you. I was feeling parched."

She accepted the cup he offered, as well as accompanying him to a couple of chairs. As she sipped her lemonade, he asked her questions about herself. She told him some about her life at Marleyfield but mentioned how much she was enjoying her visit to Surrey.

"I have always been close to Lucy, and I am becoming extremely fond of Ariadne."

"Will you be here long?" he asked.

"I cannot answer that. Lucy and Judson have told me that I might stay as long as I wish, even until next spring when they return to town for the Season. I am supposed to make my come-out then."

He studied her a moment. "You do not sound happy about that."

She shrugged. "I will admit that I have mixed emotions. To be honest, Mr. Hollis, I have not seen myself with a husband and children, at least not until I came to Surrey. Watching how happy my sister and cousin are in their marriages has convinced me that I should make my come-out and see what happens from there." She paused. "Will you attend the Season, Mr. Hollis?"

"I have never done so. I doubt I will because it is not something my uncle chooses to do. Eventually, after I have taken up the viscountcy, I plan to do so when I become a part of Polite Society."

"Will you seek a wife at that time?"

He did not answer for a long moment and finally said, "My younger brother wed several years ago. I believe I mentioned to you that he already has two children. I thought it best to wait until I came into my title until I sought a wife, however."

"My brother has decided to do the same," she said.

"In my case, the ladies of my acquaintance only know me as a solicitor. They are the daughters of other solicitors, doctors, and even tradesmen. I do not mean to sound prejudiced against the middle class, but those women might not make for a good viscountess, not having come from the world of the *ton*. I would hate it if I chose to wed and then my wife had trouble being accepted into Polite Society."

"But you will mix in a more gentler society if you remain with Lord Tilsbury," she pointed out. "You might even find someone in the neighborhood with whom you would suit."

His gaze intensified, and Dru felt compelled to look away.

"I know we have both danced quite a bit, my lady. Would you care for a less strenuous form of exercise? We might stroll the lawns."

Wanting to break the serious mood, she agreed. "Yes, thank you. A stroll would be lovely."

He helped her to stand and she accepted the arm he offered. They walked around the perimeter of the dancing and then went farther afield. He told her some about his life in London and a few of his current cases.

"One thing I have done my fair share of is negotiating marriage settlements. I am in demand for that. I pride myself on doing a fine job, making certain that whichever party I represent has fair representation within the contracts."

By now, they had drifted a good distance from the others. While she could still hear the music, the dancers were merely dark shapes.

Suddenly, he turned, taking her face in his hands. "Lady Drusilla, I must tell you how ardently I do admire you. You possess a good deal of maturity for one of such a tender age."

Before she could reply, he bent, his lips pressing against hers. She decided to allow the kiss, mostly because she wished to compare it to those of Lord Martindale.

Mr. Hollis kissed her for a few minutes, growing bolder, finally easing her mouth open and sweeping his tongue inside. While his kiss was pleasant, Dru had no desire to return it. She felt none of the magic she had experienced when Lord Martindale kissed her.

He broke the kiss, smiling down gently at her. Apparently, he had not noticed her lack of enthusiasm—or he believed it was her first kiss and she had no idea how to respond.

"Would you—"

"Save your question, Mr. Hollis," she interrupted, worried he was about to spontaneously offer marriage to her.

"But I—"

"If you would excuse me."

Dru took off, hurrying away. Perhaps she was being over-hasty, and he merely wished to ask if he might court her, but panic filled her, nonetheless. She did want to think about Mr. Hollis as a possible suitor, now or ever. She didn't want any suitor.

Unless it might be Lord Martindale.

Oh, she had turned into some foolish fluffhead. "Bloody hell," she said aloud, traveling as fast as her feet would carry her, away from the others gathered.

She needed to get notions of Lord Martindale out of her head. She was not for him. He was not for her. Despite how happy she had been at Huntsworth, it might be time to make arrangements to go home to Somerset. She could write Con and see if he could arrange his schedule so that he might serve as her chaperone back to Marleyfield. The thought of being around Mama, however, caused dread to rise within her.

Which would be the lesser of two evils—butting heads with her mother or pining over a man who would never considering wedding her?

Dru found herself at the stables and ducked inside, wanting a quiet place to be and think. Everyone at Huntsworth, including the grooms, should be at the celebration, so this should serve as a brief sanctuary for her. The comforting smell of hay and horse greeted her, something she was familiar with and found solace in. She paused a moment, trying to catch her breath.

A horse nearby nickered, and she moved to it, stroking the velvet nose.

"There's a good pretty," she said absently.

Then she heard a low moan and froze.

Someone was here.

She held her breath, waiting. When nothing sounded, she decided she had imagined the noise.

Until it came again.

The keening started low and then rose in volume. In it, she heard both sorrow and suffering, and it tore at her heart. Then it magnified into a loud wail, causing fear to shoot through her. She knew someone was in distress and must help them.

Resolve filled her, and Dru hurried down the row of stalls until she located the source of despair. Glancing into the stall, which was empty of any horse, she saw a man curled up in the hay, his body twitching. Surprisingly, Toby nestled against him. Pity filled her, especially when his head whipped about and she caught sight of his face.

It was the Earl of Martindale.

CHAPTER NINETEEN

PERRY LEFT THE merrymaking, his heart rending in two. He hurried toward the stables in order to reclaim Zeus.

What was it about Lady Dru that spoke to his soul?

He only knew that he would be poison to her, his problems becoming hers, if they wed. She deserved far better in life than a broken-down soldier who feared the night. If Mr. Hollis did not please her, then she would certainly find another gentleman who would suit her come next Season.

Suddenly, he stumbled, taking a spill to the ground. His knees took the brunt of the fall and stung like the dickens. So did the palms of his hands. Thankfully, it did not seem as if he had broken anything. That would have been disastrous, especially with more of the harvest yet to be claimed. He swore softly under his breath, knowing the fall warned him of just how weary he was.

When he reached the stables and found no one inside them, he decided for his sake and the safety of his horse that he should lie down for a few minutes. It would be dangerous to be out on the road and fall asleep in the saddle. Harm might come to him and Zeus if he did so. Thankfully, the grooms were all dancing in the moonlight so that he might nap for a short while.

Perry walked down the row, stalls on each side of him. He came to one near the end. It was empty, devoid of everything, and he continued looking, finding the next one empty but with hay scattered about the ground. This would do.

He entered, feeling something brush against his leg. Glancing down, he saw Lady Dru's cat.

"What are you doing here, Toby?" he asked.

The cat's loud purr sounded, so he added, "I need to rest my eyes a bit. You are more than welcome to keep me company."

Quickly, Perry brushed the hay into a corner, making himself a bed of it. He was too tired to even slip off his coat as he curled up, Toby snuggling next to him. He closed his eyes, sinking into oblivion.

Once more, the nightmare came. The fear. The horror. The blood. Death. It was as if he knew it was a dream that he must succumb to, knowing he had no control to keep it at bay.

This time, the fierceness of the fighting seemed magnified. He fought hard, leading charge after charge, each one turning into a bloodbath. He thought it would never end as the nightmare became more vivid, the smell of death more intense.

Then the faint whiff of gardenias reached him, and he thought of Drusilla Alington. Her image gave him a courage he had never experienced before. Calling to his men, he rallied them for one more charge against the enemy.

His horse was shot out from under him, and Perry leaped from it, landing on his feet, shouting for his soldiers to follow. His pistol in his left hand, he drew his sword with his right, swinging it, cutting a swath through the thick column of French bastards. A bullet pierced his shoulder, and he let out a hoarse cry. Still, he moved forward, urging his men to do the same.

Yet, one by one, they fell, their cries for mercy falling upon deaf ears. Blood now poured from his shoulder wound, and he found himself weakening as he came face to face with a French officer. They engaged in combat, swords arcing, profanity spewing, cuts to their torsos bringing cries of agony. Perry fought on, the scent of gardenias encouraging him, a warmth filling him.

Then his opponent kicked him in the knee, and he went down on his back, the breath knocked from him. The officer hovered over him, a smile of pure evil on his face as he lifted his sword and jammed it into Perry's eye.

He awoke, shrieking, pain filling him. But something—no, someone—silenced him. He grabbed, holding fast, another mouth on his, the smell of gardenias surrounding him.

Lady Dru . . .

Forcing his eyes open, he realized she held him tight, her body sprawled atop him, her mouth fixed to his. His arms went about her, and he took charge of the kiss.

And oh, what a kiss it was.

Perry drank hungrily from her, need for her filling him. The kiss went on and on, in endless bliss. There had never been a more perfect moment than now. With her. His hands roamed her back, grasping her buttocks, kneading them. He felt her breasts swell against him and knew he had to taste them.

With a bit of regret, he broke the kiss, his lips sliding downward as he rolled so they lay on their sides, facing one another. Her gown had a low, scooped neckline, and he slipped his hand inside it, bringing one breast out and freeing it. Immediately, his mouth went to it, and he sucked hard. She wriggled against him, her gasp loud. She began moaning low as he continued sucking hard, devouring it.

He lifted his head a moment, needing to see her. Her eyes were glazed, but she managed a few words.

"Do that. Again."

He fought for control, starting more gently this time. Licking. Blowing cool air gently. Licking again. Grazing his teeth against her raised nipple, hearing her cry out. He began sucking on it again, feeling it swell, even as his hand traveled up her calf. Suddenly, the need to taste even more of her overwhelmed him. He pushed her to her back and moved lower, finding the hem of her gown and pushing the gown to her waist.

Gripping her knees, he moved between her legs, dipping his head, licking the seam of her sex. She was already dripping wet with desire.

Hearing her gasp, he lifted his head. "I assume you want

more of the same," he said huskily.

Her eyes large, she nodded eagerly. "Yes. Oh, dear heavens, yes!"

Pinning her gaze, he told her, "I am going to satisfy you as no other man has."

He moved between her thighs again, once more licking her seam, tasting her juices. Then he began a game of cat and mouse, inserting his tongue, lapping at her, sucking, teasing her, removing it and beginning again. Though he held her knees firmly, she began to quiver, and he knew she was close to orgasm.

Once again, he plunged inside her, now using teeth and tongue, teasing her pearl, feeling—and hearing—her eruption like a volcano.

"Yes!" she cried. "Oh, yes. Yes. Yes!"

She came undone, her hips pumping, her fingers thrust into his hair, tightening almost painfully. Still he kept on, and she rode wave after wave of pleasure until she stilled. He released her knees, and they fell to the hay.

Then Lady Dru lifted her head, her smile like that of a siren. "You are one very wicked man, my lord."

"Perry," he prompted, needing to hear her call him by name. He couldn't recall the last time anyone had used it.

"Perry," she said, trying it out. "For Peregrine, I assume?"

He nodded, suddenly shy around her.

For her part, she sat up, hay sticking out from her hair. "That was marvelous." Then panic suddenly filled her eyes. "Did we make a babe?"

He smiled gently at her. "No, we did not."

She bit her lip. "I would not have minded if we did. I think I would like your babe growing inside me."

His ears burned, and he seized her mouth with his, kissing her long and hard and deep. His hand went between her legs again, stroking her, but she grabbed his wrist.

Breaking the kiss, she said, "No. I want to pleasure you instead."

His cock, already full and aching, begged for her attention.

"You need to tell me what to do," she pressed, reaching and beginning to unbutton his trousers.

"Are you . . . certain?" he rasped as she freed it, grasping it in her hand.

"Oh, this is large. Hard and yet smooth as silk," she mused, her thumb rubbing its head.

"God's teeth," he said through clenched teeth of his own.

A wicked smile played about her lips. "You like that, don't you, Perry?"

He liked it. He wanted it. He wanted her.

"Yes," he managed to say.

"Lay back as I did," she instructed, taking charge. "I will try a few things and see how you like it."

"Oh, I will like it," he guaranteed.

Her fingers danced up and down his shaft, sometimes holding it, stroking it, rubbing it. She instinctively seemed to know what to do, and soon he was swelling, ready to come.

Then she kissed the tip of his shaft—and licked it.

"Bloody hell, Dru," he said as he jerked away from her, spending on the hay, groaning and moving and smelling that scent of orange blossoms. He would never inhale that scent again without thinking of her—and this moment.

For her part, she watched in fascination. She even dipped her finger against the hay and smoothed his seed between her thumb and index finger, causing him to groan.

"Did that make you feel wonderful?" she asked expectantly.

"It did," he said, pulling her back to him so that her head rested against his chest.

He brought his arms around her, holding her tenderly, yet possessively. Closing his eyes, Perry savored this moment.

Until he heard a voice.

"Stay there, Uncle," Mr. Hollis said. "I will fetch our horses."

"Nonsense," the viscount replied. "I can lead a horse from a stall, young man."

Perry placed his finger against Dru's lips. She nodded silently. To be caught in such a compromising position would be scandalous.

And lead to her ruin.

"Lord Huntsberry should have insisted at least one groom remain in the stables," Mr. Hollis said.

"It would be hard to deny anyone a chance to feast and dance," Lord Tilsbury said. "I knew there would be no servants here. That is why I suggested we bring the barouche. It is easy to attach the horses to. Ah, come, Starlight."

He heard a stall door open and assumed the viscount led one of his horses from where it was housed.

"Did you enjoy yourself this evening?" the viscount continued.

"Very much. I kissed Lady Drusilla."

Anger seared through him. He felt Dru stiffen against him.

"You like her."

"I do, Uncle. She is unpretentious. Young but an old soul. She did not know how to kiss, which told me that she never had been kissed before."

Their voices faded as the two men led their horses from the stables. Still, he waited a few minutes before speaking.

"So, your Mr. Hollis kissed you, did he?"

"He is not *my* Mr. Hollis."

Curiously, he asked, "Why did he think you had never been kissed?"

"Because I did not wish to respond to his kiss," she said saucily. "You have taught me enough about kissing, Perry. Mr. Hollis' kiss was meaningless."

"And mine aren't?"

She sighed, a dreamy look coming into her eyes. "Your kisses, my lord, are heavenly."

Her hand went to his nape, bringing his lips to hers. They kissed for a long time, lazily at first, then more heatedly.

He broke the kiss. "You should get back. You will have been missed by now."

Perry pushed himself to his feet and then held out a hand. Dru took it, allowing him to help her stand. Quickly, they both repaired themselves, even picking hay from one another's hair and clothes.

He started to open the stall, and she caught his wrist. "What is to happen next between us, Perry?" shea asked softly.

"Nothing," he said sadly. "I must promise myself not to touch you again."

"Why?" she demanded, her brows knitting together. "I know you have feelings for me, just as I have for you. Why can't we explore them?"

He framed her face in his hands. "Because nothing can come of it, Dru." He brushed a kiss against her brow. "You are not for me."

Anger sparked in her eyes. "I am not good enough to be your countess?"

"That is not what I meant." He caught himself just in time, almost calling her *my love*. "I am flawed. My time at war changed me in ways I still do not understand."

He began stroking her cheeks with his thumbs. "You deserve someone whole, Dru. Someone worthy of you. I can never be that man."

His hands fell to his sides. Suddenly, the sting of a slap sounded, his cheek burning.

"You are everything I could ever wish for in a man, Perry," she told him. "You cut me to the quick, denying what is between us. You would have us both suffer in silence—apart—rather than be together."

Though his heart warred with his head, he knew he must do what was best for her. Because he loved her. "Yes, I think that is best."

"And what about what *I* think? Oh, you are like every other man. Only what *you* say and feel counts. You disregard my feelings without a second thought."

"Dru, I—"

"When you are ready to tell me that you love me as much as I love you, come to Huntsworth and say it to my face," she declared. "Until then, I do not wish to have anything to do with you."

She pushed him aside, sweeping up Toby, who had remained inside the stall, and stormed off. He watched her, thinking she was the most magnificent creature he had ever seen.

And she loved him.

He shook his head. He would not ruin her life by wedding her. She would eventually get over him. Either this coming Season—or one after that—she would find a man worthy of her love.

All the while, he would live on the crumbs of knowing that Drusilla Alington had once loved him.

His heart heavy, Perry saddled Zeus and rode back to Beauville, determined to avoid seeing Dru at all costs.

CHAPTER TWENTY

DRU PACED THE bedchamber, her eyes grainy from lack of sleep. She berated herself for her behavior last night. But she would not take back a single word she had said to Perry.

Why did the man have to be so bloody stubborn? It was obvious they had feelings for one another. She had even blurted out that she loved him, something he had not echoed in return. Still, if he did not love her, she knew he did hold some feelings for her. They could not have been so intimate together last night otherwise.

Once more, he had cracked open the door to a new world. The way he had touched her. Reverently. Lovingly. He had stirred not only physical feelings within her, but strong emotional ones, too. It was love on her part. That she knew beyond a doubt.

Yet a part of her could understand his reluctance in making a commitment to her. He admitted last night that the war had damaged him irreparably. He might not carry the physical scars of a soldier, but his soul had been injured.

And it was up to Dru to help him to learn how to heal.

Of course, that was going to prove to be difficult, especially since she had given him an ultimatum. She had told him he must come to her and admit his love, or else she would have nothing more to do with him.

How could she help him begin to heal if they weren't even speaking?

She tossed herself onto the bed, frustration filling her. She knew how stubborn she could be, and she might have met her match in Perry. She needed to find a way to break down the walls he had built about him. To let him know he was not alone. That they could face whatever fears he experienced together. Yet she was not one to be intimidated, either. He needed to understand just how strongly she felt about him. Dru had declared her love. She could not force him to love her, in return.

But if he didn't, her heart told her that she could never love again. That her heart would always belong to the Earl of Martindale, whether he claimed it or not.

Her stomach grumbled. She decided to go to breakfast. Only Judson was in the room when she arrived.

As she helped herself to the buffet, she asked, "How is Lucy this morning?"

A self-satisfied smile crossed his lips, and she knew immediately Lucy and her husband had coupled this morning. Dru already knew they spent their nights in the same bed, so it didn't surprise her. "Your sister is well this morning," Judson told her. "Since we stayed until the end of the celebration last night, however, I told her she must get extra rest today. I had a tray sent upstairs so that she might breakfast in bed."

"That was very thoughtful of you, Judson." She paused, and then asked, "Are you a proud man? Even a stubborn one at times?"

He grew thoughtful at the question. "I am proud in the marriage I have made," he began. "Sometimes, I feel as if my life did not begin until I met Lucy. She is my everything, Dru. I am nothing without her. But yes, I do have pride in not only my marriage, but also in Huntsworth and the work we are accomplishing here. I know I will be proud of the children my wife bears. Already, I think of the one growing in her belly all the time. I see how Julian is with Penelope, and I will venture to say that I will be as enchanted with any child Lucy births."

He paused. "Why do you ask?"

She did not want to confide in him with two footmen and the butler standing nearby. Servants gossiped tremendously, even beyond their households, and she would not wish for word to travel from Huntsworth to Beauville regarding her feelings toward Perry.

Instead, she said, "I was merely impressed by the bounty of the harvest collected at Huntsworth, and I assumed that you take great pride in what you are accomplishing here with your tenants."

He studied her a long moment and then said, "Perhaps you might like to see some of the early tallies. Come with me to my study after breakfast, and you can review them."

Though Dru wasn't interested in the numbers regarding the yield, she smiled politely and said, "Of course, Judson. I would like very much like to see that."

As they ate, they talked about last night and how much the tenants and staff seemed to enjoy the food and dancing.

"Lord Tilsbury told me last night that he and Mr. Hollis have decided to emulate us and begin a similar tradition when they collect their own crops next week."

"Oh, that reminds me." She felt her cheeks warming as she said, "Lord Martindale told me the same. He met with his cook yesterday to discuss what they might serve. I volunteered to bring a list to Beauville today, a copy of the one Lucy made regarding the dishes Cook prepared last night, for Beauville's cook."

"Then I suppose we can meet later to discuss our yield."

"Yes, thank you, Judson."

Dru finished her breakfast and went to Lucy's parlor. A desk stood in the corner, where her sister kept up with her correspondence. She found the list of foods prepared by Cook and sat, copying it item by item. She would ride to Beauville now and deliver it to Perry's cook. Since he should be out in the fields, she doubted she would run into him.

The ink now dry, she folded the list and slipped it into the pocket of her breeches before leaving the house to head to the stables.

On her way there, Judson joined her and asked, "Might I walk with you?"

"Certainly," she replied. "Why do I have the feeling you were waiting for me to leave the house in order to speak with me?"

"You are not the only one aware of servants listening to our conversations, Dru. I believe you wish to address something with me. We are alone now. Speak freely."

Her eyes misted with tears, and she blinked rapidly several times. "I am not certain how to begin."

"Then I shall begin for you. You are in love with Lord Martindale."

She stopped in her tracks. "How did you guess?"

"I have had my suspicions," he shared. "Watching the two of you together, I noted the spark between you."

A tear ran down her cheek, and Dru wiped it away hastily. "I do love him, Judson. I cannot say exactly what his feelings are for me since he has never expressed them. What I do know is that he does not see a future with us together," she said, her voice cracking.

He took her hand and squeezed it gently. "Why do you say that?"

"Because he has told me so himself," she said dully.

Judson's eyes darkened in anger. "Has he touched you, Dru?"

"We have kissed," she admitted, keeping the rest to herself. "He is the first man I have ever kissed, and those kisses took me to a place I have never been. But his war experience has colored his outlook on life, Judson. He has admitted to me that he suffers from nightmares. I believe this is the reason he refuses to commit to me. He has spoken of being damaged by the horrors he has witnessed."

Her brother-in-law grew thoughtful. "It would be kind of him if he did steer clear of you, Dru. I have heard some terrible tales of how the war has affected soldiers. Because of his experiences, Lord Martindale might not make for a good husband."

"Yet he plans to go to the Season next spring and peruse the

Marriage Mart!" she declared. "Why would he wed another woman and yet reject me?"

Their gazes met, and he said, "It may be because he has tender feelings for you and that he does not wish to trap you into a marriage which would prove to be unsuccessful. Lord Martindale is looking out for your wellbeing and happiness. Do not get me wrong, Dru. I like the earl. Quite a bit. But I would not see you bound to someone who would eventually make you unhappy, through no fault of his own."

"I will be most unhappy if I do not wed him," she said. "I love him. I believe he loves me, yet he is too stubborn and full of pride to cast it aside and seek a marriage with me."

Judson looked at her sadly. "I know from Lucy how tender your heart is when it comes to animals, especially injured ones. That you have nursed many of them, either sick or injured, back to health, and then released them into the wild once more."

He paused. "Not everything—or everyone—can be mended, Dru. Lord Martindale has seen horrors you and I could never understand. He has lived through experiences he can never forget. Most likely, he even suffers from survivor's guilt. As an officer, he led men into battle, and not all those men returned. Obviously, what happened to him on the Continent has changed the man he once was. Whether you understand it or not, he is doing you a favor by keeping you at arms' length. Because he is honorable, he does not wish to drag you into the mire with him."

She pulled her hand from his, not liking what he had said. "It is too late for that. My heart is already engaged, Judson. I do want to try and help him to heal. I do not know if that is possible, but I would do my best to help him. I realize that the war was life-altering for him. While I might not be able to make him into the man he formerly was, I am desperate to share my life with the man he now is. But fool that he is, he will not let this come to pass."

"Your feelings appear to be strong for him, Dru. As strong as mine are for Lucy. If Lord Martindale's feelings toward you are similar, he will not be able to stay away from you for long."

His words gave her hope that she could make a life with Perry.

"Be careful for what you wish for," he warned. "While you obviously have a physical and emotional attraction to him, he may not be able to make you happy in the end."

"I would rather be wed to Lord Martindale and experience various ups and downs than be with another man, Judson. Mr. Hollis kissed me last night," she revealed. "He is a very nice gentleman, and yet his kiss left me cold. I believe the earl has ruined me for any other man. Either I wed him—or I become a spinster and doting aunt."

"I respect your feelings, Dru. You are still young, however. If things are not settled between you and Lord Martindale, will you consider attending the Season and making your come-out?"

She thought of all the glittering balls, which held absolutely no appeal to her, and how hard it would be to attend them and see Perry dancing with someone else. It would eat away at her, seeing him move from woman to woman, trying to find his countess.

"I cannot look that far ahead. I will make no promises regarding the Season at this time."

"Guard your heart, Dru," he advised. "Feel free to come to me anytime if you wish to talk about Lord Martindale. While I know you and Lucy are close and discuss everything, she is seeing the world through her own optimism these days. She is happy with me. We are in love. She is expecting our child. Naturally, she wants the same kind of life and happiness for you."

"Lucy would worry if I shared how traumatized Lord Martindale is. She would want better for me. I will keep your words in mind, Judson, and if I wish to speak about these matters again, I know I have a friend in you. Thank you for letting me unburden myself."

"Are you still riding to Beauville?"

"Yes. I promised Lord Martindale that I would deliver the list to his cook, and I intend to keep my word. He will be out in the fields for harvest, so I will not have the occasion to see him."

"Then let me ride to Beauville with you," he said. "I can use the excuse that I wish to see how his harvest is coming along. It will keep him occupied while you are speaking with his cook."

She smiled. "I feel I have inherited another brother to care for me. It is the very thing Con would do for me. Yes, you may ride to Beauville with me. I will not be long with the cook, so I will make my way back to Huntsworth alone."

They continued to the stables, where their horses were saddled for them and they rode directly to Beauville, parting ways. Dru headed toward the main house, while Judson rode in the direction of the workers in the field.

She stopped at the stables, handing off her reins to a groom, telling him that she would return shortly.

As she approached the house, she saw two maids beating a carpet. They greeted her, and she explained that she wished to speak to the cook regarding the feast Lord Martindale would hold tomorrow evening.

"If you would like, my lady, I will take you straight to the kitchens," one of the maids offered.

"Thank you," she replied, following the servant to the back door and entering.

The maid took her to the cook, and she introduced herself.

"I am Lady Drusilla Alington. I have brought a list of the dishes our cook prepared last night for our harvest feast at Beauville, my brother-in-law's estate."

She handed the paper to the older woman, and Cook accepted it, a smile on her face.

"His lordship told me at breakfast this morning that you would be dropping off this list. He also shared with me the numerous dishes prepared by your tenants, as well."

"At . . . breakfast?" she echoed, thinking Lord Martindale most unique for even bothering to have a conversation with his cook.

"Yes, my lady. Lord Martindale and I ate together yesterday morning and again today, as well. He told me in detail about the feast at Huntsworth."

Cook's eyes skimmed the list. "So, this is everything your kitchen staff prepared?"

"It is."

"This will help me and my scullery maids in readying for tomorrow night. His lordship has also asked the tenants' wives to bring food of their own to the celebration, much as was done at Huntsworth." Cook set the list on the table nearby. "His lordship was very complimentary of you, my lady. He asked that when you stopped by, that I invite you to Beauville's celebration tomorrow evening. Lord and Lady Huntsberry, too."

So, Perry had had enough faith that she would bring the list this morning. She wished she could ask what he had told this servant about her, but she refused to stoop to gossiping.

"If you do not have any questions of me, Cook, I will return to Beauville."

"This gives me a good idea of what needs to be prepared, my lady. Thank you again for bringing this to me, and please thank your own cook for sharing."

"I will do so. Good day."

Dru left the kitchens and returned to the stables, claiming her horse. She rode back the way she and Judson had come, seeing the Beauville workers in the distance as they toiled in the fields. She wasn't ready to see Perry yet. In fact, she did not know if she would come to Beauville tomorrow night. Just because an invitation had been extended did not mean she must accept it. After all, she had told him he would be the one who needed to reach out to her when he was ready to declare his love for her.

She wondered if he did love her. If he would be willing to tell her so. And if he could gather his strength and try to recover from the memories which tortured him. Dru was willing to meet him.

But only halfway.

CHAPTER TWENTY-ONE

PERRY APPRECIATED LORD Huntsberry stopping by to check on him and the Beauville harvest. The marquess even tossed off his coat and rolled up his sleeves, helping out for several hours. Although they worked side by side, he refrained from mentioning Dru, not wanting to involve Huntsberry in his problems.

When Rankin called a halt to work and men began moving to the tables set with food and drink, Huntsberry said, "It is time for me to return home. My own steward will be wondering what happened to me."

"Was yours a productive harvest, my lord?" he asked.

"Very much so. I am pleased with Wayling. This is the first estate he has been in charge of, after spending many years under his father's tutelage. I could not ask for a better, more creative steward."

"Rankin mentioned how he is impressed with Wayling, as well. I believe they will become fast friends and consult one another when they run into problems or seek an opinion different from their own." He paused. "I am beginning your tradition of feasting and dancing tomorrow evening. I would be most appreciative if you and Lady Huntsberry might join in our celebration. Lady Dru, as well," he added, wanting the invitation extended but doubting she would accept it.

"I must check with my wife to see if we are available," the marquess said. "I gave her strict orders to remain in bed and rest this morning since we were up so late last night. Since she is with child, I do not want her to overtax herself." He paused. "As far as my sister-in-law is concerned, I will pass along your invitation. She actually is at Beauville today."

His heart slammed against his ribs. "Did she come to speak with my cook?"

"Yes. We rode over together. She will be long gone by now."

That had to be the case because Huntsberry had been here all morning. Still, he regretted not seeing her, which was absurd. She had made her wishes clear to him last night. That she had no interest in seeing him.

Unless he came to see her—with a declaration of love.

How could he do so, knowing what he did about himself? He might look the picture of health to any outsider, but he was emotionally scarred. Dru deserved much better than he could ever give her. Yet the thought of her belonging to another man caused anger to bubble within him. How could he attend next Season and see her blithely dancing the night away in another man's arms? Or hear word of her betrothal? It had been hard enough overhearing that Mr. Hollis had kissed her. That image had been one which had danced in his head all night, preventing him from sleep, as had Dru's ultimatum to him.

Collecting himself, he said, "I hope to see you and Lady Huntsberry, my lord. Lady Dru, as well."

The marquess gazed intently at him. "You know she has given no other leave to call her by that name. Not even Mr. Hollis."

It was true. From the beginning, he had felt a strong connection to her, and she had asked him to address her more informally as Lady Dru instead of Drusilla.

"We are friendly, my lord. Or should I say I hope that we are friends."

"Friends who kiss?"

Perry was taken aback and sputtered, "What did you say?"

"You heard me, Martindale. I know the two of you have

kissed. That Dru has deep feelings for you." Huntsberry paused. "And that you have yet to share your feelings with her."

Thankful that the other workers around them had already retreated to eat and no one heard their conversation, he said, "I am a bit surprised Lady Dru shared this information with you."

"She is on the verge of a broken heart, Martindale," the marquess chided. "Either tell her how you feel—or let her go. No more of being wishy-washy. That is simply spineless. Either be a man and tell her the depth of your feelings, or let her know she is free to seek the company of other gentlemen. You cannot play with her affections any longer." Huntsberry paused. "Or you will deal with me."

He swallowed. "I do love her, you know," he confided. "I think I did from the first time we spoke. She is unlike any other woman. Unique. Vivacious. Spirited." He frowned. "But it is wrong of me to wish to pursue her. There is . . . something wrong with me, my lord. I returned from the war not quite myself. Some call it blue-deviled. Others refer to it as used-up or worn-out."

Huntsberry eyed him with sympathy. "I have heard of this. How does it affect you?"

"Not as badly as it does other fellows, thank goodness," he shared. "Sometimes, those bothered drink far too much, or they behave recklessly. My only problem is with sleep. I have a hard time falling asleep and when I do, I am plagued by terrible nightmares. Each night, it is as if I am at war again, reliving the worse parts of every battle I fought in. I awaken frightened. Covered in sweat. Crying. Screaming." He shook his head. "How could I push my problems upon Lady Dru? She deserves far better."

"What my sister-in-law deserves is an honorable man. From everything I have seen, you are one, Martindale. Dru needs someone who is kind. Someone who would be respectful toward her. Who would honor her and the marriage. Most importantly, she warrants a man who will love her unconditionally. She is not a woman who loves indiscriminately, my lord. She is a remarkable woman—and she would make you a better man."

"But I—"

"Yes, you have problems. They seem unsurmountable to you now, but I have learned that sharing a burden, especially with someone you love, is a way to lighten that burden. A marriage is never evenly divided. At any given time, one spouse gives more than the other. I believe Dru could help you conquer your demons, Martindale. And once she has helped you, I know that you would be the best husband possible to her." Huntsberry sighed. "But it is up to you. Not me. You must believe enough in yourself and Dru, as well. If you do, I think you both would be very happy together."

Perry's mind raced with what the marquess had said.

"Dru confided in me," the marquess continued. "Lucy knows none of this. We should keep this between ourselves. I only hope you will do the right thing and tell her that you love her. Give her the power to decide her future. And yours."

He swallowed hard. "I will take your words under consideration, my lord."

"I do not offer them lightly. I only know that I did not believe myself good enough for Lucy. That I would dim her light. Instead, she has taught me how to shine beside her."

Tears stung his eyes. "Thank you for being frank with me."

"No matter the outcome, I offer you my friendship, Martindale. I only hope that you will come to the conclusion that your future would be better with Dru in it than without. Good day."

Lord Huntsberry left him, rolling his sleeves down as he walked away, retrieving his coat. He even accepted a tankard of cider from a farmer's wife and downed it in one, long gulp, causing those nearby to cheer.

The marquess' final words stayed with Perry.

Would his future be better with Dru?

PERRY LEFT THE house, going down to where the tables were being set up. Cook barked orders at various maids and footmen, telling them where things should be placed, and then she rearranged several. Foster and Mrs. Foster were also bustling about, instructing where tables and chairs should be placed.

He gazed about, satisfied with the productive harvest and how hardworking his tenants had been. Rankin had gone over the early numbers with Perry, declaring this to be a record harvest at Beauville. Pride swelled within him as he thought back to where he was this time last year. While he had given his all to the army and would have laid down his life for his men, being back at Beauville was infinitely better than being on the battlefield.

The nightmares had come again last night, as usual, but this time, Perry seemed to fight them. When he awoke, he was not nearly as depleted as he normally was. In fact, he had fallen asleep quickly again and slept until past dawn, which was unusual for him.

He had spent several hours in his study today, thinking on Lord Huntsberry's words. Anyone could see how happy the marquess was with his marchioness. It was something Perry wanted for himself.

With Dru.

Despite his many misgivings about bringing her fully into his life—and into his bed—he knew his life would be bleak without her in it. Because he had finally admitted this to himself, he was ready to ride to Huntsworth tonight if she did not arrive as a guest.

Lord and Lady Aldridge made an appearance, minus Penelope this time. For a moment, that brought Perry a moment of sadness, which surprised him. He had enjoyed holding the babe, which had made him eager for ones of his own. He let the couple know how much he appreciated them coming tonight.

Lady Aldridge thanked him for the invitation saying, "As you see, my lord, we have no babe with us tonight. My husband will need to dance at least thrice with me." Her eyes gleamed with mischief.

For his part, Lord Aldridge took his wife's hand and kissed it. "You know I adore dancing with you, love. We will dance as many numbers as you wish this evening—and then dance a bit more at home."

Perry had a good idea just what kind of dancing would occur once the couple returned to Aldridge Manor.

Lord Tilsbury and Mr. Hollis arrived next, and he was thrilled his friend had come. Perry also greeted Mr. Hollis graciously, knowing he would one day take his uncle's place. He wanted to shout to Hollis that Dru would never be his, but he kept his head and behaved graciously, knowing they would be neighbors for years to come, hoping they would enjoy a friendly relationship.

He did his best to maintain a pleasant face when Hollis inquired, "Will any of your other neighbors come this evening?" Perry knew Hollis was only interested in *one* neighbor.

"I did invite Lord and Lady Huntsberry, along with the marchioness' sister. I do not know if they will be able to attend, however."

Disappointment flickered across Hollis' face. "I see."

A few minutes later, the Huntsberrys did arrive, minus Lady Dru. Lady Huntsberry apologized, saying that her sister had developed a sharp headache.

"I sent her to bed. My maid is attending to her."

"I hope her health will improve soon," he said, knowing there was no headache and that Dru was refusing to come to him.

So, he would go to her.

Perry addressed those gathered, much as Lord Huntsberry had done two nights ago. In his brief speech, he thanked the tenants for their hard work and belief in themselves—and him.

"We can do great things together," he promised. "Keep doing what you are doing. Mr. Rankin will help us stay the course. For now, though, eat up and drink your fill before the music begins!"

A celebratory cheer went up, and he felt a deep fulfilment, having fully settled into his title and life at Beauville. The only thing lacking was a countess—and hopefully he would solve that before the night ended.

He made certain everyone's plates were filled before slipping away. He did not think he would be missed. Perry did hope to be back, Dru in tow, by the time the dancing commenced.

Making his way to the stables, he saddled Zeus, telling the horse, "There is a certain lady we are off to see. Get us there as quickly as you can."

His ears pricked up, and he seemed to understand the urgency, taking off at a brisk pace. They arrived at Huntsworth, and Perry rode straight to the stables, giving a groom Zeus' reins.

"I do not plan to be long," he said. "I do need to speak with Lady Dru, however."

"She just came in from a ride, my lord," the groom volunteered. "I saw her heading to the gardens."

"Thank you."

Perry went straightaway to the gardens, entering them and hurrying down the path, hoping to catch up to her. Then he spied her, bending down, inhaling the scent of a bloom, her rounded bottom tempting him in her tight breeches. Silently, he crept up behind her, slipping his arms around her waist, drawing her back into him, his lips nuzzling her throat.

"Perry!" she cried. "Whatever are you doing?"

"Kissing you," he murmured, his lips trailing to her nape.

She wriggled against him, trying to escape, but he held fast.

"Let me go," she demanded.

"No. Not until I say what I came to say."

She stilled. Looking over her shoulder, she asked, brows arched, "And what might that be?"

He turned her in his arms because he wanted to face her as he spoke.

"You told me not to grace your presence again until I came to tell you that I love you. Here I am, Dru, ready to do that very thing."

Her breath hitched. Her eyes widened. He thought her the loveliest creature on earth.

"I do love you," he began. "I have for the longest time. That sounds odd because we have only known one another for a short while, but it seems as if we have always known each other. I know the person you are, down to the depths of my soul. I realize there is still so much to learn about you, but I want to do that very thing."

"Am I dreaming?" she asked uncertainly.

"No, my darling. This is real. My love for you. Your love for me. You have an inkling of why I refused to commit to you. It is serious, Dru, these memories which have stayed with me long after I have left the battlefield. I revisit them in my dreams each night. They are the worst of nightmares and haunt me every time I close my eyes."

"I heard you when you were sleeping in the stables." Concern filled her eyes. "The noises you made. The sheer terror that seemed to fill you. I want to help you, Perry. Do I think I can chase away all these nightmares? Of course not. But you no longer have to face them alone."

"I thought you would think less of me. Think I was unfit to be a husband because I could not vanquish them."

"Your suffering from these bad dreams is not a character flaw," she said gently. "I think you are an honorable, kind man. A man I have come to love a great deal." She paused, a teasing light entering her eyes. "And not merely because you kiss so well."

He grinned. "Well, there is that. We do have a spark between us. I believe if we fan those flames, we might possibly ignite."

"I would gladly burn with you," she declared, her hands framing his face. "As it is, I burn for you. I feel a physical connection with you, Perry, but it runs more deeply than that. Frankly, I cannot see myself marrying anyone but you."

Dru took the initiative, pulling him down for a long, leisurely kiss. He wanted things to become official, however.

"Will you promise to spend the rest of your life with me, Drusilla Alington? I want you by my side. I want to laugh and cry with you. Get to know everything about you. And hold on tightly to you when the nightmares become too much. I hope they won't chase you away."

She caressed his cheek. "I love you so much, Perry. Nothing, especially your nightmares, could vanquish my love for you."

They kissed again, and a calm blanketed him.

"I feel both euphoric and contented," he confessed. "It seems an odd combination, but you do incredibly odd things to me, Dru."

"I want you to teach me all the things I do not know about intimacy," she told him. "I feel we have barely exposed what is to come. I look forward to coupling with you. Having your babes."

"Our babes," he corrected. "You will be responsible for the greater part of that process." He kissed her again, hard. "I do love you so much. I cannot imagine a life without you. Will you accompany me back to Beauville now? Let me announce our betrothal?"

"Oh! You are missing your harvest celebration."

He smoothed her hair. "This is no celebration to be had unless you are a part of it, my darling."

She grinned wickedly. "Then we should hurry back to Beauville."

He laced their fingers together and led her from the gardens back to the stables, placing her atop Zeus and climbing up behind her.

Wrapping an arm about her, he said, "I must write to your father tomorrow morning to request your hand in marriage. I would ask that they come to Beauville. Or that we go to Marleyfield. And that the banns be read this coming Sunday."

"I rather like the idea of wedding at Beauville. Besides, Mama will be impressed with your estate. I say you show it off—and I will show *you* off." Dru laughed merrily.

They arrived at Beauville and stopped at the stables.

"I will send a groom back to tend to Zeus and rub him down. I want to be there before the dancing commences."

They did so, sending a groom to Zeus. A few tenants had picked up their instruments, and it was obvious they were looking for him to see if it might be time for the dancing to begin.

Perry went to where the musicians stood, his fingers entwined with Dru's. He looked out over the crowd.

"I have already told you how proud I am of you all and that we are here to celebrate our autumn harvest tonight. We also have another reason to celebrate." He paused. "Lady Drusilla has agreed to become my wife."

A loud cheer sounded, with his people showing their approval. He caught sight of Lord Huntsberry, who nodded approvingly at him.

"Let the dancing start!" he shouted, and the musicians began tuning their instruments as groups formed on the lawn.

The music began, and he said, "We should speak to your sister before dancing."

He guided Dru to the Huntsberrys, and Dru fell into the marchioness' arms, tears of joy coming from both of them. Lord and Lady Aldridge joined them, as did Lord Tilsbury and Mr. Hollis. The latter looked wistfully at Dru, and Perry hoped Hollis would find love himself someday.

"We want to wed at Beauville," Dru told her sister. "Lord Martindale will write to Papa tomorrow. I will write to Con."

"I assume this wedding will take place soon," Lord Huntsberry said.

"We will start the reading of the banns this Sunday," he shared. "Of course, Lord Marleyfield will need to give consent. That would mean the banns only need be read here in Surrey."

"Oh, we have so much to do," Lady Huntsberry fretted. "You need a wedding gown, Dru. A new wardrobe."

"Might we host the wedding breakfast?" Lady Aldridge asked.

He looked at Dru, and she nodded enthusiastically. "That

would be a wonderful gift to us, my lady," he said gallantly.

Mr. Hollis spoke up. "Since things are progressing quickly, I will remind you that writing up marriage settlements is one of my specialties. I would be happy to represent Lady Drusilla's interests."

Lord Huntsberry said, "I think it would be wise to begin the process, Dru. If you wish to wed by the last calling of the banns, it would be wise to have the marriage settlements recorded beforehand. I am certain once your parents arrive, your father would concur."

"I agree," Perry said. "My solicitor is Mr. Chapman. I will notify him of our upcoming marriage and have him come down from town to work on them with you, Mr. Hollis."

"I know both Chapmans and would be delighted to work with them regarding the marriage contracts," Hollis said.

"Then for now, things are settled," he declared. "And I am ready to dance with my betrothed."

Perry led Dru to where the dancing occurred. He slipped an arm about her waist.

"We should wait for the next tune to begin before entering the fray."

She smiled radiantly. "My first dance since becoming betrothed. This is not a night I will soon forget, Perry."

"And my vow to you, dearest Dru? It will get better every day. I promise you that, my darling."

He brushed his lips against hers, everything finally right in his world.

CHAPTER TWENTY-TWO

NERVES FLITTED THROUGH Perry as he guided Zeus toward Huntsworth.

This morning, he would meet his future in-laws for the first time.

Dru had done the best she could in preparing him for this occasion. He understood that Lady Marley was the true power in the family and that it would be her approval he must win in order for their marriage to take place. If she convinced her husband to halt the proceedings, then they would have to wait until Dru's twenty-first birthday, when she would no longer be under a guardian's care and could consent to the marriage herself. He couldn't imagine waiting any length of time; it was imperative that he impress the countess.

He reached the stables and handed off his horse to Harry, going around to the front of the house and being admitted by Brown.

"Lord and Lady Huntsberry are waiting for you with their guests in the drawing room, my lord," the butler said.

He followed Brown up the stairs, slowing his breathing as he had learned to do before riding into battle. While he did not want to liken meeting Lord and Lady Marley to engaging with the enemy, he couldn't help but be a bit on edge after Dru's frank description of her mother.

At least he had taken to her brother. Viscount Dyer had come down from town a week ago in anticipation of the upcoming nuptials. Perry found Dru's brother to be most affable. They had found they enjoyed one another's company and had gone riding and played chess during the past week. Even Dyer, though, had warned him about how difficult his mother could be. Both Dru and Dyer had said that Perry should stand his ground when it came to Lady Marley. Politely, of course, but that he should not be intimidated by her.

He heard Brown announce his name and entered the drawing room. Immediately, his eyes went to Dru, looking lovely in a periwinkle gown. She nodded encouragingly at him as he crossed the room.

It was Dru's sister who took the lead in making the introductions. "Mama and Papa, I would like to introduce you to Lord Martindale. My lord, these are my parents, Lord and Lady Marley."

He took the countess' offered hand and kissed her fingers. "The pleasure is all mine, my lady. You have raised two lovely daughters, and I have gotten to know your son a bit, as well, this past week."

Lady Marley assessed him. "It is good to meet the man who has caught my daughter's eye, Lord Martindale. I feared I would have to drag Drusilla to town in order for her to make her come-out and hope some gentleman might take to her, despite her quirks."

He gazed levelly at her. "I am fortunate in that I was able to come to know Lady Dru before others in the *ton* did. She does me a great honor in accepting my offer of marriage. I will be proud to take her to town this coming spring so that we both might have a taste of Polite Society."

Perry turned to the earl and offered his hand. "Lord Marley, I am delighted to make your acquaintance. Lady Dru has spoken so fondly of you."

The earl, looking as genial as Dru had described him, smiled broadly. "Has she, now? Drusilla and I have always had a special bond. It is good to meet you, Lord Martindale. If our daughter is taken with you enough to agree to wed you, then I know you are truly a special gentleman."

Lady Marley sniffed. "We still have yet to grant permission for this wedding to take place, despite the fact the banns have begun to be read. We must see your estate, my lord, and speak to you at greater length before we consent to the marriage."

Perry was glad Dru had predicted this very thing, telling him that her mother would have a good number of questions which needed to be answered. In the long run, however, it would be Lord Marley who must voice permission for his daughter to wed.

Deciding to take charge of the situation so that the countess would see he was no weakling, he said, "If you are well rested enough after your long journey from Somerset, I would be happy to guide you about my estate now."

Lady Marley looked slightly taken aback, but met his gaze. "That is exactly what I had in mind, Martindale." She looked to her son-in-law. "Huntsberry, can you provide horses for us to tour Beauville?"

"My stables are yours, my lady," the marquess said cheerfully. "Dru can even help you choose mounts because she has ridden several of our horses."

"My daughter's presence is not required," Lady Marley said dismissively. "Lord Marley and I are the ones who will ride out with the earl to his estate." She glanced to her son. "Constantine, you may come along to keep your father company."

He hated that Dru had been excluded from their party, and he looked to her now to see if he should intervene on her behalf. She looked pleadingly at him, and Perry decided he would not upset the apple cart.

"Then we shall leave at once," he declared. "Lady Huntsberry, thank you for your hospitality. I will take good care of your parents and see them safely home."

They headed to the stables, and Viscount Dyer fell into step beside him.

"You did not back down, Martindale. Good for you. Mama can subdue the mightiest nobleman with a few cutting remarks. Keep standing your ground, and you might just gain her respect."

The reached the stables, and two grooms readied horses for them. As they waited, Lady Marley turned to him and began peppering him with questions. She wanted to know the size of his country seat. The number of tenants residing upon it. How long his steward had been in service at Beauville. The type of crops grown and the yield from the most recent harvest.

Perry was able to answer all her questions with ease, but he understood now just how shrewd the woman was.

"We shall ride through Alderton in order to reach Beauville," he shared as they mounted their horses. "The village is larger than most and offers many shops to residents in the area."

"We came through it on our way to Huntsworth," Lord Marley said, and Perry noted that the earl rarely spoke unless directly addressed. "How far is Beauville from Alderton?"

He explained the distance and then mentioned, "My closest neighbor is Viscount Tilsbury of Tilsbury Manor. He is a widower who has offered good advice to me ever since I came into my title. My father was not often at Beauville, and so Lord Tilsbury has helped me settle into country life."

Lady Marley condescendingly said, "I know of your father and his reputation." She paused, scrutinizing him closely. "What of Lady Martindale? I would think with the wedding imminent that she would have already left town."

His gaze steadfast, he coolly told the countess, "My mother prefers town. She will not be at the wedding." He didn't wish to get into the complications of their relationship and semi-estrangement with this woman.

"I see," Lady Marley said, spurring her horse.

He did the same, keeping pace with her, subtly letting her know he was the one who led this party—and not her.

Once they reached Beauville, Perry gave them a complete tour of the estate for the next two hours. When they occasionally paused, Lady Marley had more questions for him. He was grateful that he was able to answer each one to her satisfaction and hoped he was winning her over.

When they reached the apple orchard, the earl lit up. "My, you have a good number of trees in your orchard, my lord."

"Yes, we will embark on the apple harvest next month."

Lord Marley smiled. "I enjoy a good apple tart now and then."

"This is the last of my land," he said. "Perhaps you would care to go to the house for a bit of refreshment."

The earl and viscount looked to the countess, who nodded her approval.

"I wish to see where my daughter will be living. *If* I consent to the marriage."

Perry bit back a smile at her words. He knew she had been impressed with what she had seen of Beauville and was merely flaunting her power.

They rode to the stables and left the horses to be tended, going into the house.

"Foster, we are in need of refreshments. Please have Cook send tea and something for us to eat to the drawing room."

"At once, my lord," the butler replied smoothly.

He led them upstairs to the drawing room, and Lady Marley said, "While we are awaiting tea, I wish to see your ledgers, Martindale."

Though the request was unusual, he smiled benignly. "Then let me take you to my steward's office, my lady." He glanced at the other two, saying, "We will not be long, gentlemen," letting the countess know he would only indulge her interest so far.

They retreated to Rankin's office. Fortunately, his steward was not there to be grilled by Lady Marley.

"You have seen my estate. I have answered every question which you have asked of me. What is it that you need to see in my ledgers?"

"I merely wished to speak to you privately, Martindale." Her gaze bore into him. "Why do you wish to wed Drusilla?"

"Your daughter is the kindest, most caring soul I have ever met. She is intelligent and nurturing. Lady Dru will make for a fine Countess of Martindale. You have seen everything, my lady. I have hidden nothing from you. I will be able to provide for your daughter, and she will lack for nothing." He paused. "Especially love."

Her brows arched in surprise. "Love? You *love* the chit?"

"Yes," he replied, resenting her referring to her own daughter in such a manner. "I love your daughter very much. I had not expected to ever love my wife. My plan was to attend the next Season and select my bride from the Marriage Mart. I assumed I would make a marriage of convenience, as my parents had."

Perry smiled. "But I am one of the fortunate ones who has found love. My life is richer for having Lady Dru in it. I did not know that love actually existed beyond fairy tales, but I have witnessed it in abundance since I have come home to Beauville. Lord and Lady Huntsberry have proven to be a shining example to me, as have Lord and Lady Aldridge. I have never been happier in my life, and I will do everything in my power to show my wife each day just how much I do love her."

"Love," she said dismissively. "Whatever is happening to this generation? A marriage of convenience has been the standard for centuries amongst those of noble birth." She shook her head. "I will be frank with you, my lord. I believed it almost impossible to marry off my youngest. If you have not discovered it yet, you will. Drusilla is headstrong. Willful. Stubborn. Combative. We have clashed over the years more times than I can say. I will be happy to grant my consent for you to wed my daughter because it means she will no longer be my responsibility."

Her words angered him, and he quickly tamped it down, not wanting her to see it. "I am sorry things between the two of you have been strained over the years," Perry said. "And I am happy to take on all responsibility for my betrothed."

There was so much more he wished to say to this woman.

How if she had shown an ounce of love and compassion to Dru, things might not have been so difficult between them. Still, he needed her approval in order for this marriage to happen, so he would do nothing to alienate her and cause her to withdraw the approval she had just spoken of.

Apparently what he said passed muster, because the countess nodded curtly.

"You will receive my husband's permission for the match, Martindale."

"I appreciate hearing so, my lady," he said gratefully. "This means a great deal to me. Come, let us return to the drawing room. You must be parched after our long ride."

The teacart had just been rolled in ahead of their return, and the countess immediately took over, pouring out for them. Perry nodded subtly to Viscount Dyer, letting him know all had gone well. He caught Lady Marley giving her own subtle nod to her husband.

"We cannot thank you enough for showing us about, Martindale," Lord Marley said jovially. "You have much to be proud of. I believe my daughter will be quite happy in making a marriage to you."

"Then it is settled?" he asked.

"Certainly," the earl said.

Boldly, he announced, "Since Lady Dru and I are most eager to wed, we will forgo the last Sunday of calling the banns. I have already spoken to Mr. Harper, our local clergyman, and he is willing to issue a common license for us."

Perry looked to Dru's brother. "Viscount Dyer, you are familiar with the area now. If you would see your parents home, I will go to the church now to obtain our license. We can wed there tomorrow morning."

Lady Marley sputtered, "Is that enough time for preparing the wedding breakfast?"

He smiled. "I have told Lady Aldridge of my plans, and she will make certain all is in hand. In fact, I will call at Aldridge

Manor on my way home from Alderton to let her know we are set for tomorrow morning at ten o'clock."

"Shouldn't you also call on my daughter to let her know when she is to be wed?"

"Lady Dru and I have discussed the matter at length. We decided once you arrived from Somerset and Lord Marley gave his consent for the marriage to occur, we would wed the next morning."

He fought to keep from bursting into laughter at seeing his almost mother-in-law left speechless.

Viscount Dyer rose. "Come. I will see us back to Huntsworth." He offered his hand to Perry, and they shook. "It will be good to have you in the family, Martindale." Dyer leaned closer and whispered in Perry's ear, "Especially since you have learned the skill of how to handle Mama."

They returned to the stables and rode as far as Alderton together before parting ways.

"Tell Dru that I love her," he told Dyer. "And I cannot wait to make her mine."

The viscount beamed at him. "I will certainly pass along that message, my lord."

Perry bid them farewell and rode directly to the church, finding Mr. Harper and telling the vicar that he was there to purchase the common license which they had previously discussed.

"I hope you are available tomorrow morning at ten. My betrothed and I are most eager to unite in holy matrimony."

The clergyman smiled indulgently. "I hear it is a love match, Lord Martindale."

"It is indeed, Mr. Harper."

"Then I will start the ceremony promptly at ten o'clock," the vicar promised.

He rode to Aldridge Manor and gave the good news to Lord and Lady Aldridge.

"I will have our gardeners collect some flowers and supervise the decorating of the church," the marchioness told him.

"Congratulations again, my lord. And now that you are family, please call us Ariadne and Julian."

A warmth filled him. He was in love and would soon wed Dru. Her family was becoming his.

And Perry hoped he would find peace for his soul once the marriage took place.

CHAPTER TWENTY-THREE

DRU HAD SMILED so much, her cheeks were hurting, but she would take this kind of joy any day.

She was now Drusilla Beaumont, Countess of Martindale.

Tenderness filled her as she glanced at her new husband. His hair, usually the color of wheat, had lightened even further with all the time he had spent outdoors during the autumn harvest. She longed to run her fingers through it and knew she would do that very thing the moment they were alone.

They had spoken their vows that morning at the church in the village in front of her family. Perry had wanted to invite Lord Tilsbury and Mr. Hollis to the ceremony, as well, the viscount being the closest thing he had to family. She had asked him about his mother attending, but he told her the door was now closed on that relationship, explaining his solicitor had found a house for her and that she had vacated his London townhouse for it. When Dru worried aloud about their strained relationship, her fiancé had told her not to worry, assuring her that his mother would be pleasant and polite when they came across her at social events, but they had agreed that would be all to their relationship, mere cordial greetings, with no visiting.

It saddened her to think their future children would not have any relationship with the dowager countess. While she knew her mother would not be interested, Dru determined that she would ask her father to visit regularly so he might get to know his grandchildren. Besides, their children would be raised with doting parents, as well as many aunts, uncles, and cousins whom they would see all throughout the Season each year. It amazed her to think of having her own children, but she was eager to do so.

Because she loved her husband so very, very much.

He had certainly charmed her mother, and Dru had thought that an impossible task. Something told her that Mama realized she had met her match in Perry and would do whatever was necessary to keep the peace in the family. In a way, she felt sorry for Con's future bride. The future Countess of Marley would have far more to do with Mama than Dru and Lucy did, now that they were both wed and living far from Marleyfield. Dru would do what she could to smooth the way once Con chose a bride. She hoped they might even become good friends. Of course, her brother still showed no interest in marriage, and she couldn't blame him. He wasn't expected to settle down for several years.

Thankfully, Con got along splendidly with Perry. Although they were very different in nature, they seemed to enjoy one another's company. She was pleased that Judson and Julian also seemed to be growing closer to her new husband. It would make not only life in the country more fun, it would also make for an enjoyable time each spring when they all went to town for the Season.

Relief filled her now, knowing she would not have to be paraded about on the Marriage Mart. She would enter Polite Society as a married woman and not have to go through a stressful come-out. In fact, she now looked forward to the Season. Lucy had described many of the social events to her, and Dru was eager to participate. Why, even balls now sounded fun to her. Not only because she enjoyed dancing—but she would be dancing with the most handsome, loving man in the world at them.

"You look like a cat who has lapped up all the cream," Lucy said, joining her. Her sister slipped an arm about Dru's waist. "I am so happy that you are pleased with the marriage you have made."

"I am. I never thought to wed, much less wed a man whom I love. Perry has changed everything about me. My life. My perspective."

"I do hope you will want to have children," her sister said. "And not just mother animals."

"I plan to do both," she said. "For now, Toby will be it. Perry said he would like to have a dog or two, beyond hunters. I am agreeable to that. Now, whether Toby is or not, remains to be seen."

"I cannot believe how that cat took to Perry," Lucy said. "His entire temperament is much calmer these days. Toby's," Lucy clarified, laughing. "Perry has also changed since falling in love with you. He is more open. More carefree."

She liked that her sister and cousin had encouraged being addressed by their Christian names and could tell it had also meant a great deal to her husband. He did seem more relaxed. She had not asked him about his nightmares, however. Dru did not believe that they would disappear, simply because Perry was happier than when he had returned to England from the war. But she would do whatever was in her power to comfort him when they did occur.

"I think it is time for you and your husband to leave," Lucy suggested. She touched her fingers to Dru's cheek. "I know Ariadne and I have prepared you the best we could so that you understand what the marriage bed is about."

"I do thank you for that. Mama did us no favors in keeping things from us."

"Mama never loved Papa," Lucy said flatly. "You will have a better marriage than she ever did. You have an attentive, loving husband, and you will learn and grow together. That includes the intimacy which passes between you. Remember, anything you do with your husband is acceptable. No limits, Dru."

She laughed, kissing her sister's cheek. "Thank you for asking me to come to Huntsworth for an extended visit. If I had not done so, I would not be Lady Martindale now."

Lucy smoothed Dru's hair. "I will take full credit for your happiness then," she teased. "Come along."

Her sister took her hand and led her to Perry, who was talking with Lord Tilsbury.

"It is time for the happy couple to say their goodbyes," Lucy said.

Perry's gaze immediately connected to hers, and Dru felt her pulse speed up.

"Everything is ready for your departure," her sister continued. "Dru's trunks, both the ones she brought for her visit and the others Mama brought with her from Marleyfield, have been taken to Beauville. The only thing lacking is a lady's maid. You will need to hire one soon, Dru."

"I can play lady's maid for the time being," Perry said. "As long as my wife tends to her own hair."

Everyone laughed, and Lucy motioned for the others present to gather around.

Perry took the lead. "I must thank Ariadne and Julian for hosting this lovely wedding breakfast for us. Your friendship means a great deal to the both of us. And thanks to everyone else who witnessed us speak our vows."

"Will you go on a honeymoon?" her mother asked.

"We have decided not to do so at the moment," Perry replied. "Perhaps after the apple crop is brought in. For now, we merely wish to settle into marriage with one another."

Her husband offered her his arm, and Dru took it, letting him lead her out to the waiting carriage. Perry handed her up and joined her, and they waved goodbye before the vehicle turned and rolled down the lane of Aldridge Manor.

Slipping an arm about her shoulders, he said, "It is good to finally be alone, Lady Martindale."

"I agree. Though it is going to take some time for me to get used to being addressed in that fashion. I am a countess. A countess!"

He kissed her, softly brushing his lips against hers.

"That is all for now, Lady Martindale," he told her. "If I continue to kiss you, I might not be able to stop. Best we leave that for the privacy of our bedchamber."

"Are you . . . certain you wish for us to share a bed?" she asked quietly.

Perry had told her that both Judson and Julian had confided in him that they slept each night with their wives in their beds and encouraged him to do the same. Of course, neither knew the trauma Perry faced and the nightmares which plagued him.

"We discussed it before," he reminded her. "While I am reluctant to expose you to what I am like when I am haunted by bad dreams, I realize now having your support to comfort me could make a huge difference."

He framed her face with his hands. "If it gets to be too much for you, do not hide that from me, Dru. I would rather you feel safe and protected in your own bed if that is what you want."

"I want to be with you. By your side. No matter what," she insisted.

"Good."

He brought her close, kissing her temple, making her feel very married.

They arrived at Beauville, being greeted by the butler and housekeeper, as well as two long lines of servants.

"Would you care to address the staff, my lady?" Foster asked, as Mrs. Foster gave her an encouraging nod.

"Yes, Foster."

Dru gazed out over the people who would be taking care of her for decades to come.

"Thank you all for the work you do at Beauville. I look forward to getting to know each of you. I hope if you have any problem, you will come to me so that we might solve it. I wish for you to enjoy working at Beauville, and I appreciate your warm welcome."

The Fosters led them inside, and Mrs. Foster said, "Your things have been placed in your rooms upstairs, my lady. Allow me to show you to them."

She looked to Perry, who said, "Once you have done so, Mrs. Foster, please see that a light supper is brought to my sitting room upstairs."

"Certainly, my lord," the housekeeper replied, guiding Dru up the stairs.

The rooms designated for the countess were large and airy. Thankfully, they were also devoid of anything which might have belonged to the now Dowager Countess of Martindale.

"I hope you don't think me presumptuous, my lady, but I noticed you brought no lady's maid with you."

"I have never had one," she explained. "One of our maids at Marleyfield always helped me to dress, and another did my hair. Mama had said a lady's maid would be hired for me once I was to make my come-out next spring. While I have been with my sister at Huntsworth, I shared Annie, her maid. I will need to hire one. Until then, I hope that I might have your assistance, Mrs. Foster."

"I am happy to assist you, my lady. What I wish to say is that my sister's girl would make for a good lady's maid for you. She is skilled with a needle and doing hair."

"Where is she now?"

"Her employer in Kent recently passed, and she is looking for a new position."

"Then I will take your recommendation, Mrs. Foster. See that she is brought to Beauville at once."

The housekeeper beamed. "I appreciate you trusting my judgment, my lady. Might I help you into your night rail now?" she asked, indicating the one lying on the bed. "I set it out for you earlier."

Dru supposed this would be a good idea since she doubted she and Perry would wish to be interrupted after their supper.

"Yes, please."

Lucy had insisted they go into town in order to see her modiste. They had commissioned a few new gowns to be made up, including the one she wore as her wedding gown today. The others would be ready soon, but Madame had also created some beautiful night rails for Dru. They were of the most delicate of materials, and she had felt like a princess trying them on.

The housekeeper helped her undress and placed the night rail on her, offering her dressing gown to wrap around her for the time being.

"You do look lovely if I may say so, my lady."

"Thank you, Mrs. Foster."

"Might I make one more suggestion? Men seem to like a lady's hair down. I could remove the pins for you."

She almost acquiesced, and then she thought how Perry might enjoy doing so.

"No, I will leave the pins in for now."

"Ring if you need anything else," the housekeeper told Dru, exiting the room.

She roamed about the bedchamber for a few minutes, seeing where things had been placed. Then she heard a light tap and looked up. Perry stood in the door which led from her bedchamber into her dressing room. They must have adjoining rooms.

"Would you like something to eat and drink?"

No words came from her. He stood in his banyan, with bare legs and feet, and though belted, she could see a glimpse of his bare chest. Her mouth grew dry. All she wanted to do was touch him.

"Perhaps a little something," she agreed.

He took her hand and led her back to his set of rooms, where a small table held a platter of fruits and cheeses. Taking a champagne flute in hand, he poured into the glass and filled a second one for himself.

Handing her a flute, he said, "To us—and a long, happy marriage."

"To us," she echoed, sipping the cold liquid, its bubbles tickling her nose. "I have never had champagne before today. Now, I have had a glass at our wedding breakfast and again here."

"It can go straight to your head," he warned. "Drink it sparingly."

He seated her, and they nibbled on the selection before them. Everything was so easy between them, assuring her that her choice in a husband had been the right one.

"I think you are the only man I could ever have wed," she told him. "You . . . complete me."

His smile made her belly do flip-flops. Taking her hand, he kissed it. "Without a doubt, you are—and forever will be—the only woman for me." He kissed her fingers, causing desire to ripple through her.

Dru set down her flute. "Enough talk, Lord Martindale. I am ready for action," she said saucily.

"Oh, you are?" he asked, coming to his feet and yanking her against him.

She could feel the bulge beneath his banyan and shivered.

"Teach me," Dru told him. "I want to learn everything from you. About you."

His eyes gleamed. "Then we should retreat to the bedchamber and begin those lessons."

CHAPTER TWENTY-FOUR

B ETWEEN WHAT HAD already passed between them and what her sister and cousin had shared, Dru had a good idea of what lovemaking entailed. Anticipation rippled through her, knowing she belonged to this man alone.

And that he was also hers.

The bedclothes had already been turned back, but Perry stopped before they reached the bed. One hand cupped her nape. The other cradled her cheek. He bent, softly pressing his lips to hers. That delicious smell of sandalwood, coupled with a masculine scent that was his alone, mixed together, intoxicated her. She slipped her arms around him, rubbing her hands along the smooth silk of the banyan resting against his back. He generated a good amount of heat, and she gravitated toward it. Toward him.

The kiss became more demanding, and he urged her mouth open, sweeping his tongue inside. He tasted of the champagne they had just drunk, and she felt the slightest bit dizzy, causing her to push against him for support. He deepened the kiss, causing her to mewl and him to chuckle.

Breaking the kiss, he gazed down at her. "I have never wanted a woman more than I have you, Livia Drusilla."

She had never mentioned her full, given name to him before today's marriage ceremony. When Mr. Harper had used it, Perry turned to her, grinning. She would need to tell him of all the unusual names in her family, all ten cousins being named after ancient emperors and empresses. But that was for another time.

"Kiss me," she urged.

"With pleasure," he said, his voice husky, sending shivers along her spine.

His mouth returned to hers, his hands now moving up and down her arms. Her back. Clasping her buttocks. Each touch caused anticipation to build within her.

He guided her hands to the knot of his belt. "Untie it," he ordered.

She did so, then pushed the banyan from his broad shoulders. He let it slide down, falling from his arms, puddling at their feet. Her eyes went wide, and her fingers immediately moved to explore the exquisite muscles of his arms and chest. She allowed her fingers to dance lightly over him, the muscles bunching to her delight. They went lower, finding his cock, and she stroked it tenderly.

Knowing how much pleasure he had afforded her when he put his mouth to her sex, she fell to her knees, licking the tip of his shaft. He groaned, his hands clutching her shoulders.

"Do you like that?" she asked, already knowing the answer.

"Yes," he said hoarsely.

Lucy had told her a bit of what to do next, and Dru opened her mouth, guiding him inside it. She licked and sucked, moving her lips up and down the stiff shaft, hearing the noises which came from him.

"Enough," he said, breathing harshly. "Or I will not be able to pleasure you."

Perry took her hands, helping her to stand. He undid the knot of her dressing gown, removing it and placing it over a nearby chair. He took her hands in his, holding her arms wide. She already knew the night rail's diaphanous material left little to the imagination. He lifted it over her head, setting it, too, on the chair.

"Do you like what you see?" she asked, worried that she

wouldn't be enough for him.

"You are perfection, my darling. Not a flaw to be seen."

Lifting her from her feet, her husband carried her to the bed, gently placing her on it.

And then the magic began . . .

They spent a good hour exploring one another's bodies. Touching. Kissing. Learning what each liked. He slipped his fingers inside her, bringing her to that height of unbound pleasure, causing her to both squeal in delight and call his name in need.

"I want you inside me," she told him as he caressed her breasts lovingly.

"Do you know what happens when we couple?"

She grinned. "That it makes us both wild for one another, and it can also make a babe."

He chuckled. "I suppose you have down the basics."

His mouth returned to hers, his touch addictive. They kissed for a long time, each kiss more heated than before. Then he rolled to his back.

"Mount me," he told her. "You are going to ride me."

"That sounds interesting," she purred, climbing atop and straddling him.

He clasped her waist, lifting her with ease, and then brought her over his cock, saying, "You will slide me into you. Do this, then we will go from there."

Without hesitation, Dru did as he asked, taking him inside her, delicious sensations occurring as she did so.

When she was fully seated, he said, "I hope you felt no pain."

"There was none," she assured him. "Lucy told me I might feel some, but Ariadne disagreed. She said as often as I ride—and the fact most of that is done astride—I should feel no pain."

He took her hand and kissed it. "I am glad you did not experience any."

"What now?" she asked eagerly.

"You will ride me. Hard. It may take a minute before you

capture your rhythm, but when you find it, it will be indescribable."

She wriggled about, searching for how to move. The sensations began growing as she figured out what felt best for her and hoped it did for him, as well. Her movements increased in speed, and her heart began beating wildly. For his part, Perry moved, too, and they began an incredible dance full of heat and passion.

And love.

That lovely climax built within her, and she didn't try to muffle herself. Her husband also was enjoying himself, and they clung to one another as their orgasms erupted at the same time. She was laughing. Crying. Living. Loving.

Dru collapsed against his chest, their bodies still joined as one. "Lovemaking is exhilarating," she proclaimed.

"It is," he agreed. "And we can do it in several other positions."

She kissed his chest and rested her cheek against it. "Then I hope we will try every one of them tonight."

He laughed, his hand absently stroking her hair. "Give me a chance to recover, my darling. It takes a man a bit of time before he can perform again. But in the meantime?"

Perry lifted her from him and began kissing the length of her body, moving up and down limbs and torso. He kissed her from her eyelids to her toes and every place in-between. His mouth moved to her core, and once more, he rocked her very existence, using tongue and teeth and fingers to bring her to the heights of heaven.

Exhausted, he collapsed atop her, quickly rolling off and cradling her to him.

"I must sleep," he murmured. "Stay."

"I will not leave you. Ever," she promised, hearing his even breathing, and then tumbling into sleep herself.

DRU AWOKE, HEARING the low groan coming from Perry. His body twitched, and she knew he was in the throes of one of his ghastly nightmares.

He shot up and she could see his wild eyes since they had not extinguished the candle before falling asleep.

Soothingly, she said, "You are with me, Perry, my love. You are safe. Nothing can harm you as long as we are together."

His body jerked once as he panted as if out of breath, and she nudged him back to the pillows, wrapping herself around him.

"I am here. Go back to sleep."

Moments later, his body stilled. Then she heard his breathing return to normal.

"That's it, my love. Sleep."

She could not imagine what he had seen during his years on the battlefield. She would never ask him about it, or what came to him in these terrible dreams. What Dru could do was be here for him.

Once more she awoke, feeling the tension in his body. By now, the candle had extinguished itself, so she lay in the dark, prepared to do what she could to calm him. A soft cry escaped his lips. It occurred to her just how much solace washed over her in church and how she loved to sing.

Quietly, she began doing so, the words of "Amazing Grace" spilling from her.

> Amazing grace! how sweet the sound,
> That saved a wretch like me!
> I once was lost, but now am found,
> Was blind, but now I see.
>
> 'Twas grace that taught my heart to fear,
> And grace my fears relieved;
> How precious did that grace appear
> The hour I first believed!

Thro' many dangers, toils and snares,
I have already come;
'Tis grace has brought me safe thus far,
And grace will lead me home.

He calmed as she sang, and by the time she had completed the third verse, he lay sleeping peacefully once more.

Dru brought the bedclothes over them and nestled close to her husband, grateful she had been able to bring comfort to him. She closed her eyes and drifted into sleep.

What awoke her next was Perry's lips nibbling her nape.

Satisfaction filled her, even as her heart began speeding up. During the night, she had turned away from him, but he now enveloped her, her back pressed against his hard, muscular chest. His hand gently squeezed her breast and then playfully tweaked its nipple, sending a jolt of desire through her. It drifted lower, teasing her core, as his finger dipped inside her and stroked her deeply.

"You are wet for me, my darling," he said against her ear, his teeth tugging on her lobe, sending fire streaming through her.

She pushed against him, wanting more, and he chuckled.

Soon, she was writhing at his touch, the orgasm shattering her. Quickly, he rolled her to her back and entered her with one, powerful thrust. They began the dance of love. Kissing. Touching. Sharing words of endearment.

"Wrap your legs about my waist," he told her.

She did so, feeling him move even deeper within her. Her hips met each thrust, even as another orgasm, stronger than the one before, racked her body.

Perry's cry of victory sounded, and then he collapsed atop her, driving her into the mattress, his weight welcome. Her limbs held tight to him as she breathed in the scent of her husband, knowing his seed rested inside her, hoping they had made a babe.

"I am crushing you," he said, rocking to his side, bringing her with him.

Their bodies still joined, they looked at one another, love reflected in their eyes. He smoothed her hair, kissing her gently.

Then he stopped abruptly. Broke the kiss. Frowned.

"What is it?" she asked, worried.

"I . . . I did not awaken last night," he said, bewildered. "I cannot recall a nightmare."

Dru was tempted to tell him he had none, but she would never lie to him.

"You did awaken, Perry. Twice."

He raked a hand through his hair. "I do not recall doing so."

She touched her fingers to his face. "It was brief. The first time, you sat up, distressed. I told you I was here and that you were safe with me. You lay back against the pillows and fell asleep again."

His brow furrowed. "And the second?"

"It was not as bad as the first. Since we were entwined, I awoke, feeling the tension in your body. I calmed you. By singing to you."

He looked startled. "You did?"

She smiled. "I did. William Congreve was right. Music has charms to soothe the savage breast."

"It softens rocks and bends oaks," he continued, finishing the line of the Congreve poem. "I have no recollection of any of this, Dru, but I have always thought you have a lovely voice."

"Then I am glad I was able to help you."

He pulled her close, kissing the top of her head. "You are a comfort to me, Wife. I could not conquer my demons on my own. I needed your help to do so."

"They are not gone completely," she reminded him. "But I do think they will lessen as time goes by."

"The comfort you provided me kept them at bay. I hope I did not alarm you."

"Not at all. I was glad to be with you and help you fight through it."

"The nightmares may never totally be dispelled, but I am

grateful you chased them away." He kissed her tenderly. "No one could have helped me through this except for you, Dru dearest. You are the love of my life. My North Star, giving me direction and purpose."

"And you have shown me such love, Perry. I could never have imagined how good love could be. You are the only one for me. Thank the heavens above that fate brought us together."

Her husband smiled gently at her. "We will live our lives in love, my darling. Of that, you can rest assured."

EPILOGUE

July—1808

PERRY LAY NEXT to Dru, one arm about her, cradling her belly. He could feel the strong kicks of the babe and wondered how his wife could sleep through them. Then again, she was coming to the end of her term and had been exhausted for the last week or so. She had told him it was difficult to inhale a deep breath. The babe also pressed upon her bladder, resulting in numerous trips to the chamber pot throughout the day and during the night.

She lay sleeping peacefully now, and he would stay with her until she awoke. It gave him time to reflect upon how much had happened since they had met and fallen in love.

Though some might have gossiped about the speed of their marriage, he had known Dru was the woman for him. He had fought against it, not wanting to trap her in a marriage with a man who feared the nights because of the terrible nightmares he had. They still came to him from time to time, but he recalled little about them. All he knew was that his wife had the ability to ease his ravaged soul. She could soothe him by singing a few lines of a song and reassure him with a loving touch.

They had gone to town in the spring for their first Season. Though they only went to a few of the social events, it had been good to try out the Season together. They had also made time for family. Of course, Judson and Lucy were present, as were Julian and Ariadne, and he was comfortable in their company. He also met Val, the Duke of Millbrooke, who brought his new wife to town, along with his sisters Tia and Lia, who had made their come-outs. Con was also present, and Perry had enjoyed trips to White's with Con and the other men in the family.

A new family member had made her appearance the first day of March, shortly before the Season began. Lucy had given birth to a daughter. Ironically, Elizabeth shared a birthday with her cousin Penelope, who was exactly a year older. Perry had grown comfortable holding the babe, and he particularly enjoyed the rapturous look on Dru's face when she held little Elizabeth. He could not wait to see their own child in his wife's arms. With two girls already in the family's next generation of cousins, he wondered if they, too, would have a daughter or if Dru would give birth to a son.

He liked that they had come home to Beauville for the birth of the babe. After six weeks of the Season, they both were ready to retire to the country. Dru was ready to stay off her feet, while he preferred the quiet of Surrey to the noisy ballrooms of town.

His wife began to stir. Her hand moved to her belly, and the babe's kicks grew fierce. She sighed, and he knew she was now awake.

"Did someone wake you?" he asked.

"They most certainly did." She chuckled. "And for once, it was not you."

Perry stroked her belly, moving his hand around, feeling the babe kick wherever he touched. It still fascinated him that life grew within her, a child whom they would raise.

And love.

His own parents had paid little attention to him, much less loved him, but he was determined to be a good parent. Dru would help him in this endeavor.

Toby came strolling up the bed. The tabby slept at their feet each night, something which had taken a bit of getting used to, but he rather liked the cat now and considered Toby a part of the Beaumont family.

Scratching between Toby's ears, he asked, "Are you ready for the whirlwind which will take over our lives?"

The cat purred, arching his back. He licked Dru's hand once and jumped from the bed.

"I suppose I must get up," she said, sounding more tired than usual.

"You may do whatever you like, my darling. You are the Countess of Martindale and beholden to no one. Stay abed all day if you choose. Your time draws nears. If you—"

Dru yelped.

"What is it? Is it the babe?" he demanded.

"Help me up," she said, urgency in her voice.

He came around to her side of the bed and lifted her. Just as he set her on her feet, a loud whoosh erupted. Water splattered about their bare feet.

"It is time," she said calmly. "Lucy and Ariadne were very specific about this."

A thousand thoughts raced through his mind, and panic must have shown on his face because Dru said, "Perry, I am fine. Ring for my maid and your valet."

He did as she requested, his heart galloping like a horse out of control. Dru had him remove her night rail and place a fresh, dry one on her. He slipped into his banyan.

Both servants arrived, and he told Grilley, "Go and bring the midwife back at once."

"Yes, my lord," the valet said, racing from the room.

To the maid, he said, "Have Cook put on water to boil. Then return here and tend to Lady Martindale." It was something Judson had told him was needed, so he wanted to have plenty on hand.

His wife seemed calm, but her demeanor changed. Her face scrunched up in pain. She let out a low cry.

"What can I do?" he asked, feeling absolutely useless.

"Stay with me until the midwife comes. Help me back to bed for now. And stack the pillows behind my back. It is hurting a great deal."

He hated that she would bear this pain alone and sat on the edge of the bed, holding her hand, trying not to look worried.

The midwife arrived and shooed him from the room. Not wanting to go far, he placed a chair in Dru's dressing room and sat next to the closed door. He could hear her cries, ranging from low moans reminiscent of a cow to the loud screeching of a crow. Each time, the sound of her anguish filled him.

Then a scream erupted, earthshattering, and he threw open the door and raced into the room. He saw his wife, her face bright red, the sweat pouring from her. The midwife leaned between her legs, urging Dru to push.

"I cannot," she said, tears flowing down her cheeks. "I haven't got it in me."

He rushed to her. "I am here, my darling girl. How can I help?"

With watery eyes, she got out, "Sit behind me."

Quickly, he moved the pillows supporting her, crawling into the bed. His long legs cradled hers. He linked their hands together as she fell back against him.

Perry glanced at the midwife, who said, "She must push the babe from her, my lord, when the pain comes. Else the child will be stuck."

Left unsaid was the babe would die.

"She will do so," he guaranteed. "Dru dearest, the next time the pain comes, bear down hard. Push with all your might. Grip my hands as tightly as you can."

She nodded, too tired for words.

"You can do this. You can move mountains. You saved me. Do this for our child."

He sensed the pain as it rocked her body and urged, "Now. Now, my love. Bring our child into the world so that we might love them with all our hearts."

Her body tensed. She squeezed his hands so hard, Perry thought she might break a few of his fingers. But he would do anything to help her. She grit her teeth, a guttural cry emerging, and pushed.

"That's it, my lady," the midwife praised. "You're doing it."

He could sense the determination rolling through her now. As another labor pain erupted, she pushed again, the growling coming from her fierce and resolute. And long. Extremely long.

Perry sensed some change in the air and then in his wife's body. The midwife gave a cry.

"You've done it my lady." She paused. "It's a son."

A lusty cry filled the room, and Perry relaxed at the sound.

"A son," Dru said, blubbering, as he kissed her temple and then brought her hand to his lips.

"A son," he said proudly. "You are a mother, Dru Beaumont."

More tears came, this time happy ones, and she said, "We never spoke of a name."

She had not wanted to do so, fearing it might bring them bad luck. He had gone along with her wishes, knowing too many times that childbirth ended in death for the mother, the child—or both.

"We need to now," he said, an idea suddenly coming to him. "Let us see our son first."

The midwife had handed the babe to a maid to clean, and she asked, "Would you step from the room a few minutes, my lord? There are things to do. You may see Lady Martindale shortly."

Reluctantly, he slid out from behind Dru, setting the pillows behind her again, and kissing her mouth softly.

"I will be nearby. Call if you have need of me."

Perry returned to the dressing room but was too exhilarated to sit. Instead, he paced the length of the room, again and again, hoping all was well with mother and child.

The door opened, and the midwife said, "You may return, my lord."

He hurried to Dru, seeing she wore a new night rail. Her hair had been removed from its braid and brushed, resting about her shoulders. And in her arms, she held their babe.

"Come, meet your son," she urged.

He sensed the others leaving the room in order to give them a moment of privacy, and so Perry slid back into the bed, slipping his arm about his wife. They didn't speak, just simply gazed down at their newborn, who quietly studied his parents.

"I think he likes us," Dru said.

He touched the babe's head, which had a soft fuzz of light hair atop it. His thumb stroked the infant, and a wave of love burst inside him.

"It is love at first sight for me," he admitted, and Dru said she felt the same.

They watched the babe for a few minutes, and then his eyes grew heavy.

"He is tired," she said. "Just as I am. But it is a good kind of tired, Perry. We are parents."

"We are parents," he agreed, pride swelling within him. "And I have a suggestion. What if we call him Alington Beaumont?"

"Alington," she repeated. "It is a big name for a very small babe."

"But he will grow into it. Better yet, we could use Alington as his given name, but we might call him Beau."

Tears misted her eyes. "Oh, I do like that. Beau," she said, gazing down at the bundle she held.

The babe opened his eyes, and they both said, "Beau," in unison.

And Perry could have sworn that their son smiled at them.

Softly, Dru began singing to Beau, her rich voice surrounding their infant. He blinked twice and closed his eyes again.

"You certainly know how to comfort all the men in our family," he told her.

"I will sing to Beau each day," Dru promised. "And any siblings he has."

He thought of the family they would raise over the years to come, and peace descended upon Perry.

"I love you, Dru. And I love you, my precious Beau."

Perry kissed the infant's head and then his wife. The kiss was sweet, almost innocent, much as the first kiss they had shared.

The years would pass, and he knew his love for this woman and their children would continue to grow each and every day.

About the Author

USA Today and Amazon Top 10 bestselling author Alexa Aston lives with her husband in a Dallas suburb, where she eats her fair share of dark chocolate and plots while she walks every morning. She enjoys travel and sports—and can't get enough of *Survivor* or *The Crown*.

Her Regency and Medieval historical romances bring to life loveable rogues and dashing knights. Her series include: *The Strongs of Shadowcrest, Suddenly a Duke, Second Sons of London, Dukes Done Wrong, Dukes of Distinction, Soldiers and Soulmates, The St. Clairs, The de Wolfes of Esterley Castle, The King's Cousins, Medieval Runaway Wives,* and *The Knights of Honor.*